GIRLS GONE ROGUE

JO LYONS

Boldwood

First published in 2024 as *Benidorm Again*. This edition published in Great Britain in 2025 by Boldwood Books Ltd.

Copyright © Jo Lyons, 2024

Cover Design by Alexandra Allden

Cover Images: Alexandra Allden, iStock and Shutterstock

A CIP catalogue record for this book is available from the British Library.

Paperback ISBN 978-1-80557-224-4

Large Print ISBN 978-1-80557-223-7

Hardback ISBN 978-1-80557-222-0

Trade Paperback ISBN 978-1-80656-032-5

Ebook ISBN 978-1-80557-225-1

Kindle ISBN 978-1-80557-226-8

Audio CD ISBN 978-1-80557-217-6

MP3 CD ISBN 978-1-80557-218-3

Digital audio download ISBN 978-1-80557-219-0

This book is printed on certified sustainable paper. Boldwood Books is dedicated to putting sustainability at the heart of our business. For more information please visit https://www.boldwoodbooks.com/about-us/sustainability/

Boldwood Books Ltd, 23 Bowerdean Street, London, SW6 3TN

www.boldwoodbooks.com

For Lindsey
Inspirational. Courageous. Fabulous.

1

Falling head over heels in love has been like someone throwing surgical gloves at me, out of the blue, expecting me to try my hand at a kidney transplant. It's exhilarating and nerve-wracking at the same time, but I'm giving it my best go because Matteo is the most excessively attractive man I've ever laid eyes on. And it is essential that I make a decent impression before he realises that I am not naturally good at this.

Be casual, Connie Cooper. Be cool.

'You know what they say about watching people while they sleep?' Matteo says, opening one eye. I am sharing his pillow and borderline stalking him with my face.

A giggle escapes from my lips. I will never tire of waking up next to this dreamboat. 'Stop making it sound weird. I've only been watching you for the last two and a half hours.'

Matteo laughs gently as he places a light kiss on my lips.

'What a week,' I say, sighing blissfully. It seems like only yesterday I was spilling scalding-hot coffee on his crotch. It has been nothing short of a wild rollercoaster. This whole week in Benidorm has flown by. I hope he feels the same.

Matteo frowns playfully as though this has been the longest week in living memory. 'I thought it would never end.'

Not exactly what a loved-up woman wants to hear. Although, he has a point.

I have developed an unattractive habit of bringing chaos to his otherwise calm and ordered life. And I'm gutted that we have only just discovered each other and are being forced apart so soon. But it is very early days. I must not appear too insecure or needy, just because I'm going to miss literally everything about him; *everything*. I give him big cow eyes, causing him to smile back at me. He's smitten with me. It's written all over his lovely face.

'I can't believe you're leaving for LA,' I say, stroking his cheek while I admire the strong line of his jaw, the dark stubble on his chin, the kissable lips. He is literally the Oxford Dictionary definition of gorgeous. 'Three months is such a long time to be away.'

'I can't believe you're flying back to the UK today,' he says, a trace of sadness in his voice. 'But it's great that you get to tour with the Royal Northern Sinfonia. That's a huge deal. I'm going to miss you singing cheap covers in Voices, though,' he jokes softly. He is trying to hide how unfair the timing feels for us. 'It won't be the same without you.'

I should hope not. Poor man. So far, I have broken his phone, given him a black eye, and almost ruined his business – all by accident. My week-long marathon of incredible personal growth and off-the-scale sexual awakening has been really tough on him. And to be fair, he has seen sides of me that not even I was aware of.

I love that he has faith in me to sing classical music with a world-class orchestra. And I love that he is going to miss me. I walk my fingers up his bare chest. 'I'm really going to miss your expert approach to successful leadership, fiscal planning and dealing with the emergency services.'

None of us are going to forget that yacht fire in a hurry. Or the way he took charge when handcuffed to me against his will, while in the middle of running a huge music festival. Or indeed, the way he proved himself to be the manliest of men when he politely pretended not to hear me yelling angrily at the universe, sobbing hysterically in the shower or demonstrating quite the unprofessional flop several times before going on stage.

'I hope that's not all you're going to miss, Cenicienta,' he says, giving me a look that sends a delicious shiver straight through me. I have fallen very hard and very fast for this glorious man. And this Cinderella nickname seems to be sticking, but I really don't mind because it's how I feel. Elated and joyful and bursting with desire.

'Well, let me give you something to remember me by.' I've also recently discovered that I can be nothing short of a brazen hussy when I'm with him. His eyes widen with desire, filling me with immediate delight. I have never considered myself sexy, but he effortlessly brings it out in me with a simple look, a simple smile. I chew my lip, slide the cover slowly from his body and take my time deciding how to drive him wild with passion. I trail my fingers lazily down his chest and hear his breath catch as they circle his lower abdomen. He closes his eyes and presses his head into the pillow, a low groan escaping from his lips. I find his attraction to me intoxicating. How are we meant to survive without each other for three whole months?

* * *

A surprisingly short while later, Matteo can barely speak coherently. I should insist on a performance review, what with me being so new to it all, but so far, sex with me seems to be going very well. He is staring up at the ceiling as though in an artificially induced coma. I poke him to make sure I haven't done any lasting damage. 'What did you just do?' he whispers, which sends a wave of tingles up my spine. 'That was incredible.' He gets out of bed and promptly trips over the rug. 'Christ, my legs feel like jelly.'

'Is that a good thing?' I ask, beaming happily at him.

He fixes me a terrifyingly sexy look as he slowly nods his head.

Oh, my.

My phone pings. It is my best friends and live-in housemates-come-therapists, Ged and Liam, who rushed here to Benidorm a couple of days ago to support my rather huge and, as it turned out, completely unnecessary meltdown over Matteo being engaged to be married – which he isn't. Luckily, the whole misunderstanding was cleared up quickly and Ged and Liam are more than delighted to be staying in my luxurious room over at the villa with the Dollz. Which means more privacy for me and Matteo in my newly acquired apartment above Voices. I decide not to read the messages in favour of following him into the shower cubicle.

I press up against him and trace the lines of his shoulders and arms with my fingers. It sends a shiver through him, causing his lips to part. He studies me silently, his eyes telling me everything. He wants me. And I want him. He inhales sharply, causing me to instinctively press my hips against him even more. We are insatiable for each other. As the water cascades gently down, he reaches out to brush the hair from my face. He strokes my lips with his thumb before trailing the back of his fingers down my neck, down, down to graze the outside of my breast. It sends a pulse of electricity right to my toes. He slips his hands beneath my bottom and gently lifts me up to straddle his waist as though I weigh nothing at all. His eyes blaze into mine as I gently rock against him, our bodies slick with soapy suds. He keeps one hand on the shower wall to steady himself as he expertly cups me with the other. Our kiss deepens as his tongue slides into my mouth, causing me to moan loudly. I tangle my fingers in his hair, kissing him back with a passion I have never felt before for any man in my entire life. The chemistry between us is crazy. My head is spinning as all too soon we are free-falling over the edge into shuddering ecstasy. We have all of two seconds to revel in this delicious miracle before we are interrupted.

BEEP. BEEP. BEEP.

'Oh no! That's the minibus!' I wail, pulling my mouth away from his. Trust the Dollz and Ged and Liam to be punctual for once. 'It must be time to go to the airport.'

I feel an overwhelming melancholy sweep through me, while Matteo is quicker to snap out of his loved-up haze as we untwine our soapy limbs.

'It's not for long,' he says in a soothing voice. 'We can FaceTime every single day if you want.'

I nod. He's such a busy man, though. I know for a fact that he has gone to extreme lengths just to fit me in as it is. He won't be able to keep his promise, but I appreciate the gesture.

As I reach behind me to turn off the water, Matteo grabs a towel and wraps it around me. I should broach the delicate subject of labelling our relationship. He is jetting off to LA for a few months to work and to be bossy and successful, and I am desperate for some understanding around being exclusive even though we have essentially just met. If it were down to me, I'm sure I'd marry him this afternoon round the back of the bins, but seeing as I'm technically the rebound after his dreadful ex cheated on him, I'd like to know his view on it all. Only a few days ago, he made it abundantly clear that he is not looking to rush headlong into a relationship seeing as he is so fresh out of such a long-term commitment and painful split.

I look up into his dark, kind eyes and instantly melt. I can feel every emotion running through him as though he's trying to transfer them to me, and I want to savour this memory forever. 'I'll miss you,' is all I can manage.

BEEP. BEEP. BEEP. BEEP.

Christ Almighty. I need to get a move on. We throw on our clothes and grab the cases, all but hurling them down the stairs in our hurry to get outside. Jorge, the bus driver, gives us a nod of acknowledgement. My support band and best friends are all scattered around waiting. They are nearly all smoking cigarettes or vaping, and getting some last-minute sun on their faces.

There is no time to have the 'exclusivity' discussion. It will have to wait.

'Connie, babes!' bellows Tash. 'You've got that top on inside out. And look at the state of that bird's nest at the back of your hair, pet. I think we all know what you two randy sods have been up to.' She cups her hands and bounces my imaginary head up and down on her groin as though she's getting the world's most vigorous blow job. She gives Matteo a huge wink, expertly emphasised by her massive eyelashes. Thick black kohl lining her eyes like an Egyptian queen.

It's so unnecessary. My cheeks flame. I can barely look Matteo in the eye. He will hate that.

Bounce. Bounce. Bounce.

Oh, my word. It's as though she was in the room watching. The Dollz burst into husky cackles as they stub out their ciggies and pile back on to the bus.

'You can tell us all the sordid details on the way to the airport. We're really friggin' late now,' complains Liberty.

Matteo rolls his eyes and swoops me into a quick embrace. 'We'll see each other soon.'

'Put her down!' yells Cherry from the window. 'And don't forget, Mr Fancy Pants, you invited us all to LA for a VIP experience.'

He looks momentarily startled. 'Did I?'

All I can do is shrug. Cherry has a gift for remembering conversations verbatim.

'Okay, sure,' he says with a resigned sigh, which only lends him an endearing quality. 'Whatever.'

A huge cheer comes from the bus.

Poor man. He'll probably live to regret that. I hope for his sake it never happens. The Dollz have really tested his patience this week. And besides, it was just me he was inviting, not my entire entourage. I'm sure they more or less invited themselves. I give him a final kiss goodbye and with tears in my eyes tell him that I will miss him terribly.

* * *

As we hurtle towards the airport in Jorge's rickety little minibus, I reflect on my week in Spain. This has been the *best* trip of my entire life. It has all happened so fast. One minute, I'm being sacked from my regular singing gig after being too miserable to perform anything other than tear-jerking ballads since my mother passed away. The next minute, my agent, Nancy, rings with a chance for me to redeem myself, and I'm being flown to Benidorm to sing cheap covers to a sea of bald heads at Voices. I meet the Dollz, my *insane* but extremely talented support band. I fall head over heels in love with Matteo. And to top it all, when I least expected it, the Royal Northern Sinfonia finally accepted me into their organisation, after years of failed auditions.

'I can't believe we'll be flying back out here in two weeks,' says Tash. 'It's a good job my boss fancies me, otherwise if he didn't give me so many holidays off work, I'd be telling him to shove it.'

As support bands go, the Dollz might be a bloody nightmare to work with, but I have grown to love and adore every single one of them. Even Cherry and Tash, who are the scariest Geordie women on earth. Liberty, Mandeep – or Big Mand, as she likes to go by – and Big Sue nod in agreement. They are nothing if not committed to their part-time singing careers.

'We're so jealous,' says Liam. 'We've absolutely loved Benidorm. It feels like our spiritual home.'

'We're thinking we might even get married out here,' Ged butts in.

This is news to me.

'How romantic,' gushes Tash. 'Are you thinking Sticky Vicky to officiate on top of one of the skyscrapers?'

Liam is quick to respond. 'We haven't reached that stage of planning yet.'

'Are you having a stag do first, though, yeah?' she asks, leaning towards them as though she's suddenly become their unofficial wedding planner.

Ged shakes his head. 'That sounds too animal cruelty or whatever. We're having a PMS.'

'PMS?'

'Pre-moon spree,' Liam says, his eyes lighting up. 'It's our pre-moon. Like a minimoon before a honeymoon but even more exciting and lavish.'

Of course. Why ever not?

'Are you sure that's how you want to describe it?' I say cautiously, visualising the invitations.

'We'll have a full week of PMS.'

It's like he can't hear himself.

'You'll be wanting all the necessary glitz and glamour required to see off your single years in style,' says Big Mand, nodding. 'Who wouldn't?'

Of course, they will need an opulent spree of Mariah Carey proportions.

'And, Connie, we'd like you to be our BEST WOMAN!' says Liam theatrically, throwing his arms wide.

Oh my!

My hearts leaps in my chest. I lean over to hug them, squealing. 'Of course I will!' I'm so full of joy I think I'll burst. I love them both so much.

'We've seen each other through the best of times and the worst of times,' announces Liam, looking lovingly at Ged. This is true. None of us will forget Ged's flirtation with lip fillers in a hurry. Liam sweeps his gaze around the Dollz. 'And obviously, you fabulous divas will all be invited.'

This causes an instant avalanche of excitement.

'We love a good stag do!' Cherry yells. 'It'll be wild!'

'We'll do our hot garbage routine,' joins in Liberty. 'That always draws attention.'

'Cherry, you do the outfits, love. Something that'll slay,' Tash says, her eyes wide. 'We need to go viral, babes.'

'We'll have a group meeting pronto to co-ordinate all the socials and get a proper strategy organised,' Big Sue says, nodding to Big Mand, who turns, beaming, to Ged and Liam.

'Drop us the MO ASAP. You two lovebirds won't know what's hit you.'

Suddenly, the pre-moon is becoming all about the Dollz. I risk a glance at Ged and Liam's alarmed expressions.

Sodding hell.

2

A week later, I'm settled back home in Newcastle, and the Benidorm trip already seems like a world away. The Sinfonia tour starts tomorrow. I have spent days shopping for gowns to wear on stage. My credit card is groaning under the weight of the expense. I even did some financial planning and it looks like, what with all the expense of travelling back and forth juggling my singing jobs, I can retire at ninety-seven and live comfortably for about eleven minutes without having to worry.

Liam snaps me from my thoughts. 'Connie, love. You've got that haunted look again. Can you stop thinking about Matteo for two minutes while we get through this Sinfonia rehearsal? I'm sure there's a good reason why he hasn't called yet today. He's like nine hours behind or something,' he says, misinterpreting my expression. 'Besides, Ged and I are in the middle of some very important couples' vision-boarding for our wedding, and he's waiting for me to decide on what colour bridesmaid dresses we want for the horses – coral or sage green. It's all incredibly stressful.'

'Yes. Sure. Sorry. I'll start again. From the top,' I say, restarting the backing music as I open my mouth to sing. Now that he's mentioned Matteo not ringing, he's given me something else to worry about alongside my poor finances and learning to ride a dressage horse in time for their wedding.

'Louder, babe. From the heart,' Liam says as though he's directing me in a Netflix movie. 'Let the audience get their hands on a piece of the real you. Not the wooden you. You're not half tree. I'm thinking use your arms more. Wave them around as if you're juggling very slowly. That's what all these opera singers seem to do. Just try to relax.'

Relax?

'Two thousand sceptical opera lovers are turning out to see who the Sinfonia have replaced their much-loved singer with,' I snap anxiously. 'You try being relaxed about it.'

Liam raises an eyebrow at me. 'Imagine you're floating in the clouds on a magical, singing breeze,' he says, waving his wand. 'Your voice is like a gust of wind wafting through the audience, light and ethereal.'

I try again but my throat sounds dry and scratchy. All the excessive drinking, people everywhere smoking, and me, bawling my eyes out unnecessarily on numerous occasions in Benidorm, have taken their toll.

The living room door opens. 'Are we role-playing?' says Ged, eyeing Liam's wand and cape jokingly. He flicks his gaze over to me. 'If so, I'd like to play the part of customer demanding a full refund.'

'Very funny,' I say, smoothing down the tight bodice of my gown. I ruffle out the heavy velvet ruched skirt to hide my bare feet. It feels like I'm wearing my own bodyweight in silk taffeta and sequins.

Ged blows me a kiss before turning to his fiancé. 'Liam, darling, is that my dragon's heartstring wand you are using as a baton? Because you know it'll only work if you wear the Sorting Hat, don't you?'

They exchange a mischievous look. They are opposites but they make an ideal couple. Ged is in the music business but can be very sane and sensible at times. Liam is a music teacher with a tendency to be outrageous and flamboyant. And while Ged stacks a dishwasher with the precision of a Swedish architect, Liam throws things in like an ape on crystal meth, but I'd trust them both with my life.

'I'm so nervous,' I say, flustered. 'I've had to learn a lot of songs very quickly. My vocal range might not be up to the job. Krzystzof Helmuth, the Swiss Maestro, is supposed to be one of the most demanding in the whole of Europe. The audience will have unbearably high expectations. And never mind trying to fit into these ridiculous theatrical costumes.'

They look at one another as though I'm being melodramatic. Which I am. I am *terrified*. My mother was an extremely successful opera singer. What if I can't fill her shoes?

'It's about confidence,' Liam says softly. He gives me a gentle, reassuring look. 'You've got this, Connie Cooper. You have nothing to worry about, my lovely.'

'Thanks.' I smile, grateful for the reassurance, but it's like telling water not to be wet. At that moment, my phone bursts to life, causing me to drop it.

'Connie, babe, you really must stop dropping your phone every single time Matteo calls,' says Liam. 'Surely you can't be that nervous around him?'

'No,' I say, scooping down to pick it up. 'Of course not.'

I jab at the phone, trying to press accept, and accidentally reject the call. It immediately rings again. My fingers have turned to mush. This is so stressful. I take a beat. *You've got this, Connie Cooper*. He's just a man. A magnificent, dark-haired, brooding, multilingual overachiever with the instincts of an MI5 special operative, the brains of a Nobel prize winner and the looks of a movie star. Why be nervous?

'Oh, hi,' I say, trying to sound light and casual – the sort of woman who doesn't sound on the edge of a substantial breakdown each time the very new love of her life calls her.

'Did you drop your phone again?' Matteo says with a hint of amusement in his voice. Thank God he can't see me. My face has gone full coal furnace.

'No, no. I just... I mean, yes. It's... slippery.'

Ged and Liam are shaking their heads at me. Unfortunately, they've had to witness this low-level deception more than once.

'Slippery?' Matteo asks.

Yes. Just like my slide into insanity.

'So, how are things in LA?' I say, anxious to change the subject.

Ged and Liam inch forward in their seats. They, too, are intrigued to hear how things are going in LA.

'I'm going to be working in the studio for the next week or so and might not get another chance to ring. How are you feeling about the Sinfonia tour?' he asks. 'I know you have some doubts about fitting in, but you'll be great. I know you will.' His comforting words immediately put me at ease.

We talk for an hour as I ask him all about LA and the artists he is working with, and he asks about my dad and how the hiking weekend at the Lakes went with his new girlfriend, Madge. It is a development that I am still trying to process. It keeps me from obsessing about *our* relationship and whether I'm merely Matteo's 'rebound' or, preferably, whether I'm his 'the one'. But more than that, our time together in Benidorm was so short, I've convinced myself it would be insane to expect him to commit to being exclusive with each other at such an early stage.

If only I were brave enough to ask him. But, of course, that would cause any man to run screaming for the hills – like my last boyfriend did.

'Say hello to Ged and Liam for me,' he says as our conversation draws to a close.

I glance over, smiling.

They are still on the sofa listening in, riveted. I entertain the idea of introducing them to a new hobby. Crocheting hats or making their own sausage or something. Liam fancies Matteo as much as I do because he is so ridiculously good-looking. Which is something I am absolutely not going to do (any more): judge Matteo on his superior looks.

'As soon as I've finished in the studio, I'm taking a few days off. Would you have time in your busy schedule to fly out to see me in Vegas?' Matteo asks suddenly. I instantly drop the phone again, cutting him off in the process.

Ged swoops down to pick it up. He gives me a baffled look and calmly rings Matteo back, handing it over when he picks up.

Matteo is laughing. 'So, is that a yes?'

Oh my life. Just the thought of seeing him again is knee-trembling.

'Yes, she'd love to!' yells Liam across the room.

And just like that, I've arranged to go and meet the absolute love of my life in Las Vegas.

* * *

Later that evening, the full reality of it all hits me as I stand at the mantelpiece in our living room. I go over the plan once more in my head. I leave Newcastle tomorrow for a one-week tour with the Sinfonia. We are performing in three major cities in the north of England. First is Manchester, then York, then back to Newcastle. Immediately afterwards, I resume my residency at Voices in Benidorm. The management are happy to be super flexible with me while I juggle all of my singing commitments. God, it sounds so exciting. I can barely believe it is me who I'm thinking about.

I blow my cheeks out at the thought of the mammoth task ahead. I will need decent clothes for Las Vegas. Standout, fashionista-type attire. Not the elaborately bouffant gowns I'll be wearing for the Sinfonia. Not the tiny, strip-per, pole-dancing costumes the Dollz insist I wear in Benidorm as part of the 'look', and definitely not the dowdy, dark, wine-stained rags I've been moping around in for two years since my beloved mother passed away.

My mother.

My lovely, kind, funny, talented mother whom I'll never hear singing ever again. I still can't believe that I'll be singing on the same stages as she did, with the same orchestra, wearing similar costumes and performing to the same audi-ences, but she'll never get to see me up on stage and I'll never get to hear what she thinks of me. Or see her. Or speak to her. Or hug her, ever again. A wave of grief engulfs me from out of nowhere. I take a deep breath in and place my hand gently on my chest as it washes over me. Sadness, pain, panic, despair, dread. I close my eyes and let the images of my mother lying ill in a hospital bed fly around. I try to conjure up some nicer images from when we were younger. Before she got sick. Before our lives fell apart. But they're not coming yet. My dad says they will come back to me over time. He says how much time it takes is different for everyone.

I feel like I've been waiting around in a numb haze forever. But at least, thanks to the Dollz and Matteo careering unexpectedly into my life, I have started feeling emotions again. I am no longer the empty husk that I've been for the past two years. Just the thought of Matteo creates a warm feeling deep within. I focus on remembering his kind eyes and the smile that lights up his entire face. It seeps through my bones like an elixir, helping the fear and dread recede until I feel back to normal.

I open my eyes at the sound of the door creaking.

'So, we've had a long talk about it,' says Liam, coming into the living room with two glasses of wine in his hands, followed by Ged. Liam gives me a glass. I'd take a guess at what he's talking about, but really, it could be anything from creamed asparagus to a colonic steam.

'We're celebrating... again?' I ask. I shouldn't be surprised. Last night we stayed up until two in the morning celebrating their one-month-a-versary as a newly engaged couple. At this rate, I'm going to turn up to the Sinfonia tomorrow looking like I spent the night sleeping rough under a bridge.

'Our pre-moon spree will be held in...' Liam says, setting down his wine glass and drum-rolling his hands on the sofa to mine the reveal for all the drama he can get.

It must be somewhere super glamorous. Thailand? Fiji? Maybe it is one of those ultra-high, super-expensive jobbies in Dubai. Liam and Ged have sparkles coming out of their eyes. They have also been to the dentist for some extra-bright whitening treatment. I'm dazzled.

They look at each other triumphantly.

'Las Vegas!' they yell in unison.

Oh, shit.

'The most romantic place on earth. The city where dreams are made. The city of love. And gay rights,' Liam sighs lovingly at Ged. I avert my gaze while they take a moment to stare into each other's eyes and clasp hands melodramatically.

'Lovely. So lovely.' I have a smile plastered on my face. 'When exactly?'

I know when. Why am I bloody bothering?

They turn their huge, excited eyes towards me as though I'll never, in a million years, guess.

'In two weeks!' they say in unison.

'As in, roughly the same time as I'll be going to visit Matteo?'

'YES!' Ged shouts. 'Isn't it bloody marvellous? You'll be there anyway, so you may as well be on best-woman duty. It'll kill two birds with one stone. And it'll save you a fortune on the flights.'

So much for their anti-animal-cruelty stance, but I do appreciate them thinking of my poor finances.

I watch them jump up and down, hugging each other. It is quite the conundrum. Of course, I am excited for them. That goes without saying. But why, when I have not yet spent more than two nights with Matteo, and we are still very much finding our feet with each other, do they think muscling in on my week of carnal passion is a good idea?

'And you've given Dubai some thought too, have you?' I ask.

They nod.

'And the Maldives? Diving with turtles? Or what about a Caribbean Disney cruise?'

Ged is folding his arms. I must tread very carefully. Liam has also begun to raise an eyebrow.

Oh God, what will Matteo think?

'Las Vegas will be perfect. So perfect,' I backtrack.

'Well, Matteo did invite us. And we thought, as best woman, it'd be easier for you to organise all the activities for the pre-moon. Because he can pull a few strings. Get us a few celebrity meet 'n' greets?'

I couldn't even organise my way to the local shop this morning. It had been my turn to nip out for full-fat milk to steam in our awesome coffee machine that you need a PhD to operate. But I was daydreaming about the last time Matteo kissed me, and before I knew it, ducks were quacking, and I'd arrived at the park. Four miles in the opposite direction. And as for Matteo pulling a few strings... I wouldn't dream of asking him. And if I'm being picky, their invite from Matteo was to LA, not to Las Vegas.

I spend the next half an hour listening to Liam and Ged excitedly list a range of must-do activities and must-see shows for me to organise, while we toast their good health, wealth and happiness. I have no idea how I'm going to balance my romantic break with such an extravagant week or how I'm going to afford it. Thankfully, my phone rings.

'Will you be needing a room in the hotel? It might not have an en suite though, and you will definitely have to share with Cherry. Or Liberty.'

It's Tash. As usual, she is carrying on a conversation as though we have been talking it through for hours.

'Hotel? Where? Benidorm?' Maybe Tash has forgotten that I have an apartment of my own above Voices.

'Vegas, babes. Where else?'

My heart has stopped. I wait for it to restart. It has forgotten that it is supposed to thump blood regularly to my brain. My brain that is playing cruel tricks on me.

'Vegas?' I gulp. 'As in Las Vegas? In America?'

'Yes. Nancy needs to know if you're staying with us. For tax and visa purposes. She's putting it all on expenses.'

Oh, my God. What is happening?

'How did you know I was going to Vegas?'

I've literally just got off the phone with Matteo an hour ago. I haven't even told my dad that I'm going.

All is revealed.

'Ged just posted on Instagram that you were all going to Las Vegas on their pre-menstrual spree thingy,' Tash says.

'Has he?' I say tentatively.

'And obviously, they invited us, but we're all too skint. Cherry is almost a single mother. Liberty has discovered vampire facials. Big Sue and Big Mand are worried about our carbon footprint, so combining work with pleasure ticks a box for all of us.'

I'm still not following but make a mental note to check up on Cherry.

'So I rang Nancy, and she's arranged for us to do a couple of gigs while we're there.'

Why would Tash do that? Nancy, our agent, is not to be messed with. Once bookings are made, they are set in stone.

'We told her you'd be bang up for it, but Nancy just needs you to confirm first. It means our flights, food, accommodation would all be free. Otherwise, none of us could afford to go.' She mistakes my silence for being overjoyed.

Tash squeals with excitement. She has no idea that she's ruining my big, special, romantic week. Instead of bonking and existing in a general loved-up haze, I'll now be working. I'll be singing in clubs while trying to keep up with the Dollz, the world's heaviest-drinking chain-smokers. And in between, I have the world's most elaborate pre-moon to organise and execute.

Deep fucking breaths.

'Thanks, Tash. That's really good of you... and Nancy.' My voice sounds distant, as though I am on a sort of polite automatic pilot. 'But I haven't got time to do gigs as well as the pre-moon for Ged and Liam. I was hoping to see Matteo that week.'

'And you will see him, Connie, babes. You will. But what's the alternative? None of us get to share Ged and Liam's big week? They'll be gutted.' Tash lets the silence hang between us for a moment.

What a guilt trip. How can I say no?

'Okay. But only if the gigs don't get in the way of me spending time with Matteo,' I say reluctantly.

Tash whoops eagerly. 'Yay! It's going to be savage. I'll tell Nancy you've confirmed.'

Savage. Oh. My. God. Now I have even less time to prepare myself for the Las Vegas trip. And even though I could really do *with* the extra money, I could really do *without* the extra pressure.

My spirits plummet at the thought of what might lie ahead. I will have to make sure I get some time with Matteo alone. Before it all turns *savage*. I will just have to be firm with everyone and learn to say no.

'All the Dollz are proper buzzing. We might need some of those upmarket showgirl giant feathers and swinging nipple tassels.'

This is getting worse by the second.

'Either way, it's going to be one hell of a messy one. We can't wait.'

Sweet Jesus.

'Anyway, gotta bounce, babes. Good luck with that snobby Sinfonia lot on tour. You'll need it. I've heard they're a complete nightmare.'

3

I must warn Matteo. I must.

But I can't.

One, he's deeply immersed in the creative process right now, and two, I'm a wimp.

'I think he'll love the surprise element,' says Ged to Liam.

They're discussing my situation.

'Imagine when he turns up to collect her, and there's all of us standing top-to-toe in full Barbie and Ken.'

This is the first I'm hearing of the trip being themed. Of course it would be Barbie. *Of course it would.*

'Wait until you see my white faux-fur coat and headband,' Ged says to me excitedly now, thrusting a phone showing Pinterest photos of Ken outfits into my face.

'Matteo will absolutely die,' says Liam.

Yes, he might.

'And he did invite us out to LA to see him,' Liam says, casually rewriting history. 'It's basically next door to Vegas anyway.'

Could a four-hour drive be considered basically next door, though? Could it?

Ged nods. He's not fully on board with Liam's obvious crush and has sensibly not allowed him to switch out Harry Styles for Matteo lookalikes as his free pass.

'And it makes perfect sense for us to be in Las Vegas,' Liam continues.

It doesn't, but go on...

'I mean, it's not like we'll take up all of your time,' says Ged. 'We wouldn't dream of it, honey. But Matteo might have an issue with all the Dollz piling over with all their drama. As much as I adore them, they can be a bit of a handful. Especially Liberty and her wandering vagina.' He shrugs casually.

He's not wrong there. I, too, adore all five of the Dollz and their loud, vampish, uncontrollable thirst for cocktails and anything on two legs, but not when I was hoping to spend a quiet week trying to impress my new lover with how low-maintenance and sane I can be.

'And it's celebrity season in Vegas right now so who knows who we'll bump into?' Liam says excitedly before fixing me with a hopeful look.

By 'bump into' he means 'who Connie will go to the ends of the earth, sell a lung or similar vital organ, do whatever is necessary to arrange for us to meet'.

Ged and Liam are famous micromanagers. Meticulous to a clinically obsessive degree. But worse than that is their absolute devotion to the flamboyant pop icon Harry Styles. I am going to have to find out if he is in town, otherwise I will never hear the end of it if we miss a sighting of him at a club. But one thing I do know for sure is that I am not asking Matteo for such a huge favour on top of everything else. Maybe Nancy will have an idea.

While I get started folding the huge, heavy gowns, a string of WhatsApps from the Dollz group chat pings into my phone.

Ping. Ping. Ping.

Tash wants to know if I can get my fella to pull some strings and get us a table at the Bellagio. Not to do any eating. Just for the Gram. She warns Cherry not to be messy if they share a hotel room. She is sick of her rolling down her knickers four times a day with each costume change and just leaving them lying around on the floor like discarded croissants. Liberty is wondering how we feel about pink Stetson hats, pink-glitter thigh-high boots and pink Daisy Dukes for the Barbie-themed week as she and Cherry are doing the outfits, and to leave it all to them. She will tot up how much they spend and send me the total.

She also reminds us that she will be getting off with as many American billionaires as she can manage. Especially if they have handlebar moustaches that she says she is craving.

God help us. I hope Matteo is understanding after I tell him I'll be working during the one week off he's arranged for us to be together. And that I'll also be dressed as Barbie when not in my stripper outfits, and our dates will be centred around trying to track down a variety of pop stars at every opportunity.

How did this happen?

A message from Matteo flashes up. It says he will be switching off his phone for most of the week, which means he can only call me at random times, depending on how long the recording sessions last. He is working with a notoriously difficult producer called Birdie, who is well known in the music industry for being a perfectionist and a tyrant. She doesn't like the creative process to be interrupted by phones pinging or by the toxic radio waves they produce. He uses an exclamation mark to signify that perhaps this is a crazy notion, but it's the word 'she' that pops out and has me all a-fluster.

My brain immediately leaps to unsubstantiated and wildly inappropriate conclusions.

Matteo then sends a short follow-up voice note to say that he is really looking forward to seeing me. He has planned lots of exciting sightseeing trips and cool places to go.

I listen to his lovely voice a few times before I frantically google music producers in LA called Birdie.

Oh. My. Effing. Word.

She is a stunning glamour puss with curves in all the right places and a face that's so perfect she could be next-gen AI. She has a string of accolades and industry awards. There are photos galore of her with famous rap artists and singers at all the cool parties.

'Who's the goddess?' asks Liam on his way to the kitchen. 'Gorgeous hair. Is that neon coral or salmon pink, would you say?'

'She's Birdie DuPont. She's a French music producer in LA,' I say, trying not to sound too jealous.

Of course she'd be cool and sexy and French. She's probably flicking her Gauloises cigarette holder and twanging her fishnet stockings at Matteo as we speak. But I fully trust him to resist the temptation and not give her stockings a second glance.

'Good thing Matteo is locked away in a music studio,' says Liam, sounding relieved. 'I wouldn't want that LA bombshell getting her hands on him.'

'They're working together,' I say, a lump forming in my throat. 'They'll be shut off from the whole world. Locked in a studio making hot Latino music together.'

Liam looks again at the image of Birdie on my phone and then back up at me. He looks devastated.

Deep breaths.

Deep breaths.

* * *

Early the next morning, Liam drops me off at the Sinfonia with my huge suitcases. I had a restless night tossing and turning, images plaguing my dreams of Birdie running off with Matteo in slow motion, hand in hand, through a cornfield at sunset. She was perfectly naked and wearing only a large, floppy sunhat and a huge, satisfied smile.

'There you go. That's all of them,' Liam says, rubbing his hands together like a cabbie. 'And try not to obsess about Matteo and Birdie. She seems very professional to me. She clearly has a thing for dark and brooding *musicians*, not for dark and brooding music *producers*. And just because she's a hot-blooded Frenchie and he's a hot-blooded Latino, doesn't mean that they'll have amazing chemistry or be instantly attracted...'

I pinch the bridge of my nose. 'Please stop talking, Liam.'

It's almost as though he is as upset about it as me. He has talked of nothing else. Has he also imagined Birdie blowing smoke rings at Matteo while lounging around in her sexy French underwear?

'And just because they are both insanely good-looking and locked away together in a creatively emotive and sensual environment does not mean that one thing might lead to another.' Liam looks at me with pleading eyes, almost begging me to agree.

'You're right, it doesn't,' I tell him. 'Because Matteo isn't the sort to cheat.' After all, I did rather find out the hard way. And by hard, I mean, of course, embarrassing. I was hurling accusations left and right at the time. I could cringe thinking about it. 'Not after that whole business with his cheating ex-fiancée.'

'Did you manage to lock in that exclusivity agreement with him? That's the crucial element,' Liam asks as though he's negotiating a peace deal in the Middle East. 'Have you landed on a relationship status?'

I shake my head glumly.

Liam instantly rallies. 'Okay. Let's just focus on the positives. In less than two weeks, we will all be in Las Vegas together where you can firm up the fine print. The sooner we get you on this bus, Sinfonia tour done and back home again, the better.'

I stare down at the many cases in a daze as exhaustion sweeps through me. Three are full of costumes, the other my day clothes, hair and make-up things. Across the car park, two coaches are waiting outside the enormous shell-like structure that is The Glasshouse, International Centre for Music in Newcastle. Ripples from the River Tyne are reflecting off its mirrored panels. Hordes of people are hurrying to pile suitcases and garment bags in the coaches' holds, before scrambling to get on board with a multitude of musical-instrument-shaped cases. Within seconds, the buses have fired up the engines ready to go. I feel panic rising from my stomach. Liam grabs my hand instinctively.

His eyes tell me he knows exactly what's going on. 'Breathe,' he whispers to me. 'Just breathe through it.'

Without warning, tears sting my eyes, causing me to take huge gulps of air into my lungs. 'Maybe this wasn't such a good idea,' I say. 'What's the point if my mam won't even get to see me?' I bury my head into Liam and unexpectedly burst into tears. I can't do this. I have too many memories of watching my mother perform on stage. It's all too raw, too fragile.

Liam envelops me in a hug. It's warm and comforting. He says nothing as I soak his jumper with my tears. I can feel two coachfuls of eyes on me.

Beep. Beep.

'I can't do it. I can't go,' I manage between quiet sobs. 'What if I'm not good enough? What if they expect me to be as good as she was?'

'There's nothing to be gained by letting them all down at the last minute,' Liam says calmly. 'Just go and do your best. It's not like they'll boo you off stage or any—'

He stops talking because he has possibly just remembered the time, not so long ago, that I actually *was* booed off stage for crying too much while singing Adele covers. It was a tough gig. Cubes of sheep's cheese and many garlic-infused olives were thrown at the stage, too. We all thought it was harsh, but Ged said that he'd be annoyed too if it was his wedding.

'You're just tired. What do we always say? Face the fear and do it anyway,' Liam says. 'You'll be amazing. Remember to smile, and you will light up the stage. You've got this, Connie. You auditioned for years. You might as well give it a go.'

He's right. I spent too long trying to follow in my mother's footsteps as a classical singer just to feel closer to her. I temporarily lost sight of what I might want from life. At least, if I give this a go and I'm no good at it, I can tick it off the career goals list.

BEEEEEEP.

Someone makes a loud 'ahem' sound. 'We are all waiting for you. Is there some emergency? Can I be of any assistance?'

A tall, impatient-looking man dressed in an expensive casual suit with a designer T-shirt, Converse sneakers and a loose scarf around his neck walks towards us.

'I'm Luke. You must be... Connie?'

I sniff up my remaining tears, wipe my nose discreetly on Liam's jumper and nod back. How embarrassing.

I'm not sure I'm making a very good first impression as his gaze very subtly flickers from my puffy face to my legs and back again. His face gives nothing away as he reaches into his breast pocket to retrieve a very soft, but more importantly, brand-new-looking handkerchief. He gives it a gentle shake, revealing it is monogrammed with swirly initials. Bowing slightly, as though he's just graduated from an 1850s school of gallantry, he offers it to me.

I gingerly take it and begin to mop at my tears in a genteel fashion. Maybe it's to do with classical music, but everyone in this world always seems to behave more formally.

Dab. Dab. Dab.

'Thank you.' I sniff. 'That's very kind. There's no emergency.'

'Well, in that case, can I prise you two lovebirds apart?' He checks the time on his phone and shows it to us. 'We do have a rather important opening night to perform this evening.'

'Oh, we're not lovers... no way,' says Liam, a tad too forcefully. 'I already have a fiancé. A much better one. I mean, a different one. A more manly one. One who's much more emotionally stable.'

I look up at him. *Who is this helping?*

'If you could say your goodbyes quickly and follow me over, we'd all appreciate it,' Luke says briskly, giving us a stern look. 'We don't want to be late, do we?'

Liam grins back. He likes this sort of moody chivalry. We watch *Bridgerton* together. He totally loves anything to do with swashbuckling, firm thrusting buttocks and men in frilly sleeves with a sense of whimsy.

But then, who doesn't? Prior to meeting Matteo, I was watching the *Bridgerton* season one buttocks scene on a continuous loop.

'I'll take these. Try to keep up,' Luke says in an authoritative manner as he heads to the coach that still has its hold door open, with two of my four heavy cases. Liam and I watch him stride powerfully away, filling out his suit as though it was tailor-made for him. The fabric strains against his shoulder blades and biceps as he carries my luggage as though it weighs nothing at all. He has the broad back tapering to a slim waist and hips silhouette of someone who has a gym membership and actually uses it. Frequently. He barks orders to the coach drivers which jolt me into action. We scurry after him.

'A week will fly by, and we can keep in touch on WhatsApp to put together the wish list for the Vegas schedule,' Liam says, helping me carry my other two suitcases to the coach.

Ah. The schedule.

The schedule that I promised to put together and send to everyone.

The schedule that can't be completed until Nancy gives me the exact dates, times and locations of all the venues we will be singing at in Vegas.

The schedule that must include a daily itinerary of pre-moon activities that we can do dressed as Kens and Barbies.

The schedule that must also include me trying to magic free time out of thin air to spend with Matteo, who has specifically taken precious time off work so that we can spend a romantic week alone undisturbed.

My heart begins to thump in my chest. At least this mild panic attack about Vegas is taking my mind off my current predicament.

'Your tour manager is a bit of a looker,' Liam says, nodding towards the coach where Luke is waiting with a phone glued to his ear. 'What is it with you and hot, bossy men? You're like a magnet. Let's hope they're not like buses.' Liam drags his eyes back to mine. 'Anyway, love, you'll be fine after a good night's sleep. It'll all work out. You'll see.'

I hope he's right.

BEEP. BEEEEEEEP.

'Christ. I nearly had a heart attack!' shrieks Liam.

Luke has raised his arm towards us and is pointing to his wrist.

'What were you saying about hot, bossy men? What a pain in the neck,' I say. 'Come on, let's get a move on.'

Liam heaves one of my cases into the hold for me, while I drag the other one, and we squeeze them in with the rest. Multiple sets of judgemental eyes are peering down through the coach windows at us, causing me to feel on edge.

Liam reaches out to give my hand a gentle squeeze. 'Ignore them.'

I hug him goodbye and assure him I'll be okay.

But when I make to climb the steps of the coach, Luke swoops in, holding out his hand to help me up as though it's a horse-drawn carriage. He might be impatient but at least he has good manners. I give him a wobbly smile and dab gently at my cheek in an endearing way. It was very thoughtful of him to give me such a high-quality handkerchief.

He clears his throat. 'If your intention is to keep us waiting so that we know you're the star of the show, then a word of warning,' he says in a low voice, edging Liam out of the way. 'We've seen it all before.' He maintains eye contact for a little too long. 'Punctuality is a mark of respect. And the Maestro does not like to be kept waiting.'

His words cause me to flinch, stopping me in my tracks. There's no need for this level of rudeness, surely? My eyes flick behind me to an open-mouthed Liam. He too looks a little alarmed.

'That was absolutely not my intention,' I say, snatching my hand from Luke's to hurry up the stairs. He has put me right off hot, bossy tour managers.

At least the bus is only half full, so there is plenty of space. I just have time to rush towards the back, to put some distance between us, when Luke follows me down the aisle.

'I hope you don't mind,' he says, plonking himself right down across the aisle from me before I can answer, 'but we may as well get this right out in the open.'

Yes, I do bloody mind.

I look around. All the seats surrounding us are empty. Instinctively, I look out of the window to see Liam watching with his mouth gaping open as though I've just been kidnapped.

I just have time to mouth, 'What the...?' when the coach engine roars to life and, with an almighty jerk, we set off.

My phone begins pinging exponentially seconds into the journey. It'll be Liam.

Luke is staring at the phone in my hand. It feels rude to answer it mid-conversation. Especially as he's just, for want of a better word, told me off. Ridiculous to think that I'm giving social etiquette top priority, but as I'm panicking over what to do, he lifts his gaze to mine.

Ping. Ping. Ping.

'Don't mind me,' he says in a facetious tone. 'You've obviously got more important things to do than focus on this tour.'

'And you've obviously got more important things to do than... than...'

'Than... than?' he mimics.

'Than manage the tour.'

This tit for tat is beneath me. I'm the lead soprano, for God's sake, but something about him has got my back up. I can't have been more than a few minutes late getting on to the bus. He studies me with an intense gaze. The azure-blue eyes are framed with thick dark lashes for such a blond-haired man. His eyes crinkle in a disarming way. He does not look impressed. 'Do I look like a tour manager to you?'

I deliberately look him up and down with a casual shrug, which seems to irk him more. He's right. Too well dressed for a tour manager, but perfectly dressed for a pompous jazz musician in the throes of a creative breakdown, or one of those brooding child-prodigy composers that this industry is obsessed with, or worse, a classical music critic. What if he's from *BBC Music Magazine* and touring with us? Interviewing and reporting on the behind-the-scenes shenanigans?

Connie Cooper, lead soprano, snivelling, emotionally unstable hot mess. Just my luck to get off on the wrong foot with someone who could make or break my career.

4

I break eye contact with Luke to check Liam's messages.

> Well, that was weird.

Liam has also texted me several ghost and musical notes emojis.

> Make sure you keep me updated, otherwise I will assume some sort of Phantom of the Opera thing is going on.

Christ Almighty. I can feel cold, sticky tears drying on my face as I attempt to smooth my hair back into place and subtly give my cheeks a wipe. This man is a professional intimidator. I really hope he is not a reporter.

Before things escalate, it might be best to check. 'So what do you do exactly?' I ask. 'Besides hurrying people on to the coach.'

'Does it matter?'

Good question. 'It does if you're a music critic. Are you?'

'I understand this is your first classical tour?' he says, ignoring my question. 'Apparently, your audition moved everyone to tears.' Luke pauses to tilt his head. 'I can see why.'

My God. Is this going to haunt my career forever?

'Is there a reason you've followed me down the aisle?' I say, changing the subject. 'Don't you have any other musicians to interview and harass?'

He seems vaguely amused at this.

'I have to say. Considering this *is* my first tour with the Sinfonia, I'm not very impressed.' I look him square in the eye, fully aware that the pot is calling the kettle black.

'Touché,' he says calmly, not rising to the bait. For some reason, probably my own nerves, I find him instantly antagonising.

I should tell him to move and give me some space. One more inch and he'll be able to tell me what type of foundation I'm wearing. Powder. In hindsight, a cream would have been sturdier against the streaking. He watches me dab at my cheek.

Suddenly, a thought occurs. Of course – his posh, monogrammed handkerchief, which is screwed up in my hand. 'Oh. You've come to get this back,' I realise, holding it out. It is filthy with black mascara.

'Keep it. You seem the emotional sort. You may need it for your... frequent outbursts.'

'How do you know they are frequent?' I'm immediately rattled by his rudeness and the fact that the BBC could subject me to this impressive level of due diligence.

'Just a hunch.'

'Perhaps you could find a seat elsewhere,' I say. I'm fraught enough as it is. I don't need this level of stalker vibe from a complete stranger. 'I'll be happy to talk to you later once I've settled.'

'Perhaps I should introduce you to Dolly. She's the tour manager and also the designated welfare officer for the tour.'

'Why would I be needing a welfare officer, exactly? I'm perfectly well adjusted and capable of doing this tour.'

He's just seen me clinging on to Liam, begging him to take me back home and weeping my way on to the bus, but I'd hate to give the impression I'm incompetent and unable to hold my own on tour. And I could do with dropping the posh accent I've suddenly acquired. Lord knows where it has sprung up from.

He continues studying me as though he's going to paint my portrait for the National Gallery. 'You don't seem okay. You seem very on edge. Very *emotional*.'

I take a calming breath in and, through slightly gritted teeth, remain polite. 'I think you'll find it is *you* that has me on edge.'

Now he's got me being rude.

With an annoying smile, he says, 'I'll ask Dolly to keep an eye on you. Just in case.'

I roll my eyes. 'If she needs to keep an eye on anyone, it should be you.' He is really overstepping for a music critic.

In response, Luke relaxes even further into his seat, elbows on the armrests. It feels like a power play. I wish he'd move. His penetrating gaze is locked on mine like a nuclear missile, unblinking and equally unnerving. He tilts his head slowly, bringing his chin to rest on his steepled fingertips. He is obviously not going anywhere in a hurry and appears to be weighing me up. Trust me to end up with the tour lunatic.

I try to will him to move through a combination of staring straight back at him in a forceful manner and the power of my mind; however, it doesn't work. He is not budging an inch.

I can just imagine the headlines now. *Police confirm Connie Cooper, classical singer, found murdered in hotel room. Cause of death 'entirely victim's fault'. Reason: 'victim too polite'. Best friend mourns, 'If only she'd insisted crazed music critic switched seats.'*

I shift to get up. If he won't move, then I will.

He exhales sharply. 'Stay,' he says in such a commanding voice it causes me to obey. 'I'll go. We have obviously got off on the wrong foot.'

He's not wrong there. Hopefully, we'll be able to avoid each other for the whole tour. He might be attractive, but his condescending manner is highly irritating.

'Well, that concludes the welcome and induction. If you don't have any questions, I'll get back to Dolly. She'll be wondering where I've gone to,' he says, getting up. 'If you need anything at all, more handkerchiefs, a shoulder to cry on, some Xanax, we'll be down the front. We should arrive in two and a half hours.'

Patronising arsehole.

Luke gets up from his seat to walk down the aisle. I glare at the back of his head as he says hello to the people scattered further down the coach and receives lots of greetings and enquiries after his health and well-being. He must tour with the Sinfonia often and he seems popular, at least, which puts me more at ease. Workplace stalkers are loners. Everybody knows that.

* * *

The journey whizzes by with many text messages back and forth between me, Liam and Ged – they are worried for my emotional safety. Me and Tash – she is worried that my singing ability will be compromised (I'll try to show off) after a week with braying toffs. Me and Cherry – she is worried that I will forget how to sexy-dance (I was once described as a singing statue). Me and my dad – he is worried that my three singing jobs (the Royal Northern Sinfonia, Voices in Benidorm and Nancy's tours with the Dollz) and the constant gallivanting is too much for me after two solid years of barely leaving the house.

Phew. By the time I have convinced everyone who cares about me that I'm at my physical and emotional best, the coach has pulled up outside a grand-looking hotel in Manchester. I rise out of my seat and peer around at the serious faces of the passengers nearest to me. I can see a group of similarly dressed young women my age, sitting further towards the back. Unlike the Dollz on first sight, they aren't intimidating-looking and are probably the chorus line, therefore, hopefully nice and friendly.

A matronly pudding of a woman bellows up the aisle, 'Everybody off! Collect your room keys at reception. Dump your bags. Back on the coach in twenty minutes for rehearsals and soundcheck at the venue. Then back here for late lunch before the evening performance.'

The women from the back bustle down the aisle, smiling and chattering away. They have immaculate, glossy, assorted-toffee-coloured highlighted hair cascading around their deeply bronzed shoulders as though they've been lined up at a car spraying plant.

'Listen to Dolly barking orders at us.'

'She'd make a great baritone. She sounds more manly than the men.'

'She looks more manly than the men too.' This causes a wave of sniggering.

'Someone needs to have a word with her about those whiskery eyebrows and that pot belly. Just because she once toured with Pavarotti, she thinks it's okay to let herself go. What Luke sees in her, I'll never know.'

My ears are burning as I pretend to check my handbag for something.

'He's like an electric bike. Smooth, silent and fully charged,' one of them explains. 'I'm going to get on that saddle and ride him for hours and hours.'

The girls stop suddenly in the aisle right next to me.

'No way, Maddy. *I'm* going to get off with Luke. *Facto benito*,' says another.

'Stop pretending you speak Italian. I had first dibs on him, Florrie. I told you on the last tour. You know I did.' The one called Maddy frowns huffily.

'You said you were going to milk him like a cow, and you didn't. He's obviously not interested.' Florrie looks down at her through thick lashes.

'Pack it in, you two. Luke has never once looked at the pair of you in his life, never mind milking him dry.'

'What would you know, Trinny? You fancy him even more than we do,' Maddy snaps.

I watch them bicker all the way to the front.

Cripes. 'Milk him dry'? They are the Dollz in posh form. All I need is for them to start heavy drinking and pole dancing, and we're good to go.

When they pass by Luke, they give him big, horsey smiles as they trot down the aisle like show ponies. Dolly scowls at them and whispers something in his ear as soon as they have disembarked. Luke shakes his head, a faint grin playing on his lips. She must have to watch him like a hawk. As I follow the rest of the singers off the coach, I avoid eye contact with the pair of them, keeping my eyes trained on the floor.

'Not very friendly, is she?' I hear Dolly say, just as I'm about to fling myself down the stairs and hurry away. 'Although, you've had many a snooty singing partner. I'm sure you can handle her.'

Wait. I'm his what *now?*

My jaw falls slightly open as I'm stopped in my tracks mid-step. I turn slowly towards them. 'You're my what?'

'Oh, didn't I mention? I'm the lead tenor,' says Luke, looking distinctly unimpressed. 'Graduate of the National Conservatory of Music, one of a handful to reach an octave above middle C without breaking a sweat. You're insanely out of your depth, but do try not to feel *emotional* about it.'

What a cheek.

Even though it's a relief to know he's not from the BBC, I'm immediately incensed.

'Celebrated in over forty countries. Televised several times,' he continues to brag.

'Wow. Forty countries. And yet you manage to remain so modest,' I say. 'It's a wonder the Sinfonia can afford such a global superstar.'

I seem to have hit a nerve. He screws his eyes at me. 'Don't come crying to me when you can't keep up.'

Dolly's eyes are pinging back and forth.

'The only crying I'll be doing is with joy, when this tour is over,' I say tightly.

'Looking forward to that day already.'

I'm not even going to dignify that with a response. Instead, I blink deliberately slowly at him, the atmosphere growing increasingly hostile. How am I ever going to get through this tour with a partner like him?

'Time to go,' says Dolly, breaking up the spat. 'We don't want to be late.'

I scamper down the steps away from them. My heart is beating wildly. I am not great at confrontation at the best of times, never mind with an accomplished international singing star who obviously now hates me.

Luckily, there is a concierge who will deliver all of our heavy cases to our hotel rooms while we are in rehearsals. I just have time to join the massive queue to collect my key at reception, scroll through a variety of messages from the Dollz on how to confront perverts, stalkers and smug singing partners, take the lift to the third floor, open the door to my room, sweep my gaze around – basic but clean – and close it again... because my twenty minutes are up.

5

My nerves are completely on edge as I make my way up the steps to enter the theatre. There was an anxious silence on the coach all the way here from the hotel. Nobody spoke a word. It felt as though it would be bad luck to break it, so I couldn't ask anyone what was going on. Even when we arrived, and the other coach full of musicians spilled out, they filed into the theatre as though it was a funeral. The feeling is very disconcerting. I've never experienced anything like it in my life. No one is even making eye contact either. It's so strange. If I wasn't nervous before, I am bloody petrified now.

I follow the stragglers into the theatre, across the grand marble foyer, through some double doors marked 'Staff Only' and down a narrow, plushly carpeted corridor lined with antiquated wooden panels. We troop silently past baroque-style paintings hung on deep plum-coloured walls, through a curtained side entrance, into the dimly lit backstage area.

Luke is standing at the edge of the stage as I approach.

'Where's your wife?' I ask him. 'I need the running order from her.'

'My wife? You mean Dolly?'

'Yes, Dolly. Your wife, girlfriend, partner, significant other, soulmate, whatever.'

'Ah, that wife. She's on the other side,' he says, pointing to far stage right. He's not going to make this easy for me.

'Well, then, could you...?'

'Hmm?' He doesn't even bother looking at me.

'Could you tell me the running order?'

He sighs loudly. 'Running order?'

'Yes,' I snap in case he thinks I'm asking for directions to Zambia or instructions on how to cook a beef Wellington. 'The running order. So that I know when I'm coming on and what I'm singing.' *God, he's infuriating.*

'Places, everyone!' barks a sour-faced stage manager. A huge shuffle occurs while the chorists take their place on stage, musicians scurry to find their seats, a blur of limbs and instruments dashing in all directions. Amid the clunking and clicking, musical devices, gadgets and utensils are produced, instruments are tuned, violins screech, and Krzystzof Helmuth, the conductor, marches down the central aisle of the theatre. Like a drop of oil in water, people scatter, clearing a path, his dark robes flapping as he walks. His highly polished shoes make the squeaking sound of brand-new leather as he climbs the stairs and crosses the stage to the podium. He is small in both height and frame but has a big aura. He smooths back thin wisps of squiggly grey hair over his balding head, as he sweeps his beady child-catcher gaze around the orchestra.

A sudden hush falls across the entire theatre as the lights dim. The conductor taps his long, beaky nose with his baton four times and clears his throat noisily before flicking the sheet music back and forth. He is deep in concentration.

Flick. Flick. Flick.

Is this code? Am I supposed to know what is going on? Who is in charge?

I stand rigid at the side of the stage, unsure of where I am supposed to be. Luke seems to have disappeared and the temperature has suddenly plummeted to zero degrees. All we can hear is the rustling of the sheet music. My nerves are wound tight as I witness everyone in the orchestra looking anxious. Suddenly, from out of nowhere, one of the chorus girls leans in to murmur in my ear, making me jump with fright.

'It's his ritual. The nose tap. It grounds him.'

'Okay. Thanks for letting me know. But next time, try not to sneak up on me. You nearly gave me a heart attack,' I hiss, keeping my eyes glued to the back of the conductor. He twists around to give me an unforgiving stare. He must have the hearing of a barn owl. He has heard us whispering, and we have broken his concentration. I rotate slowly to find the perpetrator has sunk into the shadows, nowhere to be seen. I swallow nervously as the conductor continues to bore holes into me with the concentrated look of a great white shark. He is livid.

He shakes his head with a sigh and continues flicking the pages back and forth before landing on one that agrees with him. He studies it in deadly silence.

He taps his nose again with the baton, throwing me a sly side-eye. I have obviously interrupted his OCD routine, and this is the price I must pay. The lights dim further.

A single bright spotlight shines down on him. He is terrifying. He's lifting his arms dramatically and pointing his wand high in the air, just as I feel the warm tickle of hot breath in my ear again. It makes me jump out of my skin.

'*Expelliarmus!*' My voice echoes out across the whole auditorium at an ear-splitting pitch.

There's a deafening silence as my voice takes an eternity to bounce off every conceivable surface. The acoustics here are unforgivably world-class. Seconds later, it's still floating around like a disgruntled ghost. '*Expelliarmus... mus... mus!*'

Fuckedy fuck.

I catch a flash of amusement on the chorus girl's face as she steps away from me. Like a scene from a horror movie, the conductor spins slowly in my direction. His eyes bulge from their sockets. I swallow the huge lump in my throat, feeling the weight of every single pair of eyes on me.

Luke steps towards me with an incredulous look on his face. 'What the fuck was that?'

* * *

Three hours later, I flop down onto the hotel bed. 'It can't have gone that badly,' soothes Ged as I bawl down the phone at him. 'Besides, that's what rehearsals are for. To get all the nerves out of the way before the big show.'

'And at least you made a lasting impression!' I hear Liam yelling from a distance. 'Although I think Wingardium Leviosa would have gone down better.'

Ged stifles a giggle. 'That was quite the knee-jerk reaction. What's the cure for magical Tourette's?'

'It's not funny,' I snap. 'I have to face the Maestro, and everyone else in less than two hours. He hates me. And it was all the chorus girl's fault. *And* I still need to get into costume and do my hair and make-up. I'm stressed to bits!'

I'm yelling. Thank God this is a decent hotel, otherwise the walls would be paper thin.

'Why did I ever apply for this bloody job? I hate it! It's horrible! Everyone is so creepy and out to get me!'

There's a thump from next door that rattles the lamp.

'Charming!' a woman yells back through the wall. They are not as solid as they look. It sounds like Dolly.

Oh, my God.

I whisper to Ged that I've been overheard by the tour manager, and this sets him off giggling even more. 'Christ, Connie, love. Why do you always turn everything into such a drama? Do you think, on some level, you're addicted to catastrophising your life?'

He might have a point.

'Or is it some sort of attention-seeking disorder? I dread to imagine what she'll be like in Las Vegas,' shouts Liam, expertly bringing the focus back to himself. 'Anything could happen! Anything from licking cocaine off Harry Styles's smooth chest at some wild penthouse party to waking up naked in the desert chained to a giant Bengal tiger.'

'No. Not on my watch,' I say, glad of the distraction. 'I will have every minute accounted for.'

'Between Connie and the Dollz, we'll be lucky if someone doesn't end up in a cell for the night or upsetting a mobster, and we have to run for our lives,' says Ged, laughing.

Oh. My. God. They are confusing a relatively mild week of enjoying the tourist attractions with *The Hangover*. They are also assuming that I've had two minutes to even think about their pre-moon.

'Can you send the schedule ASAP, please? I need to know how much gambling time you've allocated between activities. And Liam is desperate to include a haunted massage.'

'Sorry? A what now?'

'Ghosts do the massage apparently,' says Ged, trying to disguise a hint of exasperation. But he'd do anything for Liam. 'Unless you've already booked us one?'

'Unless I've already booked you a *haunted* massage?' I repeat. What type of pre-moon are they expecting? 'Guys. Maybe it's time we managed your expectations. I'd hate for you to—'

'Ignore him. He's trying to micromanage again. Ged, you promised me you wouldn't. Just let Connie get on with it. But you have included a helicopter ride though, haven't you, babes? And a celebrity house tour?'

They are as bad as each other.

I hurry them off the phone and get to work on my outfit, nerves shredded like confetti. The last thing I need to think about is spending the whole time in Las Vegas at the police station or at a seance or at the morgue identifying chewed body parts because they've been eaten by a bloody tiger.

I'm very much praying that I will be spending most of my time with Matteo.

PING.

Matteo has sent me a message to say good luck. He has called me his Cenicienta and has signed off as Mr Window Seat, our nicknames for each other. My heart skips at the thought of seeing him again. Lovely, reassuring Matteo with his high standards and his moody stare and his incredibly toned abs. I daydream about how we first met on the plane to Alicante. How I spilled scalding-hot coffee on his crotch, how I kicked him in the face trying to impress him with my pole dancing, how we ruined nearly all of his shows with our unprofessionalism, and how utterly and devastatingly thoughtful, kind and gorgeous he is. My mind wanders back to the moment he first kissed me. As soon as he cupped my face, a current swept through me so strong that I had flinched in surprise, and when I gazed into his eyes, I could see he had felt it too. When he leaned in to softly graze my lips with his own, it was as though we became lost in each other. It was a truly enchanting moment that seemed to last forever.

Christ. I hope he does not want to kiss Birdie like that with her honey-skinned face and smooth, plumped-up lips. *I must refrain from repeatedly googling images of her.* I have heard the French like to get their tongues in there, like a dentist exploring the roof of the mouth for signs of gum disease. I couldn't possibly compete!

I snap myself out of the trance.

Gah! Half an hour! Disappeared just like that!

* * *

By the time I hurry out to the coach, everyone else is already on board. Luke is tapping an imaginary watch on his wrist, and Dolly is sullen. The mood is tense. She purses her lips as I slide by. 'It's a baton, not a *wand.*'

'Thanks,' I say, attempting a smile. 'I'll try not to cast any more spells with it.'

I'm relieved to see her face soften a fraction. I continue my walk of shame up the aisle, hot with humiliation as no one dares make eye contact with me. I find an empty seat and plonk myself down. As soon as the coach sets off, the layers of chatter begin among the choir members, and I feel myself calm.

How did my mother enjoy doing this? She never once mentioned nose-tapping, humourless conductors or overbearing, time-obsessed singing partners.

Good job I can be tough and resilient when I need to be. Just because I've upset everyone on my first day does not mean I'm a quitter. I will show them exactly why they hired me. I have the voice of an angel and a vocal range second to none. I will own that stage tonight and mesmerise my audience. I will leave them captivated and begging for more.

That's the plan anyway.

Fifteen minutes later, we are pulling up outside the centuries-old, grand-looking stone theatre. I'm last to get off the bus, and Dolly and Luke are waiting for me.

'Connie,' she says. 'We haven't been properly introduced. I'm Dolly. The tour manager. I just wanted to say...'

Here we go.

'Despite getting off to such a bad start, we're all excited to see what you can do.'

The surprise at her kind tone makes my nerves lessen. 'Thank you. And sorry about earlier. The shouting. And the name-calling. And the ruining of the rehearsal.'

A smile tugs at her lips. 'The first tour is always difficult. There's a lot to get used to. The Maestro has... his process. And he can be intense.'

He's not the only one. I'm very aware of Luke towering silently over us. Without looking at him, I explain, 'One of the chorus girls thought it was funny to spook me while the Maestro was trying to prepare himself. It threw me off guard.'

Without missing a beat, Luke agrees. 'Yes. I'm sure she did.'

He doesn't believe me.

'You certainly sounded *off guard*,' he says, his face unreadable. 'Now, I have a reputation to uphold. Just because you act like an amateur, could you at least try not to sing like one?'

I immediately tense. 'Excuse me? That's a bit rude.'

Dolly seems to sense a falling-out. 'The chorus are very good at that. Distracting people. Some more than others.' She elbows Luke in the side good-naturedly, but he doesn't react. He continues glaring at me.

We watch Dolly clamber down the steps.

PING.

Luke raises an eyebrow, almost daring me to check my phone.

A message has popped up on my screen. It's a reassuring mantra from Tash.

> When you're up on stage, don't just picture the audience naked, picture the leading man naked because that's how he'll be picturing you, babes. You've got this.

Oh, my word.

'What's so important?' he snaps.

'Nothing. Nothing at all,' I say, clamping my phone to my chest and trying not to picture him naked.

'Well, do you think you could possibly put your phone away for two minutes and do the job you're being paid to do?'

For someone so accomplished, he's incredibly hostile.

6

Once I've warmed up my voice, humming do-re-mi up the scale and back down, a few lip trills and yawn-sighs, am in costume and ready to go on stage, I snake my way through the back corridors and up the steps to the wings. The orchestra is doing a final last-minute tuning of instruments. The chorus girls are in place, standing in front of the full choir. They will harmonise, blend and complement my vocals where needed to elevate the overall impact of a song and be backed by the choir for those big set pieces where we need depth, richness and complexity for the wide range of musical compositions we will perform throughout the show. They are all in variations of black dresses. Long, short, sparkling and chiffon. They are in stark contrast to me, in my ruby-red gown with its heavy skirts and sequined bodice. My shiny hair is swept elegantly over one shoulder, cascading waves undulating down to my waist, thanks to some false hairpieces and a whole can of hairspray. My make-up is glamorous, like a 1950s Audrey Hepburn. After I asked for her help, Dolly had gasped admiringly when she fastened up the back of the gown and I stood looking at my reflection in the mirror. I barely recognised myself.

Liam is right. It's all about confidence. And even though I don't have much of it at the moment, I need to find some before I step out on that stage tonight. A noise to my left distracts me. It is the Maestro, half hidden by a sweeping black curtain, hunched over a large packing crate of some sort. He is flipping through sheet music while picking up batons from a leather case and brandishing them, flicking them in the air sharply before carefully replacing them in the box. I owe him a humungous apology for the terrible first (arriving late and weeping on to the bus) and second (destroying the rehearsal with my accidental outburst) impressions.

'Excuse me, Mr Helmuth,' I say gingerly. 'I'd like to apologi—'

He jerks violently at the sound of my voice as though I've zapped him with a thousand volts. It sends the box of batons crashing to the ground. I gasp loudly, instantly flinging myself down on my knees to gather them up as they begin to roll away like unruly chopsticks.

'Sorry. I think that's them all,' I say, looking up at him as I place them hurriedly back in the box. He is drained of colour as I rise slowly to my feet, the billowing gown weighing heavily and impeding my progress. I put the box in front of him and notice his bony fingers now balled into tight fists, a sheet of music scrunched in each hand.

'I wondered if we might try a high C in the final aria when—' I say, interrupting the terse silence.

'No,' he snaps. 'Absolutely not.'

'It's just that changing suddenly from—'

'Can't be done!'

'But if you...' The words die on my lips at his unnerving death stare. I step backwards and scurry to the opposite side of the stage.

Literally everyone hates me.

My nerves are wound as tight as a snare drum. I sweep my gaze around and spot Luke immediately. He is standing by the curtain, peeking out to see the audience filling up seats. I can't sing with him while he dislikes me so much. I need to tackle him head on. Plucking up some courage, I tap him gently on the shoulder. I'm expecting animosity but his eyes widen like saucers when he sees me. He looks me up and down several times before saying, 'Good God, Connie. Is that you?' I have no idea whether he is being sarcastic.

I take a deep calming breath, ready to be the grown-up here. 'I'm sorry I ruined the rehearsal,' I say to him. 'But I assure you, I'll be fine once I'm on stage.' *If the Maestro doesn't kill me first.*

Luke absorbs this information, studying my face, perhaps for signs of nerves.

'You're right. I am nervous,' I confirm. 'It's my first time singing with a partner. It's my first time on a classical tour. And it's the opening night. Now, I know you don't like me but you either work with me on this or' – I look up at him in earnest – 'or the show is going to be a huge flop.'

I see him visibly swallow. Perhaps his international reputation is being ripped to shreds and is floating before his eyes. Whatever it is, he nods curtly and clears his throat. 'No. I'm the one who needs to apologise. I've been terribly rude,' he says tightly. Then with a sigh, he rakes a hand through his hair. 'I guess I'm nervous about singing with you too.'

'You're nervous? About singing with me?'

He nods.

'Why?'

'Because you're unpredictable. You're reckless. You have no idea what you're doing.'

How depressingly accurate. But that sliver of vulnerability is all I need to connect with him. I smile and lean in. 'You've every right to feel nervous. I'm going all out to reduce you to tears.'

For the first time, I see a genuine smile pull at his lips. He almost looks as though he is blushing. 'I deserve that. Sorry I've been so harsh towards you. I have a lot going on in my life at the moment. I guess you're not seeing the best version of me.'

He thinks *he* has a lot going on! Try organising a pre-moon spree for two divas and sourcing tasteful nipple tassels for a string of Las Vegas shows you don't want to do. Still, I'm warming to him.

'Let's start over. I'm Connie. Classical singer by day. Netflix and wine enthusiast by night.'

He tentatively shakes my hand. 'Luke. Highly acclaimed and decorated tenor by day. Renowned international Lothario by night.'

I roll my eyes.

An unexpected chuckle escapes from his lips as the house lights dim. Suddenly, the orchestra springs to life and the curtain begins to rise slowly. Butterflies invade my stomach as I ball my fists and clench them to my sides. I watch the world's current leading conductor, Krzysztof Helmuth, walk calmly onto the stage to take a bow. Like lightning he whips his baton in the air and the show commences.

Deep breaths.

Deep breaths.

My chest is rising and falling but I can't seem to get enough air. Luke steps towards me, his face serious. He is mouthing, 'It's okay. You'll be fine.'

In the next moment, the Maestro is introducing us while I successfully manage to avoid his gaze. Luke holds out a steady hand. 'Come and meet your audience.'

We glide onto the stage. I try not to panic when I see how many people there are. They look just the sort to be picturing me naked. I curtsy to the audience, and Luke bows before we turn to each other. His eyes lock on to mine, forcing my attention to stay on him. I hear the opening bars of my aria and open my mouth to sing.

Oh, God. I'm too quiet, too gentle.

Luke guides me expertly into the duet, matching my tone, and before I know it, he has me belting out the song at the top of my lungs. I don't know how he is managing it, but we are in perfect harmony. Not a note out of place. You can hear a pin drop at the end of it. It is the most thrilling experience I've had since the Benidorm music festival. The Maestro looks begrudgingly surprised. He gives us a half-smile before carrying straight on to the next movement.

* * *

Three and a half hours later, it's all over. I peer out at the audience.

Luke keeps looking at me and shaking his head in disbelief. We are holding hands in a strictly professional manner and taking our fifth and final bow, to a standing ovation. Even the Maestro has a smile hovering on his lips as I accept a ginormous bouquet of flowers.

'From the theatre,' Luke explains at my surprise before he bellows to the audience, above the roaring applause, 'Maestro!' to which the conductor takes a solitary bow. We all clap dutifully towards him. The choir beams radiantly as they applaud him, and we are rewarded with a thinly arched eyebrow raise. The musicians take a collective bow after we walk off stage, and finally, the curtain goes down, and the house lights come back on.

Luke stares at me. 'Well, aren't you full of surprises?'

Before I can reply, he is mobbed, and I am roughly elbowed out of the way.

'Luke, you were amaze, hun. Amaze,' says Florrie, one of the three lead chorus girls who stand in front of the main choir on stage. 'Everyone, wasn't he just *amaze*?'

'As were you, delightful ladies. Flawless backing vocals as ever,' Luke says smoothly.

'We're celebrating the opening night at Chinawhite,' says Maddy, thrusting herself at him with wide, slow-blinking eyes. 'They've given us the whole VIP section.'

'We're going to let off steam,' croons Trinny. She is giving him some serious eye contact too. 'You coming?'

Luke takes a while to respond, keeping them in suspense. He lets out an audible sigh. 'Sure.' The girls shriek excitedly and cling to him as though he has just agreed to shower them with highest-grade, flawless diamonds. I've suddenly become invisible. Not one of them has commented on my performance. Nor our five standing ovations.

'But only if Connie will come too.' Luke stands, waiting for me to reply. He has something like a sheepish look on his face.

'Who?' says Trinny, following his gaze to me.

'That's okay,' I say, a little caught by surprise. 'I thought I'd... sort of have an early night. Rest my voice. Besides, I'd hate to get pranked again.' I don't need a pity invite and I certainly don't want to hang out with these chorus girls. I can see Trinny eyeing the others with relief.

'Sorry, I wasn't thinking,' says Luke, seeming flustered. 'Of course you need an early night. I just wanted to, well, apologise for my behaviour earlier today, and to celebrate what is probably the most spectacular opening night we've ever had. All thanks to you.'

'Wow,' I say, thrown by his change of demeanour. 'Erm, that's very kind of you to say.'

Luke shrugs. 'You were exceptional, Connie. Truly exceptional.'

I gulp, not sure how to respond. 'You were very good too.'

A puff of air escapes from Luke's mouth. 'Thank you. You're too kind.'

It causes me to giggle. I have a ridiculous amount of adrenaline coursing through my veins. 'Sorry. I meant you were brilliant. Amazing. Amaze. Very amaze.' I'm being sarcastic towards the girls, but I can't help it.

Luke's face instantly softens. His smile transforms his face. 'Perhaps I should have an early night too then. Save myself for tomorrow.'

Trinny lets out a noticeable groan of frustration and digs Florrie in the ribs. 'But it's a Sinfonia tradition.' She raises her voice as the entire ensemble trundles past us with their instruments. 'You have to respect the customs, I'm afraid!' she shouts at me as though I've insulted them all. 'It's terribly bad luck if you don't come, Connie.'

'Please come with us!' yells Florrie, changing her tune. 'It'll be fun. I'm sorry I pranked you. Besides, you'll get free drinks.'

'Only because Luke buys bottles and bottles of champagne for us,' says Trinny, tugging at his arm. 'Because he's so kind and generous.'

The girls start giggling while Luke looks uncomfortable. 'How about we do an hour of obligatory backslapping, for the sake of Sinfonia tradition, while you protect me from these chorus girls, and then I promise to return you to the hotel?' he says to me. 'I'm sure the Maestro would appreciate it. You certainly gave him a run for his money tonight.'

'Please?' the girls say in unison. Even though they clearly would rather I didn't, I'd hate to keep upsetting them all. I've done enough of that already. They are looking up at Luke with big cow eyes, which immediately reminds me that they all want to get their hands on him and milk him dry.

I shake the image from my mind. 'Okay. I'll go get changed,' I say, turning to leave.

* * *

My ears are still ringing as I flop down into my dressing room chair and stare at myself. I have my own dressing room! The light bulbs framing the mirror give me an ethereal glow, which makes my skin seem other-worldly. My eyes sparkle with energy. The ruby-red sequins of my fitted, full-length costume are twinkling. They highlight my matching ruby-red lips, made to look plump and glossy under the stage lights. I could be in any decade. Timeless. I understand now why my mother loved her career with a passion. It was like I became possessed while I was on stage. One minute, I was petrified, and the next, I was shining so brightly that I dazzled the audience into rapt attention, feeding off their energy, my voice soaring to the furthest reaches of the gods. I was consumed with the need to fill every single bit of space in the theatre. I may have accidentally missed a few cues and come in a split second late, but I doubt anyone except the Maestro would have noticed.

And then suddenly, it was all over. Like a dream.

I whip out my phone to take a selfie and send it to Matteo with the caption, *Smashed it.*

Luke's wife bursts through the door and shouts at me. 'Constance Cooper! I have been tour manager for over twenty years, and I can honestly say...'

Oh, Christ. Here we go. What have I done wrong now?

'...that was the best performance the Sinfonia has ever seen! It was like having your mother back on stage. You were exquisite.'

I stare at her as she visibly catches her breath.

'Really?' I manage, with a slight choke. That is the best thing anyone could say to me. I immediately warm to her. 'You knew my mother?'

Her face lights up. 'She was lovely to me when I first started out as a trainee. We toured together many times. I was so sorry she passed. I came to the funeral, but I guess you won't remember.'

I shake my head. That is one day that I'll only ever remember fragments of. It passed slowly, seconds ticking by while I walked about in a horrible, numb fog, not knowing what to do with myself.

'She'd be so proud to see you up on stage.'

I smile back, grateful for the compliment.

'Luke will have to seriously up his game after tonight. He won't want to be outshone like that every night,' she says, lightening the mood. 'The way you sang "Mi Amore Mi Amore",' she gushes. 'There wasn't a dry eye in the house.'

She holds a hand to her chest. 'You were mesmerising. Just watch out he doesn't fall head over heels in love with you.' She rolls her eyes in a jokey fashion.

'Who do you mean?'

'Luke. You're just his type. Unpretentious, supremely talented...' Breathing under control, she looks me up and down. '...and so beautiful.'

What is going on here?

I'm reminded of the chorus girls wanting to ride him like a bike. It must be a constant struggle for her.

'You've no worries on my account, Dolly. I'm sure your husband won't ever feel that way about me.'

'Husband? Husband? As if!' Dolly sounds appalled. 'I'm not his wife. Who told you that?'

I'm slightly taken aback.

'Erm. He did.'

7

'Aren't you coming to the club?' I ask Dolly as we make our way to the side entrance.

She shakes her head. 'I need to be up early. Loads to do. You go ahead. You earned it.'

'But I thought it was bad luck. Everyone in the ensemble has to toast the opening night. It's a tradition.'

Dolly shrugs, confused. 'Never heard of it. Anyway, remember what I said about—' I follow her eyes to Luke, who is waiting at the taxi rank nearby, surrounded by girls. She has already warned me to take what Luke says with a pinch of salt – the whole 'wife' misunderstanding as a case in point, as he is prone to charming everyone around him and saying things they want to hear.

'You've no worries there, Dolly. I'm pretty sure we won't get along off stage. We're too different. He's too...'

As though he has sensed we are talking about him, Luke suddenly turns in our direction. He smiles warmly at Dolly before being distracted.

'Luke. Come with us in our taxi!' shouts one of the chorus girls. They are dressed in skimpy outfits and towering stilettoes. I lose sight of them in the hustle and bustle, as more and more musicians pile out of the door as though a starter gun has gone off and the last one to get a cab has to walk home over flaming-hot coals. The line of waiting taxis is rapidly disappearing.

I look pleadingly at Dolly. 'Please come.'

Florrie suddenly appears beside me to tut loudly. 'Who, Dolly? She never comes. She hates dancing and having a good time. Hurry, Luke doesn't like to be kept waiting.'

As she drags me away, Dolly smiles tightly. 'Have a great night.'

We battle our way through the remaining crowd, Florrie darting ahead. I can't see, but I can hear car doors slamming and engines roaring and quite a lot of beeping, as people spill out in front of the opera house. Its huge stone pillars are packed with theatregoers and Sinfonia singers and musicians. I'm just about clearing the crowd when I'm knocked sideways by one of the musicians carrying a double bass over his back. I go careering into the people at my side, only to realise at the last second that they've parted ways to let me fall right through them onto the road. I'm toppling backwards into actual moving traffic when two things happen at once. A massive horn blows, which appears to be from the vicinity of the headlights hurtling towards me, and a strong hand swoops from nowhere to grab my arm, yanking me back from being mowed down by a passing double-decker bus.

Loud shrieks from the crowd drown out my own choked attempt at a scream. My hand flies to my chest. I can barely catch my breath. My eyes travel up to meet those of my saviour, and in that instant, I know that things will never be quite the same between Luke and me again.

* * *

'He's love-bombing you,' explains Ged on a video call later that evening. 'Why else would he buy you the most expensive champagne and insist on a limo to take you back to the hotel? Now, tell me again how he's suddenly gone from zero to hero in the space of a few hours?'

I put Ged on speaker as I sit and take off all my make-up. He's playing devil's advocate because Liam has gone full-on man-crush crazy for Luke since he saved my life.

'Well, he began by saving my life... so there is that, of course. He *was* quite the hero.'

'I can't believe he saved your life! It's textbook romcom!' Liam appears and yells excitedly into the phone. 'You'll have to bloody marry him now.'

'I think you'll find she's wildly in love with Matteo, Liam. Don't confuse her,' Ged says, as though my head could be turned so easily.

'And he also said that because of me, the Sinfonia had had the best opening night in recorded history.' I can't help gloating.

'What if meeting him is fate? Destiny?' asks Liam. He's become very invested, very quickly.

'Hmmm.' Ged frowns. 'Or... maybe it's too much of a coincidence how he just happened to be in the exact right place at the exact right time. What are the chances that Luke fought his way through the crowd at breakneck speed to become a have-a-go hero?'

Liam inhales loudly. 'What are you insinuating?'

'Another option could be that he's a highly functioning sociopath,' Ged says, throwing himself into the role.

What an exhausting night it has been. Euphoric in one way and completely overwhelming in others. 'It felt heroic and *coincidental* at the time, if that helps. I mean, it all happened so incredibly fast, I can hardly believe it either, but he was the perfect gentleman all night. I swear.'

'I'll be the judge of that. Let's start from the beginning.'

'Well, by the time I got changed and went to the stage door, most of the musicians had already left in the taxis. Fortunately, Luke waited for me.'

'Convenient.'

'He means gallant,' says Liam.

'Then, after he saved me from going under a bus, he insisted on taking me back inside the theatre to sit down because I was a bit shaken.'

'Like a stalker isolating its prey, yes, yes...'

'Like a gentleman, he means.' Liam is having none of it. 'Ignore him.'

'But I didn't want any fuss because literally everyone was staring at us, so we got in the next taxi. And when we arrived at the club, he went straight to the bar to get me a stiff drink.'

'I think I can guess where this is leading,' Ged says. 'Was it spiked?'

I ignore him. 'Then, he introduced me to some dame or other, who is patron of the Royal Opera House in London, and she asked if Luke and I would consider an exclusive performance in front of the Royal Family for some anniversary they are organising.' My mind is still blown.

'Where did this conversation take place exactly?'

'In a private room at the club. It made sense to sit together... in a booth... away from the noise. Because of the shock from earlier.'

'Cosy. Go on,' Ged says, suddenly sounding like a chief inspector. 'What happened next?'

'I tried to make casual conversation and mentioned that Dolly, the tour manager—'

'Is Dolly the woman who looks like a pudding?'

I nod guiltily. I'm a woman's woman. I need to start thinking like one. I will start by being more charitable towards Dolly. She has to be everything to everyone all at once.

'Dolly, the woman who previously claimed that she was not his wife? Yet conveniently failed to testify if he was married or unmarried?'

This is not the time to pull him on his semantics. 'She has a really busy job. It's like herding cats, she says. Especially now she has to help me get into my costumes. I should have gone for dresses that didn't require me to be double-jointed.'

'Let's stick to the facts.'

'Ged, this isn't a police report.'

'Tell that to the judge when all of this goes to court.' He's transforming into Judge Judy before my very eyes. And, by his admiring expression, Liam seems to quite like it. 'We need clarification. What did he say?'

I peel off my eyelashes and put them in the pot beside me for tomorrow and make a start on wiping off the strong eyebrows with cotton-wool pads and glance down to see their faces, cheek to cheek, on my phone. 'Well, I said to Luke, "Dolly told me she wasn't your actual wife." And he said, "No, of course she isn't. It was you who called her my wife. Anyway, she's gay." Then I said, "Oh really? That's nice." Because now I think back, I did refer to Dolly as his wife, but then he did play along with me, which was a bit misleading. So I said, "You really must be clearer when declaring your relationship status." Then he looked confused and turned back to talk to Dame whatever she was called. He thinks we should definitely do a private performance for the Royal Family because it would open all sorts of doors for me.'

'And you still don't know if he is married?'

I shake my head.

'Does he wear a ring or give off married vibes?'

'No, but I suppose that isn't evidence of being married these days. Anyway, like I said. There's nothing to worry about. He saved my life; I'll be forever grateful, and we're singing partners. Nothing more. Hardly seems relevant anyway, seeing as I'm not interested in him like that. He's no match for Matteo.'

Ged ignores me. He's seen how ridiculously good-looking Luke is for himself. 'Well, it's great that he was there to save your life, but I'd watch out for him. Something doesn't add up. And his eyes are too far apart. Still, well done tonight. I knew you'd smash it. We're very proud of you. Can't wait to see you at the end of the tour.'

'Now get plenty of sleep,' Liam says, blowing me a kiss. 'You have a big day of avoiding temptation tomorrow.'

'But I don't find him remotely—'

Ged has clicked off the call.

* * *

The next morning, I drift down to the hotel breakfast room feeling a little smug with myself. I really did give a top-notch performance last night. I wish I could ring Matteo and tell him all about it. Instead, I left him a rather excitable voice-mail. Hopefully, the Sinfonia will feature me on their website today, and I can send him the link. I hope they have a photo of me singing in that ruby-red costume. It was divine. I looked amazing in it.

'Hey, Constance,' Dolly calls over to me. 'You're late. And what did I tell you last night about not getting involved with Luke? Now BBC Radio Manchester wants an interview with the pair of you later this morning. Maestro is not pleased, let me tell you.'

'Is this about Luke saving my life?'

'Saving your life? No. He never mentioned that. It's the other thing.' She shakes her head as though I've done something I shouldn't and returns her attention to the plate piled high with eggs and sausage in front of her.

I have no idea what she means, but as I walk towards the buffet counter and pick up a hot plate, a hush settles across the dining area, and I feel like I'm being watched. I circle slowly while musicians and choir members whip their heads away, busying themselves, poking food around on their plates. There is definitely an atmosphere.

The only people not inspecting their continental and full English breakfasts are the group of chorus girls who are regarding me with cold and hostile expressions.

I grab a few pastries and sit down at Dolly's table. 'You haven't seen the reviews,' she says. 'Have you?'

'No, not yet.' I won't bother telling her that I didn't think newspapers covered opera any more. Who reads them anyway?

'They're over there.' She nods to a table covered in today's newspapers.

I get up and go over to the table. Nobody is even trying to pretend they're not watching me. The papers are spread out, open at the appropriate review sections.

Shitting, shitting hell.

* * *

Once back in my hotel room, I'm straight on the phone to Ged. His lovely face pops up on my screen immediately, and I sweep the camera over the newspapers so he can take in the headlines.

'Oh my God! What will I do?' I plead.

'Calm down. Matteo's in LA. He's not going to see you making out on stage with the UK's most fanciable tenor. Although, those headlines are a bit much.'

'I can't believe this is happening. It's a nightmare. And I wasn't making out with him. We were acting. Immersed in the part. "Mi Amore Mi Amore" is quite demanding, emotionally.'

'Hmmm. I'm sure it is, love. But the pictures do make it look like you're about to kiss.'

'It's the angle. I don't even know who took those pictures.'

I stare blankly at my face glowing up from the tabloids. The reviews are incredible. It's the headlines that are the worry. And the accompanying pictures of me gazing lovingly at Luke mid-song that they've chosen to print. *Ravishing Royal Rival.* The gist of it is opera's newest power couple brings the house down while Lady Hermione Greene, who just happens to be related to the Royal Family, looks forlornly at us from the imperial box. I examine the pictures of Luke and me on stage, practically in each other's arms, singing, while she gazes at us with a wistful expression on her face. She was probably caught up in the emotion. You could hear a pin drop once that aria was over. The article insinuates that the three of us are swept up in a royal love triangle. There are false accusations that I have stolen Lady Hermione's first love away from her. There is hardly any mention of the world's current leading conductor, Krzystzof Helmuth, or the world-class Sinfonia musicians.

'That's certainly one way to get yourself noticed,' says Ged.

Judging by the hostile reaction of everyone downstairs, after only one night I have alienated the entire ensemble of singers and musicians, the tour manager and our precious Maestro yet again.

'Is any of it true? Did Luke mention that he went to school with one of the Royals?' Ged asks, still collecting evidence. 'Were they really childhood sweethearts? Does she still have a crush on him?'

'How would I know? I only met him yesterday! We're not at the "can you list your entire previous relationship history in chronological order starting from age seven" or "how do you feel about throuples" stage yet. Besides, I haven't seen him today. He could be furious about it.'

'Or he could be the one behind it. Orchestrating his own publicity. Like you say, we don't know him.'

'What if Matteo sees it?' I say. After all, we never did discuss whether our relationship is exclusive or not.

'Matteo isn't daft. He'll know it's just clickbait. You could try ringing him to explain.'

'He said his phone will be switched off most of the week. Do you think this is important enough to disturb him?'

'Depends. Which artist is Matteo working with? Did he say?'

'No. It's top secret. He's signed an—'

'An NDA! Fucking hell, Connie. Please let it be Harry. Or Tay Tay! Birdie produced two songs on her last album. Las Vegas is literally five minutes away from LA.'

Oh, dear. Here we go. 'I'm sure it is if you go by private jet, and even if it was, there's no way either of them will want to be invited to the stag do.'

'Pre-moon spree, dear. And could you at least try to get on board? You are best woman,' Ged reminds me.

Suddenly, the colossal number of things I need to do hits me. Costumes, hair, nails and song lists to sort for Benidorm next week. Costumes, song lists, pre-moon spree venues and activities to sort for Las Vegas the week after that.

At least it will keep me busy and out of the press.

'I'll try and find out.' I blow him a kiss and see his face light up. 'I will make sure you have the most amazing time ever. I promise.'

We are disturbed by a gentle knock at my door.

'Who is it?' I call out.

'It's me, Luke. Can I come in, please?' He does not sound happy. 'There are a few things we need to discuss.'

I turn back to my phone screen. Ged is very concerned. 'Connie. Do not let him in, whatever you do. Okay? I know he saved your life but I have a bad feeling about him,' he warns me. 'Send him away. This is no time for politeness or manners.'

8

The knocking continues. 'Connie?'

Oh, God. I gingerly open the door and poke my head through the crack.

'I wanted to check you were okay,' says Luke with a serious expression.

'I'm fine. Just a little disturbed at the, um... headlines.'

He studies my face before exhaling loudly and clamping his hands together on top of his head. I try to keep my eyes away from his T-shirt riding up to reveal a glimpse of taut stomach. 'It sure is quite the story. Can we talk about it?'

Cripes. I'm battling with the urge to be polite. It's not Luke's fault he's so photogenic and everyone fancies him. He's just been blessed with one of those faces that, the more you stare at it, the more good-looking it becomes. Especially when you're singing romantic ballads on stage together, and your noses are an inch apart. He's a little overwhelming, to be honest. If only that musician had watched where he was shoving his massive double bass, then there wouldn't have been any need for anyone to save me. I open the door a fraction wider.

His face softens. 'I'm sorry you got dragged into it. I don't know where they got their information from.'

'Me neither.'

'You look incredible, by the way.'

'Sorry?'

He points down at the newspaper in my hand. 'In the papers. You look vibrant. Timeless.'

I've always responded well to flattery. Especially from distinguished, international opera singers. Singers who have performed in over forty countries. I can literally hear the horn section trumpeting in my brain. Bunting is being liberally strung up around my cerebral cortex. Brass bands are on the march across my cranium.

'So, should I come in?' Luke tilts his head. 'We may need a game plan.'

His manners are impeccable. And yet alarm bells are ringing faintly somewhere in the distance.

'No. Absolutely not,' I say a little too forcefully. 'I mean...' What do I mean? My mind is like scrambled egg... 'Maybe. Yes.' We probably should at least discuss the article. *Gawd.* Or perhaps not. 'Actually, no. I'm busy at the moment.'

He raises his eyebrows as though he doesn't believe me. 'You are aware that you just gave every possible answer there is to that question.'

How did I not notice his blue eyes have flecks of gold in them?

'I don't think that would be a very good idea under the circumstances,' booms Dolly. She has appeared out of nowhere, with my ruby-red dress over her arm. 'Here. It's been dry-cleaned ready for tonight. Krzystzof... I mean, the Maestro, has suggested you do not go out today in case any press are lurking.'

Relief floods through me.

'He's not happy with either of you and doesn't want any more unnecessary gossip. He feels you are deliberately stealing the limelight from the Sinfonia. So perhaps, Luke, being seen coming out of Constance's hotel room wouldn't be such a great idea.' Dolly hands me the dress and folds her beefy arms. She stands guard as though she's a bouncer recently released from a ten-year stretch in the world's toughest prison.

Unfazed, Luke gives us a little bow. 'You're quite right, Dolly. As always.'

They exchange a friendly look. 'Connie says you saved her life last night when she was knocked into the road,' Dolly says more softly. 'That's incredible. Thank God you were with her.'

Luke immediately blushes. 'It was no big deal. I just happened to be in the right place at the right time. If not me, someone else would have pulled her back. Or the bus might have swerved or something.' He looks directly at me as though waiting for a response.

'It was a big deal to me,' I say, smiling up at him.

'It'll be an even bigger deal if the press get wind of it,' says Dolly. 'Especially when they realise who you are, Luke.'

I'm confused. 'Who you are?' I say, repeating Dolly. 'What do you mean?'

Luke immediately turns into a Hugh Grant-type figure. 'Ah. Righto. That'll be my cue to leave. A hero's work is never done. Lives to save and all that. Dolly, would you happen to know where my cape is? The one I use to fly, not the bulletproof one.'

I immediately burst out laughing, causing a smile to spread across his face. Dolly waits for him to walk down the corridor away from us before squinting at me.

'What? That was funny,' I say.

'Just because he stopped you from falling under a bus, please don't encourage him by flirting.' I open my mouth to protest, but she cuts me off. 'He does this every time. He'll reel you in. Just because he's filthy rich, and Norwegian royalty, he thinks he can get away with anything. There's always drama whenever he's around. Trust me.' She spins on her heel and marches away, calling over her shoulder, 'You'll only end up with a broken heart, and the Sinfonia will have to begin searching for a replacement all over again.'

* * *

So, after a lot of intensive searching on the internet, I have found out that Luke is not really Luke. He is from the House of Glucksburg on his father's side and the Swedish Bernadotte dynasty on his mother's, making him very posh and very titled.

'He is distantly related to King Harald,' Ged is telling me as we video chat. He, too, is scouring the world wide web for pictures. 'Here's one of him with the Royal Family. *Our* Royal Family! And here's one of him skiing with the Beckhams. Oh, my God! How did the Royal Northern Sinfonia even afford him for this tour? Here's one of him singing with Bono for charity.'

It gets worse.

Luke has several titles and is actually called Count Nikolai Olav Magnus. Which Liam finds extremely sexy. 'Jeez, he's like the James Bond of opera.'

'He sounds more like a Bond villain to me,' says Ged. He is not warming to Luke in the slightest. 'Never trust a Royal. Not even a Scandinavian one. That's what they say.'

'Literally no one has ever said that,' I argue. But where do I go with this new information? It changes things. I feel like I should be learning to curtsy and walking around my room with books balanced on my head. My nerves are on end at the thought of singing with him tonight.

Ping. Ping. Ping.

It's Tash. She wants to remind me that she is technically still sort of single because Sister Kevin, her bearded 'nun' from Benidorm, seems to be dragging his heels where pinning down an agreed relationship status is concerned, and she'd like to keep her options open. She wants me to get David Beckham's number from Luke. She is after a sugar daddy.

Not happening. Although, she has my every sympathy with the uncertainty around her and Kevin's relationship status. Fixating on that can make any normal, easy-going woman borderline psychotic.

'Why don't you take your mind off it all and go shopping?' suggests Ged.

'I'd love to, but they've got me under a kind of house arrest,' I explain.

'That wouldn't stop me,' Ged says firmly.

He's not wrong there. Who could forget the lengths he went to for that paisley Gucci tank top? Two wasted trips to London and a flight to Germany, in case you're wondering.

'Plus, you'd be helping the local economy,' adds Liam before we end the call. 'It'll be fun. Just limit yourself to a few key pieces.' This coming from the man who recently went out to buy gloves and returned four thousand pounds lighter.

This has all really thrown me. Which is a shame because I was looking forward to exploring Manchester today and going on a lovely shopping spree for outfits. Romantic outfits for my romantic trip to Las Vegas to stay with Matteo. A vision of his gorgeous face pops into my head. Dark twinkling eyes with a thousand stories in them.

I lie back on the bed and conjure up images of Matteo and his dreamy smile. He has a way of making music come alive, infused with his energy and passion. He has a way of making *me* come alive, infused with his energy and passion. I've never known anything like it. He is a man of many talents. And I want to look nice for him when I get to America. Really nice.

Ping. Ping. Ping.

Big Sue has heard that I am being illegally held against my will. She is a social worker and very high up. She is asking whether she should call her comrades in the Manchester office. Freedom, she reminds me, is the corner-stone of a civilised society.

One glance out of the hotel bedroom window tells me that not only is it perfect shopping weather out there, but that we are very central and Big Sue is right. I can see the main high street from here. It's only across the square. A two-minute walk. There are crowds of people. No one will notice if I slip out of the hotel to quickly try on a few see-through nightwear items or a glamorous showstopper dress for the stag do. I mean pre-moon spree.

I text Big Sue to confirm that Elvis is leaving the building.

Within minutes, I've slipped past reception, and I'm outside. What a rush. I feel like a spy. Keeping my head down, I cross the square and head straight for the shops. They are heaving with shoppers. And not one of them realises that I am in the newspapers today. Involved in a salacious scandal that is not based on any truth whatsoever. Me and two Royals, mixed up in a passionate Scandi love triangle. One of whom saved my life. I must not get distracted. Especially not by singing dignitaries.

My phone pings, so I step to the side of the pavement to read it. It is as if Liberty senses my predicament. She has texted to ask if I am really fooling around with Prince Charming behind Matteo's back. I tell her that I am not. Then she asks if Luke is single and, if so, to pass on her number.

I don't think so.

I'm not sure why exactly, but I don't want to do that. I've seen her ruin greater men than him. I'm not even sure Liberty, with her wandering vagina, is his type.

'Hello.'

I glance up in shock to see Luke grinning down at me. He's very tall. But then all Norwegians are. I briefly wonder if Big Sue is part Norwegian before snapping to my senses. How can this be possible? Luke was ordered to stay at the hotel and keep out of sight.

'I followed you here,' he says, answering my unasked question.

I frown in response. This is so not cool.

'I followed you so that I could explain myself properly. Before we perform together tonight.'

'Couldn't you have simply waited until we leave for the theatre?'

'No.'

'Why not?'

'Because you'll know by now who I am. I don't want this to put you off. It will affect the way we sing together. It always does.'

I take a moment to swallow. He's not wrong.

'I think we have chemistry, don't you?' He has a warmth and steadiness to him that makes what he is saying sound very provocative. 'Our voices harmonise perfectly. I don't want that to change.'

'I'm fine, honestly.' I raise my gaze to meet his. I can feel the heat rise up my neck. 'It won't affect my performance tonight.'

Oh, but it will.

For the first time since we met, his face lights up. 'You were magnificent last night. Not just your voice but your whole... your whole being. It was like...'

I watch as he visibly struggles to find the right words to say. His eyes fly around before settling on mine, his arms out wide, palms up as though he's about to burst into song. 'It was like being on stage with the aurora borealis. You lit up the entire fucking theatre with your talent.'

I am literally going weak at the knees.

'It was an honour to share the stage with you. And I've never said that to anyone. Believe me.'

I peer shyly up at him. I do believe him. I have yet to see him give anyone, apart from Dolly, the time of day.

Luke points to the café we're standing outside of. 'Coffee?' He is gazing back at me in an impossibly engaging way. The sort of way you'd react to a newborn puppy, eyes yet to open, poking its tongue out for the first time. Ironically, between the two of us, he is the one now behaving out of character. Maybe it is him who feels different around me. But he's dead right about one thing: we do have excellent chemistry on stage. It's making sure we don't develop chemistry *off* stage that could be the problem.

'What's the harm?' he says in the low, soothing voice of a man who doesn't know when to give up. He casually puts his hands in his pockets, drawing attention to his athletic physique and slim legs.

And like I'm shaking myself out of a trance, I say, 'That's very kind but... it's fine. There's no need to explain, Your High— yourself. I don't feel different around you.'

Lies! Lies! I almost called him Your Highness. I need to get a grip. 'Besides, I have a lot of shopping to do,' I say, readying myself for escape. 'For outfits.' I need to put some distance between us.

'Need any assistance? I have a good eye for putting pieces together. Gucci, Versace, Armani. I have accounts with them all. They'd be happy to oblige you with a personal shopper to help speed things up.'

'Hmmm.' I pretend to consider it. 'Do you have an account with George at Asda by any chance?' I joke, trying to relieve the tension between us.

While Luke throws his head back to laugh, my mind fast-forwards to me trying on cheap, sexy thongs and lacy underwear from Primark. It's a world away from what he's used to, and I don't need a personal shopper or any help for that. And God forbid the press catch us doing it.

'Anyway, it's not *that* kind of clothes shopping that I need to do,' I blurt without thinking.

'Stage costumes?'

I shake my head. 'No. Just more, erm, personal items of...' *For the love of God.*

And as though he is reading my mind, a smile tugs at his lips as his eyes twinkle with mischief. 'Oh. I see. That just happens to be my area of expertise.'

If things weren't awkward before, I am definitely making things awkward now. My cheeks are on fire. Actual flames.

9

Oh, God. There's been a frisson between me and Luke ever since I ran off from him earlier like an Olympic sprinter hearing a starter gun go off. I ran straight back to the hotel and didn't even get my shopping done because I was so flustered. Luke then messaged me to apologise for following me and that he hoped he did not overstep with his comments. I replied to confirm that he did not overstep, and that I was looking forward to singing with him tonight. He replied with one word – 'likewise'.

Now I fear that he thinks I fancy him. When I don't.

To make things worse, Dolly has knocked on everyone's doors to let them know the Royals are in attendance again tonight, and the Maestro wants everyone at the theatre earlier than usual and to play their best.

It took me four attempts to do my make-up after Ged and Liam had Face-Timed me to wish me luck. The conversation went like this:

Liam (gasps): Christ alive, what have you done to yourself?

Me: Whatever do you mean?

Ged: Your face is collapsing in on itself, like a melted welly. Why the radioactive blue streaks?

Me: It's for the stage. I need heavy make-up. The lights are strong. I thought I'd try something new for His Royal Highness.

Liam: The one that's coming to the show? Or the one you're singing with?

Me: Ha ha, very funny.

Ged: You look like Barbara Cartland having an extremely bad day. Perhaps tone it down a bit?

Me (very childish): No, Ged. You tone it down a bit!

* * *

The journey to the theatre on the coach does nothing to help matters. Luke and I, for some bizarre reason, choose to ignore each other completely, which causes raised eyebrows from all on board. The ambience backstage is hostile at best. The chorus girls are refusing to speak to me because their chances of milking a Norwegian count have been severely reduced. Dolly says nothing as we make our way to the dressing rooms.

'I'm so sorry to drag you away, Dolly, but I can't manage these ridiculous costumes on my own.'

'It's fine. Just don't tell the others or they'll all expect special treatment.' She helps me into my first gown while I diligently run through all my vocal warm-up drills and tone down my make-up (Ged was 100 per cent spot on – my attempt at thin wings would have put even Amy Winehouse to shame) and accompanies me to the stage. Luke is already waiting in the wings. He nods at me, his face unreadable. The musicians have taken their places, the lights are about to go down, the Maestro has scowled at both of us because he can sense somehow that there is a spark, a tangible electric current flowing between Luke and me. And he was extremely displeased that members of the press were swarming around backstage, and none of them wanted to interview him. They were after Luke. They have found out who he is and have become obsessed with making a story out of nothing. To make things worse, the Royals have returned, again, but in droves. Apparently, according to Dolly, everyone, royal cousins, aunts, sisters-in-law, etc, are intrigued to see what all the fuss is about.

Who knew singing for the Royal Northern Sinfonia would be so full of drama... or Royals? And I thought Benidorm had been bad.

'Break a leg,' whispers Luke, finally turning to look at me as we stand waiting at the edge of the stage. 'Wait. You've got...' His fingers lightly graze my cheek as he reaches out to remove a smudge. A smile tugs at the corner of his mouth when he sees his thumb is now blue. It's such an intimate gesture, and in front of the watchful glare of the entire ensemble. I blink rapidly. *Why would he do that?* To add fuel to the fire? And, worse, why do I have a stomach full of butterflies?

My eyes roam the full length of him. He's wearing a custom-made tuxedo like he was poured into it. It clings perfectly to his lean frame. His body language is supremely confident. His blond hair shines in the stage light. His chiselled looks are classic and manly. He's got a voice to die for, and the stage presence of an A-list celebrity. The more I see of him, the more I realise that he is talented and charismatic to a criminal degree. He catches me studying him. There is a dangerous glint in his eye.

I hurriedly tear my gaze away and wait for the Maestro to introduce me on to the stage.

Deep breaths.

Deep breaths.

I can handle this. It's just a form of Stockholm syndrome. I'm reacting to Luke because I'm new, and I've never had a singing partner before, and he saved my life, for Christ's sake, and I'm also missing Matteo like crazy. That's all. My heart is thundering in my chest as I hear my name called, but my whole body is frozen to the spot. There's a deafening silence while the Maestro holds out his baton ready to welcome me.

My legs won't move. I find the Maestro terrifying. His beaky nose is pointing skyward while his cold eyes slide over to meet mine. He arches an eyebrow at me. I see a tic pulsing in his left eye as he pierces me with an unfriendly glare. He, too, seems suspended in time.

What if I peaked too soon last night?

'You've got this,' Luke murmurs in my ear.

And like a cattle prod, I am jolted into action. I glide onto the stage, relieved to hear the audience erupt into applause.

It's showtime.

* * *

A few hours later, it is all over. We bow to the Royals. They are the only audience members not standing. The thunderous roar of applause rips through the auditorium. We have brought the house down, as they say.

'Unbelievable. Incredible. Insane!' Luke is repeating himself over and over to anyone who'll listen.

Tonight's performance went ridiculously well. Both of us were on top form and we had the highest recorded number of standing ovations the theatre has ever seen. It was a massive success.

Adrenaline is pumping through my veins like rocket fuel.

I'm giddy.

Drunk on endorphins.

Dolly is charging towards us as we come off stage. 'What a performance! It was out of this world. You two have unbelievable chemistry together. I've never seen an audience react like that. Connie, you had them in tears again with your lament. In actual tears! I thought even Maestro was going to well up at one point.'

She is ecstatic. I will not burst her bubble and tell her that I have a strong history of reducing my audience to tears, especially at weddings and birthday parties.

'Thanks, Dolly.'

'Your mother would be so proud.'

This makes me immediately choke up as we share an understanding look.

'Your father will be very proud of you, too. Is he coming to see us in Newcastle?'

'Yes,' I say, swallowing back my emotions. 'He's coming to both performances.' My father will be in bits. I know he will. He's also bringing Madge to the final evening, which might be strange. Seeing him with a woman who isn't my lovely mother will take quite a bit of time to get used to. But I'm very happy to see him smiling again and doing things that spark joy. Even if it is hiking across lumpy fields and staying in B&Bs with chintzy pelmets. I wish he had been here tonight to see me.

The chorus girls rush up to Luke, all but pushing me and Dolly out of the way. They get busy kissing his cheeks, praising his magnificent singing abilities and trying to drag him away to speak to the paparazzi who are waiting outside. I imagine they will want to be photographed at his side. I will have to think of a way to sneak past them when I leave.

As if sensing my turmoil, Luke bats them away and swoops in beside me. 'Hurry. Grab your stuff, and let's get back to the hotel to decompress. I have a private car waiting at the side exit.'

I nod, grateful for the chance to calm my nerves. I still feel like I'm floating on air in some incredible dream.

'I'll deal with the press,' Dolly is telling everyone. 'No one is to make any comments. There'll be no attempts to seek a quick buck on my watch. No selling stories or telling lies online just to get more followers. Do you understand?'

The three chorus girls protest loudly, but Dolly screws her eyes as though she suspects them of being behind the leaks.

'Wait!' comes a sharp instruction. 'Not so fast.'

The Maestro is hurrying towards us. 'The Royals have requested a private audience with myself and Count Nikolai. Come with me,' he orders Luke. Luke just has time to give me an apologetic smile before they rush off.

The chorus girls are quick to turn their attention to me.

'What's going on?' Florrie accuses openly.

'Yeah,' chips in the one that sings in the middle and whose name I can no longer remember. 'You know he's spoken for, don't you?'

Ah, it's the one who is hoping to pull on his teat. As opposed to the one who is hoping to ride him like a bike.

'Just because you throw yourself at him on stage, doesn't mean you can do it off stage. He'd never be interested in someone... so... council estate, no offence,' Florrie says in her posh, plummy accent.

Whaaaat?

I stand up straight. I am the lead female singer on this tour. More than that, I'm a proud Geordie woman, and I don't give a flying fuck what they think. They can't tell me what to do. I won't stand for this kind of attitude. It's time to put the people-pleasing wimp in me to one side. Besides, I'm high on endorphins and confidence. I jut out my chin, ready to put them firmly in their place.

'Ladies. Whatever is or isn't going on between me and Luke is absolutely none of your fucking business.'

They seem immediately shocked at me standing up to them.

'I'm not in the habit of milking my leading man like a farmyard animal,' I say very loudly, using their own vulgar terminology, so they know that I'm on to them. 'But my point is... if I want to pull on Luke's big, hairy udder till the cows come home, I will!'

There, that's them told.

The chorus girls are standing with their mouths hanging open. Dolly is standing with her jaw also wide open. They appear to be staring past me. A sinking feeling invades my stomach as I twist slowly round.

My eyes come to rest on the Maestro first. He looks livid, as always. Behind him, Luke appears vaguely amused. He is quick to interject. 'Excuse me, but I think you'll find there's nothing hairy about my udders.'

Some polite coughing alerts me to some shocked yet familiar faces whom I slowly recognise as famous royal figures, and finally, my eyes are drawn to a scruffy-looking man who leaps towards me with a microphone in his hand.

He thrusts it towards me. 'So, you're admitting that you'd like to... did you say "milk the Count like a cow"?' He is doing air quotes with his fingers. 'Is that a sexual reference? Does he wear a costume when you do the milking? Do you sit on a stool? Are you two having an affair? How long has it been going on?'

Fuck me.

* * *

It only took the Maestro to snap his baton in half, grab the nearest sheet of music to crumple into a ball and shriek, 'Get her out of my sight!' for the entire backstage area to empty as though a nuclear warning had sounded. Dolly grabbed my arm and whisked me away before I had time to set the journalist straight. Half an hour later, the whole ensemble is crowded into the hotel bar for a nightcap. Tomorrow morning, we will set off for a three-night run in York, and Dolly has ordered everyone to have an early night. Especially me. They all think I have caused enough trouble for one day.

'I'm so, so sorry.' I have been apologising non-stop to Luke since we arrived back at the hotel. I can only imagine the dreadful headlines.

'These things happen,' he says. He still has a dangerous sparkle in his eye, as though he is thoroughly enjoying the attention but doesn't want anyone to know it. 'The Royals have heard worse, believe me.'

'And I didn't mean to say...' *That your schlong is big and hairy.* I mean, how would I know?

'Don't worry about it. It'll all blow over.' He starts laughing suggestively. 'No pun intended.'

Oh my fucking word. What if he thinks I want to blow him like a trumpet? *I don't! I don't!*

My eyes are popping out of my head. *How do I explain? How?* A hot flush envelops me as I turn to face away from him.

'It's sweet how embarrassed you are,' he says. 'I'm just joking around. Take no notice. I know exactly what those chorus girls are like.'

'Thanks,' I mumble.

I should mention that I am with Matteo, and I'm simply not interested in Luke that way. Who would be, with Matteo waiting for me in LA? Gorgeous Matteo. I know we have only been together for a week, and under any other circumstances, perhaps if I was single, I might be attracted to Luke, but right here and now, I only have eyes for one hot guy, and that's Matteo.

'I'd hate you to get the wrong idea. Especially when I have a commitment to—'

Luke cuts me off. 'Forget it. Even if you did have a crush on me, I'd be fine with it.'

'I don't!'

'But even if you did, it would be okay, really. I'm used to it.' He pantomime-winks at me.

'But I don't. I absolutely don't.'

He smiles maddeningly, then blinks slowly while he relaxes further into his seat, oozing self-confidence. 'Okay. I'm sure you don't. But even if...'

Grrr! This conversation is going nowhere. I throw my hands in the air. 'Goodnight!' I swirl round and stomp over to the lifts in the reception area and start jabbing at the buttons. My heart is thumping out of my chest. I'm both infuriated with him and mortified that he thinks I fancy him. I don't!

Gah! Trust the hotel to have a million floors. I continue to jab at the lift button.

He's insufferable.

Jab. Jab. Jab.

He's arrogant.

Jab. Jab. Jab.

He's too cocky and full of himself.

I risk a sly glance over.

Oh God. He's watching me with a huge grin plastered on his face.

I. Do. Not. Fancy. Him.

I do not.

10

The next morning, I skip breakfast because I cannot bear to face Luke, Dolly, the Maestro or anyone else. And also because I had such a troubled sleep. Plagued with terrible visions and sordid dreams where Matteo was doing delicious things to me. He'd bring me to a sweaty conclusion, only for me to open my eyes and see Luke. I woke up panting, with an ache between my legs, and couldn't get back to sleep for the guilt.

I toy once more with ringing Matteo. But it is three in the morning over there. I'd truly love to hear his voice. See his face. Hear him tell me again how excited he is to see me in less than a couple of weeks.

Less than a couple of weeks.

A girl should be able to withstand a mild attraction to her singing partner and not put her brand-new relationship in danger for the sake of a ten-day wait. I can't help wondering if Matteo is experiencing the same attraction to Birdie. They will be huddled over a mixing desk together. Speaking into the microphone. Their lips inches apart. Their hands might accidentally touch. Their faces might be cheek to cheek. They might be sharing inside jokes and becoming very close.

These things can happen.

Ping.

It's the Dollz group chat. Cherry thinks she may have gone off her husband. She has awoken this morning to a startling realisation that he is thinning on top, and she very much prefers a man with a full head of hair. She is wondering if she should get out now while she still can. She is wondering about the suitability of Luke and asking about the likelihood of his being a step-parent to her two feral offspring.

Big Sue demands more information. What does Cherry mean when she says 'while she still can'? Big Sue wants to know if Cherry feels unsafe in the marriage or trapped in any way.

Cherry explains that while she is still in her prime, looks-wise, and her two children are young and barely recognise her husband, because he is always playing fantasy football when not at work, her chances of securing a richer, second husband with more hair are substantially higher.

Liberty warns Cherry to stay put. She has been through all of the dating apps, and there are no decent men on the market, especially not ones who are rich and good-looking with lots of hair but who are also legally unmarried. We find out that her last date had declared upfront that he'd just come out of a three-year relationship with an inflatable animal (she never said what type and no one dared to ask) and the one before that had produced an engagement ring before they'd even arranged a second date. The long and short of it being that Luke is off limits because Liberty has already put in a prior claim. She is making out that there's some sort of waiting list, and I am in charge of it.

This is exactly the kind of distraction I need. I have been extremely lucky to find Matteo at just the right time in my life. I should not be throwing away this opportunity on a whim. I send him a message to say that I am missing him and really looking forward to seeing him soon, and that I hope he and Birdie are managing to make some great music together. Then I delete the last part in case it puts ideas in his head. I make a coffee in my room, pack up my things and go down to reception before anyone else.

The concierge meets me with all my cases and helps me to the coach. It is completely empty, so I walk towards the back, putting my handbag next to me to discourage anyone sitting beside me. I slide down in my seat and do a search for the local news headlines.

Oh, no.

Oh, no, no, no.

The *Manchester Evening News* is running with the headline, 'Star of the Royal Northern Sinfonia threatens to milk her leading man like a cow'. I scan the article, a lump the size of a turnip in my throat. It says the Royal Family have the hump. It makes out I am chasing Luke down with the intention of 'nabbing myself an heir to the throne of Norway', and that I'm a 'gold-digging nobody' after the advancement of my singing career. 'Where has she come from?' they are asking.

Someone has leaked that I am nothing but a two-bit, cheap covers tribute act from Benidorm, way out of my league, with unrealistic working-class aspirations to fit into the elitist classical music crowd. Someone else is accusing the classical music industry of being classist and that I am not to be treated like cheap meat just because of where I come from.

Feckedy feck! They have illustrated the article with a picture of me pole dancing in Benidorm wearing one of my carefully selected stripper outfits that the Dollz made me wear. They have taken it straight from Nancy's website. Tash must have snapped it moments before I accidentally kicked Matteo in the face and sent all the drinks on the table crashing to the ground. Now, that would have made a good front-page picture. Thank goodness for small mercies, I suppose.

I sink lower into my seat as people start to get on the bus. I'll be lucky if I'm not sacked from the Sinfonia for this and sent packing.

It's a proper shitshow.

I stare at the image. My leg is hooked high around the pole, while I lean as far out as possible, my hair tumbling down into people's drinks. My boobs are straining against the flimsy bustier, and my sky-high stripper gladiator sandals are screaming, 'Have sex with me right now – up against this pole'. It is a very provocative image.

Dolly is thumping her way up the aisle towards me, peering at the seats as she goes. 'Is she here? Is Connie on board? Where is she?'

I let out an enormous sigh. Here we go. Might as well face the repercussions. I sit back up and pop my head above the headrests. She spots me immediately and hurries sternly up the aisle to fling the newspapers down next to me.

Is there any point in denying it's all lies?

'I can explain,' I say before she starts on me.

'No need,' she says.

Crap. 'What do you mean? Am I getting sacked? Because, honestly, none of it is true. Well, the pole-dancing bit is, but the rest isn't. Except the singing covers in Benidorm, that's true too, but… we're not having an affair, and I'm not after Luke's money, and I absolutely do not want to milk him like a cow.'

'That's a shame.' Luke appears behind Dolly, waving a copy of the newspaper. His comment stops us both in our tracks. He flicks his hand against the photo. 'Is that outfit... the George designer you mentioned yesterday?' he says dryly.

'Very funny,' I say, turning back to Dolly. 'If the Sinfonia don't like the fact that I have a life outside of work, then too bad. I'm just sorry the press are making up all these lies about us.'

'No worries. My family is squeaky clean to the point of tedious,' Luke says. 'They'll be loving all of this salacious attention.'

Dolly faces me. 'And so are half the Sinfonia Trustees.'

'I'm not following,' I say, confused.

'Sex sells. So do scandalous headlines. Did you know that, thanks to you, the rest of the tour has now sold out?'

They're both smiling at me.

'So, I'm not being sacked?'

'Far from it, my dear,' says Dolly.

I gulp. I'm not sure this is what I had in mind when I joined. *What will my dad think? What will Matteo think?*

'Well, I'm not deliberately doing anything at all. I just want to finish the tour and go home. I'm afraid you can tell the trustees that there will be no further spicy headlines from me.' It's time to be firm. 'Unless the headlines are about how fabulous the show is and how brilliant the musicians are, I'm not interested in making a spectacle of myself in front of the entire country.'

'Fair enough.' Dolly makes her way back down the aisle, barking orders and counting heads. She informs the driver we are all on board.

Luke remains where he is.

'Are you sure you're okay?' he asks, his voice thick with concern. He is about to sit down next to me. 'If you want to talk about it, I'm...'

'No!' My voice is ten octaves higher than it should be. 'No, thank you. I'm fine. I just need a bit of time to get my head round everything, that's all.'

He takes the hint and heads back down the aisle. Now it is as though I have leprosy because everyone is sitting in the front half of the coach, and I have the whole of the back half to myself.

I text Ged and Liam the link to the tabloid gossip only to get an instant reply that Tash was way ahead of me and has informed everyone. They tell me to check out her socials as she is mining her close celebrity contact for all it's worth. *Charming.*

I text Dad to warn him. He, too, has received Tash's memo. He rings me immediately while we hurtle along the M62 towards York.

'Connie, love, don't worry about it, because things have a habit of working out well in the end.'

'Thanks, Dad,' I say, relief flooding through me. 'That's exactly what I need to hear.'

'Just concentrate on your singing and getting through the tour. I can even drive down to York for the day to keep you company if you need a shoulder to cry on, love.'

Oh, my dear, sweet, lovely father. He'll be worried that I can't cope with it all. It's essential that he believes I can. Even if I feel at times I can't. And I must remind him that I'm a lot sturdier now, since my epiphany in Benidorm.

'Thanks, Dad, but I'll be too busy rehearsing. And it's only a few days until we'll be back in Newcastle at The Glasshouse. I'll see you then. I mean, how much worse could things get?' We share a laugh, and he seems happy with that. I love him. He has such a kind-hearted, generous soul.

By the time I carry out all the different WhatsApp group messaging – Cherry has agreed to give her husband's hair a second chance, Tash is experiencing an exponential growth in followers, Liberty has bought us all pink gingham Barbie dresses (for Cherry to alter and make them extra, extra short) to wear in Las Vegas, Big Mand has delivered fourteen babies in one shift, Big Sue has reported three domestic abuse violations and a heartbreaking story about an abandoned toddler on their social services doorstep – we have arrived in York.

We pull up outside the very grand Gray's Court Hotel overlooking York Minster Cathedral, which towers above it into the glorious blue sky. My gaze is drawn to the fabulous, manicured hotel gardens. They are dotted with peculiar-shaped trees and bushes in vibrant greens and ancient stonework, while sumptuous garden furniture sprawls across neatly clipped lawns. This can't be our hotel. It is way too upmarket and expensive. I wonder if the Maestro is being upgraded.

'First stop!' yells Dolly down the bus, staring directly at me.

As I make my way hastily to the front of the coach, no one appears to be moving or willing to make eye contact with me. Except Luke, who is standing at the front grinning.

'What do you think?' he asks.

'It's magnificent,' I say. 'Some upgrade, huh? I've never stayed anywhere nearly this posh before, Dolly.'

Dolly arches an eyebrow and purses her lips by way of acknowledgement.

'I can't believe this is where we're all staying,' I say, jumping down off the last step. 'The Sinfonia must be really raking it in if they can afford posh hotels like this.'

Dolly gives Luke a strange look.

'The hotel's a Grade One listed building with parts of it dating back a thousand years. Just wait until you see inside,' he says quickly, hurrying me away from the door. 'The acoustics are miraculous, if you'd like to practise before the performance tonight?'

I nod enthusiastically at him. 'Who wouldn't want to show off their vocal chops in a place like this?'

Luke laughs. 'Come on then, let's check in.'

The driver lugs our cases from the hold and heaves them over to a concierge who is walking towards us with a rather elaborate gold and dark green velvet-covered trolley. He loads our cases onto it. 'Reception is this way, sir, madam.'

I spin round at the hissing of the coach door closing. 'Why isn't everyone getting off? Wait. Where are they going?'

I make out Dolly frowning at us, and then suddenly, three annoyed faces press up against the window as the coach leaves the grounds.

A huge penny drops in my brain. 'The Sinfonia only upgraded the two of us?'

Luke shrugs nonchalantly.

My eyes fly back to the coach to see the world's most famous Maestro twisting in his seat to glare at me.

No. This cannot be happening.

'But why? How?' My instinct is to run after the coach. I don't want to be treated any differently. We're supposed to be a team. One big happy family. Well, except for the poor musicians who are herded into the Premier Inn everywhere we go. And their coach doesn't have a toilet or TV screens or a drinks service. And they don't get anywhere near the pay that we singers do. But apart from that, we're all in it together. Now it seems only Luke and I are in it together. Segregated from the rest. 'There must be some mistake. Quick, call Dolly. Tell them to come back.'

Luke gives me a sheepish smile. 'Well, I'm happy to stay here. It's an amazing hotel. There's a spa. A music room for practising. A private dining room. Massage therapy treatments. Hot tubs. Serene grounds to walk in. We are here for three nights, remember? Back-to-back shows can be very demanding. This place has everything we need.'

I gulp. It certainly does have everything. As I cast my eyes around, it has everything that a couple of loved-up, randy honeymooners could possibly need. The place is positively oozing charm and lavish decadence. And it would be a complete first for me. Liam is always saying I should step out of my comfort zone. And this is as far from a comfortable, budget hotel as you can get.

Once we're checked in, the concierge shows us to our rooms. Big old wooden doors creak open as we pass along ancient corridors lined with warm, plush carpets and stone walls. Windows offer peeks of the beautiful grounds and glimpses of York Minster as we walk along. Talk about atmospheric. This place is fit for kings and queens. No wonder Luke seems to fit right in. We come to an abrupt halt.

'Your room keys, madam. And sir.' He holds out two old heavy metal keys, each with a leather-covered key ring embossed with the hotel logo and room number in gold leaf.

Our rooms are right next to one another.

'When the luggage arrives, freshen up, and we'll take a tour of York together before lunch. There's something you must see,' Luke says, disappearing into his room with a loud creak as the door shuts behind him.

I glance at the concierge. He must be used to wandering dignitaries issuing orders. Well, I'm not. I won't be bossed around by anyone. Especially not handsome co-workers with a potentially hidden agenda.

'Maybe,' I say to the closed door. 'I'll see how I feel.'

The concierge smiles politely as my words hang in the air, and he walks me into my room.

Oh. My. God.

The walls are lined with expensive-looking mustard wallpaper with beautifully drawn branches, flowers and brightly coloured peacocks. Bookshelves line the main wall on either side of a grand fireplace. A huge deluxe four-poster bed dominates the room with gleaming walnut pillars and soft silk drapes at the head. It is like something out of a swanky wedding magazine.

'Are you sure this is the right room?'

The concierge says nothing but walks over to the bookshelf to the right of the fireplace and presses on it.

I see that it is not a bookshelf but a secret door leading to a very sumptuous en suite. It has a huge, deep, free-standing copper bath in front of a massive sash window overlooking York Minster. What an incredible view. I'm drawn to the neat rows of bottles. Expensive hair and skin products line the shelves. Piles of fluffy white towels tower beside the bath. More soaps and potions sit by the large double sink. The smells blooming out are incredible. It's like wandering through Fenwick's perfume counter. I feel like running a hot bath just so I can pour them all in and soak in the expensive bubbles.

'The rest of your luggage will arrive imminently and be unpacked for you,' says the concierge. 'Anything you need, just ask.'

As soon as the concierge has gone, there's a knock at my door. It must be the porter with my luggage. I will ask him if all the chocolates by the tea and coffee machine are free because they are from an artisanal chocolatier and must cost a fortune. Ditto the bathroom things and ditto the minibar. I have no idea. I also need my dress dry-cleaned and ready for tonight now that Dolly is not here to sort things out for me. I pull open the door, expecting to see a trolley with my cases, but Luke is leaning casually in the doorway, slightly unkempt, messy hair, an unnecessarily sexy air about him.

'Room okay?' he asks, casting his eye around.

I will stop him in his tracks. There's no way I have time to go exploring. Not when I have a Vegas pre-moon to organise on top of everything else. He's about to step across the threshold when I yelp, 'Ready to go?'

Oh my word! I didn't even *want* to go exploring with him, but I feel that's a better option than him coming into my room. My bedroom. Where there's a huge four-poster bed everywhere you turn.

Luke bows elaborately. 'As you wish.'

Like this is somehow my idea? I am panic-deciding instead of being more focused and standing my ground. I have a million things to do and not much time to do them.

I lock the door behind me. I will sort the dry cleaning out later. And the shopping for the Las Vegas outfits. And the research for the pre-moon spree will have to be done after the performance tonight. Things will have to be booked in advance, so I need to check in with Nancy about which nights we are singing and where, so that I can book restaurants and VIP areas for us. I will also have to check that we will be allowed into America looking like porn star versions of Barbie and Ken. The list is endless!

'Okay, what did you want to show me? But make it quick because I have things to do,' I say, sounding a bit like an ungrateful brat.

I see a hurt expression cross Luke's face.

'Sorry,' I quickly apologise. 'I didn't mean it like that. I guess I'm still on edge. It's not every day you're accused of... being in a love triangle. In the national newspapers. It's just all been a bit surreal.' I chew my lip as I study him. Suddenly, the weight of the past two bonkers days and the next few bonkers weeks that lie ahead falls heavily onto my shoulders.

Luke remains quiet for a while.

'I'm truly sorry you've been dragged into this. I'd like to explain.'

'Sure,' I inwardly sigh. I'm not sure in the slightest. The more personal distance we can keep the better. 'Okay.'

* * *

A short while later, Luke and I are wandering through the cobbled lanes of York, taking in the sights, the beamed architecture on wonky old houses and shops that are centuries old and straight out of Harry Potter. The place is so charming and atmospheric that I forget he has yet to explain himself. I am catapulted back to a time when my parents first brought me here. We had such fun finding the many cat statues that dot the rooftops and chimneys.

'Did you know some of the cats date back to medieval times?' Luke says, catching me staring at one of the cats on the eaves of a shop as I'm lost in thought. 'Supposed to scare off rats and pigeons, but I like to think they are there to bring good luck.'

That's what my mother once told me. A warm image of her hugging me pops into my mind. I can almost feel her arms around me.

'How come you know York so well? Do you live here in England? Have you been with the Sinfonia long?' I'm curious to know. 'I can't trace any Norwegian accent.'

'I'll tell you over lunch,' Luke says with a warm smile.

'I am starving,' I say. 'I skipped breakfast.'

'Also, probably my fault,' he says. 'Bet you didn't think these classical tours would be so full of drama.'

'Or scary Maestros. What is his deal?'

'Ah, Krzystzof. He's not without his own salacious gossip either. The tales I have heard about him!'

I have to admit, Luke is very easy company. Maybe I have been too hasty to judge. Maybe the frisson between us is all in my head. Maybe he views me as nothing more than a platonic co-worker that he once saved from being flattened by a bus.

'Seeing as it is such a lovely day, would you like to take lunch al fresco?' Luke asks.

'Lovely,' I say. The more open and public the space, and the more platonic, the better.

'The hotel has great private dining options.'

Gawd. I'm about to protest politely when he qualifies his statement.

'In case there are press lurking around with microphones,' he says, gazing about. 'You can't be too careful.'

It sounds too reasonable to object to, so I walk with him back to the hotel. When we reach reception, he asks for the summer house private dining. We are shown through the elaborate grounds to a glass gazebo with a beautifully made-up dining table for two. Ornate flowers weave in and out of strings of lights strung up around the antique-looking brass and glass structure. The menu is as exquisite as the surroundings.

Once we have ordered elaborate-sounding salads containing quail eggs, pomegranate seeds and mozzarella pearls in a cress and cucumber foam, Luke picks up his napkin and gently shakes it out. I find myself doing the same. I sit up straight and try to appear interesting and posh. This whole place is a bit much and has me on edge.

'Wine?' he says. 'Just a tiny drop to cleanse the palate?'

I really shouldn't, but I feel nervous around him now that we are enduring what many would call intimate fine dining for two. Plus, I'm still vaguely haunted by that rude dream I had last night that he featured pretty heavily in.

I nod. 'Just a small one.'

There's no such thing. I know this. I live with two highly functioning wine enthusiasts. There is no such thing as a small one when it comes to wine, and oh my God, I take a sip of the cold white wine that the waiter pours into my glass. It is divine. I feel my eyes balloon with excitement.

'Madam?' he asks, waiting for me to decide whether it is any good. My taste buds zing to life as the velvety smoothness of dark berries infused with a hint of bitter chocolate and rich cinnamon rolls over my tongue. If this is what proper wine tastes like, what the heck have I been drinking all my life? Paint stripper? This wine is incredible.

'It's delicious, thank you,' I tell him as he pours Luke and me very hefty measures. I remind myself that this does not mean that I have to drink it all. I will sip like a lady.

'I'm so glad you like it. This is my favourite wine,' Luke says, holding it up, twirling the glass, inspecting the liquid as it rolls around.

'Mine too,' I say without thinking.

'Really? What a coincidence.'

I have not thought this through. It is probably six hundred pounds a bottle. There were probably only two barrels ever made.

'I mean, it is now. It's delicious.' I relax when Luke starts to chuckle.

'I was a little surprised. It's not to everyone's tastes. Or budgets. No offence.'

'None taken. As long as the Sinfonia are paying, I will drink it.'

Tiny pink spots appear on his cheeks. 'Connie, tell me, where have you been hiding all this time? How did you come to have such an extraordinary gift for singing?'

Oh, my. He's brought up my favourite subject again. Luckily, I'm wise to these tactics. 'I'll tell you all about me, right after you explain why I'm caught up in some royal love triangle and why you led me to believe Dolly was your wife.'

I watch Luke's cheeks redden even further. Embarrassed, he dabs his lips with his napkin before putting it down.

'Firstly, I'm sorry about calling Dolly my wife. I just went along with you at the rehearsal because we'd got off on the wrong foot and, well, because I see more of Dolly than any other human on this planet.' He clears his throat. 'As for the articles in the press about Hermione and me. Our families go way back. She and I were at school together in Switzerland.'

Of course they were. Of course.

'We haven't seen each other for a while. Until recently.'

Luke fidgets with his napkin.

'And the old flame has reignited?' I say, finally relaxing. This is brilliant news. Luke is spoken for, and I am off the hook tabloids-wise. 'I'm very happy for you both.'

'She's very... How do I put this?' Luke throws me an earnest look.

'Shy?'

'No. She's the opposite of shy.'

'Rich?' You do hear about these billionaires wanting to keep it all in their billionaire circles.

'No. Not that. Well, obviously, yes, she is, but...'

He seems uncomfortable, as though he's hiding something. Something big.

'She's very...'

'Oh,' I whisper, leaning in. 'She's very pregnant?' He'll be wanting to avoid a royal scandal.

'Can you be *very* pregnant?' He throws his head back and sighs loudly. 'No. She's not pregnant.'

'Well, what is she then?'

'She's very gay.'

I did not expect that. 'Can you be *very* gay?' I ask stupidly. Of course you can. Just look at Ged and Liam.

Luke gives me a half-smile. 'She's an avid member of the all-women's rowing club. Chair of the women-only wrestling society. She founded the women's Vote Minge annual jamboree, and she lives in Hebden Bridge on a barge with a woman called Stevie. They share several cats and want to get married. I'd say yes, she's very gay.'

That all makes sense.

'She's not very happy about the article, but the palace seem pleased to have her linked to a man. Especially one from my family. As I said, we all go way back. My father has insisted I play along.'

I'm appalled. How awful. 'What can you do about it?'

He shrugs in a way that suggests he has already tried to get out of it.

'Is that why she came to see you perform last night too?' I ask.

He nods his head. 'She relies on her trust fund, so... we may have to play along at a fake relationship for as long as it takes, perhaps years.'

'Sounds like she doesn't have much of a choice. It's not very progressive, is it? Personally, I think you should make a stand. It's not your sacrifice to make. What if you fall in love and want to get married yourself some day?'

Luke fixes me a strange look. 'Exactly what I was thinking.'

I sip at my wine, but I can still feel his eyes on me. 'I have to say, you seem to be a magnet for gay wives. Dolly, Hermione... There has to be a less gay wife for you somewhere.'

'Precisely. What if I'm already engaged to be married?' he says, smirking. 'To a non-gay wife. Then they'd have to find someone else.'

'Are you engaged to a non-gay wife?'

He puts down his knife and fork and leans back in his chair, regarding me with a doe-eyed look. 'Not yet. But finding myself a beautiful, extraordinarily talented fiancée would be a great way to put an end to these fake wedding rumours, wouldn't it?'

'Oh. I guess it would. Yes.'

And just like that, there's a bit of tension.

12

Once back in my glorious bedroom, I reflect on the lunch with Luke. After his confession, he sat looking at me with a huge question in his eyes. I panicked and made a joke about having the perfect wife in mind for him. I told him all about Liberty and her relentless pursuit for a man, any man, as long as he has eyes that can point in the same direction and a full set of teeth.

I wander over to the desk by the bay window in my room. There's a brochure with pictures of a spa and people having relaxing massages and hot stones placed on their shoulder blades. In my current on-edge state, it looks very inviting. There's also a hot tub, and I experience an instant flashback to Benidorm, and me riding Matteo like a bucking bronco, without a care in the world for health and safety or public hygiene.

I ring reception to see about the Scandinavian-style spa. The receptionist quickly tells me that all I have to do is turn up. It's all complimentary.

'Complimentary?'

'Yes, madam. Free of charge. Your bill is completely taken care of.'

The Sinfonia are incredibly generous.

'We have complimentary towels, slippers and a range of swimming costumes at the spa reception,' she says. 'But most patrons opt to go naked.'

'Naked?'

'Like they do in Finland,' she explains casually as though it's the most natural thing in the world. 'You can also book a slot for a facial and de-stress massage if you so wish?'

'I do wish that,' I say. 'I do wish that very much.' Where has my Geordie accent disappeared to? I sound like I'm from Buckinghamshire. 'I wish to avail myself of all that is on offer, thank you so kindly. Except the going naked bit. I'm not Scandinavian enough for that.'

I have six hours before I am due on stage. Plenty of time to sober up by way of steaming it out of my system. 'Oh, can you also send the concierge up to collect my costumes for tonight, please? I need them express dry-cleaned.'

'Certainly, madam. I'll send up some swimwear options too. What size do you require?'

* * *

By the time the girls at the spa have run their hands lightly over my face with essential oils and massaged my back and shoulders, I am all but asleep. Soft music is lulling me into a deep state of relaxation and happiness. Wine fumes are escaping from my every pore.

'Hot tub, madam?' one of them asks and, without even opening my eyes, I nod gratefully. She laces up the back of the new bikini I chose from the fabulous selection that was sent to my room, wraps me into a fluffy robe and places a pair of brand-new slipper-type sliders on my feet and leads me over to the spa area. She points out the hot tub, sauna and steam room.

'Then perhaps a swim to cool off,' she whispers, indicating a picturesque waterfall splashing into a rock-lined plunge pool. 'You have the entire place to yourself. Enjoy.' The lights are very low, like a tropical oasis. Gentle, relaxing music is playing while the scent of bergamot and jasmine fills the air. The heady concoction of the aroma and half a bottle of delicious wine is putting me into a trance.

I step gingerly down into the hot tub as she takes the robe from me. The bubbling hot water sends a soothing warmth straight to my bones. I sag against the seat, flopping my head backwards. I have never been so relaxed in my entire life. As the jets of water massage my feet, I allow my mind to wander back to that incredible night with Matteo. The feel of his lips. The touch of his hands. The electricity surging between us, whipping up a wild and out-of-control lust for each other. A small, desirous groan of longing rumbles from my throat. Only one week and three days until we are reunited.

But it feels like a lifetime. I wonder if Matteo would be up for some phone sex. I've heard from Tash that it is the next best thing.

'Penny for your thoughts?'

My eyes snap open.

Sodding hell.

'Sorry to interrupt.' Luke is standing by the hot tub, glistening, towel in hand. 'They told me the place was empty.' He shrugs, causing droplets of water to run down his bare chest. 'Glad you seem to be enjoying it so... thoroughly.'

I swallow an imaginary lump in my throat. It's as though he is in my mind. My filthy, filthy mind. 'How long have you been there?'

'Long enough.' His eyes cloud.

I know a lustful look when I see one. And Luke has one plastered all over his face. I sink a little lower into the bubbling water. My boobs are bursting to be free from this skimpy bikini. My nipples are poking through, reminding me of the two pickled quail eggs we ate at lunch. I choose my words carefully so as not to encourage him. 'I was practising my tongue trills.' I've managed to make it sound sexual. 'I mean, I was blowing, erm... lip bubbles.' *Sounds just as dirty.*

Luke's eyes grow wide. 'You can blow whatever you like. I'm very open-minded.' He waggles his eyebrows and takes a step towards the tub. 'Can I join you? I find the steam great for the larynx.'

This is very true, and while I think the two of us sharing a hot tub is a terrible idea, I'm at a loss for words as to how to tell him *no*. But he starts to get in before I can say anything. I hastily look away as he climbs in and sits down opposite. Steam billows around us, making me feel light-headed and dreamy. I try to sit up straight. I must act normal, so he doesn't think I'm encouraging him. Just because we are both tipsy, and he is sitting across from me looking like a sexually depraved catwalk model, doesn't mean anything needs to happen between us.

He seems to inch a little closer.

It causes my pulse to react. 'I was thinking around, erm... around 5 p.m. for a light dinner?' I hear the break in my voice as I busy myself, collecting up my hair. I twirl it into a bun and rearrange the clip.

He watches every movement intensely.

My boobs thrust towards him as I lift my arms. It had seemed like a good idea in the moment. Now, it feels as though I'm inviting him to knead them like lumps of dough.

I watch him swallow. He seems mesmerised by my every move. I watch him lean back, resting his arms casually on either side. Droplets of water rolling casually over his biceps.

Electricity crackles between us.

'You are... simply breathtaking,' Luke says, his voice barely audible. He shakes his head. 'Sorry. That was wildly inappropriate.' His eyes flick down to my quail eggs before he tries to disguise it by inspecting the surroundings.

I have butterflies raging inside me and my voice has become low and husky. I turn coyly away as I feel heat rise to my already flushed cheeks. My blood pressure is skyrocketing. *Where does one go with that?* What is the social etiquette around two work colleagues sharing a giant bath when one of them is clearly attracted to the other? This is wrong on so many levels, not least professionally, but I am equally alarmed to be enjoying the attention. However, I must discourage this thing before it goes any further.

'I blame my upbringing,' he says. 'Norwegians are very open and honest about things. And I did go to a French boarding school in Switzerland where anything goes, so that hasn't helped.'

I am reminded that he probably speaks French like a native. And we all know what else Frenchmen are famous for.

'I don't want to be the cause of any embarrassment. And I'd hate to make you uncomfortable.' He is impeccably polite. 'But I've never met *anyone* quite like you before. You are truly *exceptionelle,* and I have a deep respect for your talent. I just need you to understand that.' The intensity of his words sends a crackle of excitement shooting through me. 'I know I'd regret not telling you.'

I. AM. GIDDY.

I am also quite tipsy. And when I am tipsy, I also become fluent in French. I have a GCSE in it. Well, I don't. It's in Spanish. Which is the only explanation I can find as to why I blurt out this next thing.

'*Non, je ne regrette rien.*'

His eyebrows shoot up. 'Exactly. Life's too short for regrets. Edith Piaf certainly had a weakness for men. Raised in a bordello, you know.'

I do know. I studied everything about her turbulent romantic history as part of my music degree. 'Although, she was no stranger to rejection.'

'Rejection? What's that?' Luke grins. He is ridiculously good-looking, especially in this flattering, dim spa light.

I take a beat. It's not my fault Luke and I seem to be drawn together like magnets. But it *will* be my fault if I allow anything to happen. Especially if I keep openly propositioning him with song titles that sound like sexual invitations. I really hope Matteo is not also on the receiving end of such blatant French temptation.

'The French have rather cornered the market when it comes to songs about love... and sex, of course,' he continues, not taking his eyes from mine.

I swallow nervously.

We are work colleagues, I chant silently. We are professional artists. We are doing nothing wrong. We are having playful conversation. All is above board and morally certifiable because we are creatives. And everyone knows creatives have a different way of doing things.

'Forbidden sex is always the hottest sex, don't you find?' he says, breaking the silence. He tilts his head, as though he's wondering how I'll react. 'The French are very good at that too.'

I nod blankly. I have no idea. Although, in this moment, I can quite imagine illicit, steamy, handprint-on-the-car-window sex with someone you really *shouldn't* be having sex with being very, very erotic.

We stare at one another for what feels like an eternity. My heart is thumping wildly in my chest. I don't want to be *this* attracted to him, but I am. I just am.

What about poor Matteo? Poor lovely, sweet Matteo. Who I am head-over-heels mad about. Just as I'm about to blurt out that my heart belongs to another, Luke stands up, the water swishing round his muscular thighs. His swimming shorts are sticking to him like cling film. My eyes are drawn to his manhood straining against the fabric like a giant, prize-winning cucumber, a few inches from my face. I gulp. This man has no sense of boundaries.

'We should go,' he says in a serious tone. He holds out his hand to help me up, leaving a tingling sensation in my fingertips. The spark causes me to let go. His eyes are clouded with lust. He felt it too. We stand inches apart in the hot, bubbling water, steam billowing around us. The only two people in the entire place. My chest expands with each deep breath. Once again, my quail eggs draw his gaze, causing a low moan to escape from his throat.

'Go? Go where?' I say, stalling. *Christ Almighty, what have I done?*

He drags his eyes to my mouth; my lips have parted with the heat as water drips slowly down my face, my neck, my chest. I can feel each individual drop. He blinks slowly. 'Upstairs.'

13

This is all my fault. I have indicated that I am a woman of questionable morals without a care in the world, albeit in a foreign language but it still counts, and now I have to backtrack out of it.

I stare up at him in panic as he climbs out of the hot tub, ahead of me. I try not to be distracted by the long, long legs, or the massive cucumber, or the six-pack, or the chiselled jawline, or his hand waiting for me to take it.

Oh, God. How embarrassing is this?

'Don't look so terrified,' he says, a knowing smile tugging at his lips. 'I meant we need to get dressed if you want dinner at 5 p.m.'

Relief floods my body.

'Yes! I knew that. That's what I thought you meant.'

He pulls me up the final step of the hot tub so that we are standing close enough for him to whisper in my ear, 'I'm a gentleman. If you want me to have sex with you, I'd at least expect you to buy me dinner first.'

I'm not sure what to say. I have no rebuff. My eyes are glued to his. They are bright and dangerous and utterly sexy.

'Besides, who would be crass enough to have sex in a hot tub?' He wrinkles his nose at me.

Yes, who would be that crass?

'I'll give you a knock before five.' He dips his head to bow.

I watch him stride away. He is in expert shape. He has an incredibly tight butt. It's like watching two bowling balls rubbing together.

What is wrong with me?

Pull. Yourself. Together.

* * *

As I race past the receptionist in my fluffy dressing gown, she waves me over with a flustered look. 'I'm very sorry but your dress is not ready for you this evening.'

'What do you mean my dress isn't ready?' I say through tight lips.

She explains about the dry-cleaners shutting early, without warning, with all of my costumes trapped inside.

'But what will I wear tonight on stage? I have nothing to wear!' I am trying my best not to create a scene. After all, it isn't her fault. Although, in a way, it sort of is.

As she tries to calm me, a few elderly patrons sitting in the lobby have the nerve to peek over the top of their newspapers to shush me.

Panic is rising from my stomach. It is mixing with the alcohol that I shouldn't have had at lunch and the encounter with Luke in the hot tub that should also not have occurred.

A quick check of the time tells me it is already four o'clock. 'So, when can I have my costumes? I need at least one of them right now. And the rest of them sent to the theatre by nine. I have to do costume changes because I change character during the performance. And the costumes match what I'm singing.' A picture of the Maestro pops into my head. He'll explode if I get into any more trouble. I'm not sure his frail frame and fragile temperament could take it. 'I will be sacked if I don't have any costumes to wear. Sacked!'

'I'm sorry, madam. Perhaps I haven't been clear enough. The dry-cleaners are closed. They aren't picking up the phone. We have no way of retrieving your costumes before tomorrow morning.'

'But I need to wear *something*!' I bellow petulantly. A crowd is starting to gather at the fracas. I am creating the scene I said I wouldn't create.

The receptionist looks startled. 'My friend has a boutique. It does brides-maid and evening wear. Maybe she can help. I'll ask her to bring some dresses round. Or I could get a driver to run you over there?'

Deep breaths. Deep breaths.

'Yes. Take me to the shop. Thank you.' I take in a large gulp of air. 'Give me two minutes to change.'

I charge up to my room like a heifer boiling with rage and yank on the first things I can find. Some joggers and a hoodie. This is 100 per cent my fault. I am to blame. I have taken my eye off the ball and allowed it to wander, and this is what I get. Just as I lock the door, I remember my dinner date with Luke. I knock on his door. No answer. I knock harder. Still no answer.

Bugger it! He'll just have to dine by himself. I'll leave a message with reception. Yes, that's what I'll do. Just as I'm about to leave, the door swings open. Luke is standing dripping wet, clutching a small towel around his waist. He looks surprised to see me.

Keeping my eyes trained on his, I say, 'I'm sorry, but I'm going to have to take a rain check on dinner. An emergency has come up. I can't make it.'

His face falls.

'Can I help?'

'No. No, it's a costume thing. They've lost all my dresses, and I have nothing to wear tonight.'

'Oh, shit. We are due to leave at six thirty.'

'I know,' I say, speedily backing away. I simply do not have time for this. 'Go without me. I'll see you at the theatre.'

* * *

'This is all you have?' I'm too upset to yell. The lady is keeping the shop open for me especially, and I feel rude and desperate and unbelievably annoyed at myself, so I'm going to have to choose three dresses from this scrawny selection. They don't all come in my size, so my choice is further limited. My heart is sinking as I rifle through the racks, silently mourning the lack of my ruby dress.

'I've got this pink satin fishtail in your size. This high-collared, frilly gold lamé, pleated knee-length,' she says. 'Or this billowy, lemon satin puff?'

'No satin, if at all possible, please.' They are three of the most horrific dresses I've ever laid eyes on. I'm only just keeping it all together.

'What about this sheer, peach blush, chiffon floaty one?'

At last. Something half decent. It is after four thirty, and I have less than two hours to buy the dresses, get back to the hotel, do my hair and make-up and make my way to the theatre. I usually need three to four hours at least.

'Or I have it in champagne mist?'

'*Yes!*' I grab the dress off her and charge into the changing room. I yank off my hoodie and joggers. The dress fits very snugly. I rip back the curtain and walk over to the full-length mirror. The material shimmers and swishes as I move, which is a good sign.

I stand, taking it all in. It has an empire-line bodice, elbow-length sleeves in beaded chiffon and a *Pride and Prejudice* vibe about it. It would do for the romantic 'Mi Amore Mi Amore' duet section.

'Do you want the veil and wedding gloves to go with it?' she asks.

What is she not getting about this horrendous scenario?

'I'll just take the dress. Do you have anything more formal in a dark colour, floor length?'

She screws her forehead into a frown.

'Anything at all.' Tears are prickling the backs of my eyes.

Suddenly, her face changes. 'Yes! We had a delivery last week that I have yet to unpack. Winter Brides. There's bound to be something for you in that.' She races off down some stairs, and I hear lots of banging while I continue to search for the showstopper outfit. The dress I'll wear for the finale and the curtain calls. It needs to scream 'Top of my game!' like my ruby-sequined, whale-boned, take-your-breath-away dress.

I hear her thumping up the stairs.

'I've got a peacock blue in full skirt and feathers and an emerald-green strapless sequined ballgown.'

She holds them both up.

'Are they my size?'

She nods. 'Almost.'

Good God. I'll look like a 1980s pantomime dame. I haven't even got the heart to try them on. 'I'll take them,' I say, whipping out my credit card. The amount almost reduces me to tears. Who would have thought three ugly dresses would cost so much? I hope the hotel will compensate me. I have barely anything left on my credit card as it is. And I still need something nice to wear to Las Vegas. At this rate, I'll be turning up in these peacock feathers.

'Thank you so much. I really appreciate it,' I gush, rushing out of the shop.

* * *

It's like a nightmare. After repeatedly interrupting my vocal warm-ups with a 'What was that? Did you say something, love?' my taxi driver finally stopped asking every time I opened my mouth to do my scales, my lip trills, my humming chants. I've arrived at the theatre to find the entire crew and cast have the hump; literally everyone is ignoring me. I race through the glazed stone arches of the colonnade, through the old Georgian folly behind the stage and round the medieval well. Dolly is waiting for me in my dressing room.

'You're late!' she barks. 'The Maestro is furious.'

'I know. I know,' I say, racing in with all of the outfits in garment bags and my suitcase full of make-up and hair things. 'There was an issue with my dresses and—'

'You haven't even done your hair and make-up! Too busy enjoying the high life, were you? I wish we could *all* stay in a fancy hotel and have room service and spa treatments.' Dolly takes the outfits from me and unzips the covers. 'What the fuck are these awful things? You can't go on stage like this! This underskirt is like a hot-air balloon, for Pete's sake!'

'That's what I'm trying to explain. The hotel made a cock-up, and now the original dresses are locked away at the dry-cleaners until tomorrow.'

She stops to eye me suspiciously.

'I've been racing around trying to find replacements. These were the best of a bad bunch. It's them or my jogging pants.' I fly over to the mirror and plonk myself down. My face looks worn out and haggard. That's the last time I daytime drink before a performance.

I get to work, furiously brushing foundation over my face and slapping on blusher and eye make-up while Dolly hangs the gowns up.

'I suppose it's better than nothing.' Dolly comes over to give me a hand. 'The dresses will be the least of your worries tonight anyway.'

I put down my mascara wand and make eye contact through the mirror as she teases my hair up into an elaborate chignon.

'What do you mean?' I frown.

'The Maestro is livid that you and Luke have disappeared off to stay in Gray's Court Hotel. Livid. And so are the chorus girls. Mind, they have been bitching behind your back since the newspaper scandal. They're jealous of all the attention Luke is paying you.'

'But I didn't ask for his attention. If anything, I have spurned him.' I feel flushed at the memory of today in the hot tub and how close we came to doing something I'd bitterly regret.

Dolly gives me a disbelieving huff and helps me into the first of my three disgusting gown options – the champagne-mist chiffon. We hear the bell ring to indicate I'm due on stage in three minutes. We scurry down the rabbit warren of corridors and take the stairs two at a time with me trilling warm-ups at the top of my voice, just as the Maestro introduces me. Out of breath, I take two steps forward onto the stage, only to feel Dolly pull me sharply backwards.

'A word of caution,' she says. 'That dress is completely see-through under these stage lights.'

Fuck me!!!

Deep breaths. Deep breaths.

14

There's a collective inhale of breath as I walk onto the stage. Not just from the ensemble of musicians visibly doing a double take, but the audience's applause is also delayed just a fraction. Enough for me to realise that Dolly is 100 per cent right.

The Maestro seems as though he is going to explode, from this distance. His eyes look like two boiled eggs. I have no idea just how see-through my champagne-mist dress is, but now I'm equally regretting having put nude-coloured underwear on.

I glance over to the chorus girls who are supposed to sing me in, but they are falling about laughing. The musicians have also come in late because they too have been distracted by my walking onto the stage practically naked. They all have their jaws hanging open. This has made a vessel in the Maestro's neck turn blue, and his eye tic has returned. The whole intro has been a cock-up. Everyone is out of time.

I will style it out. I make the brave decision to start singing, in order to give the ensemble and the chorus girls some time to get over themselves and start acting professionally.

The Maestro glares at me. I have made the wrong decision. I am now so terribly out of sync that we all sound dreadful.

The chorus girls keep coming in too soon, cutting me off. The brass section is out of time with the string section. The screeching sounds like they are warming up, not playing a beautifully crafted, two-hundred-year-old piece of music.

The audience has no idea how to react to this farce. And they clearly have no idea how to react to the Sinfonia's lead classical singer appearing on stage in the nude. A low rumbling can be heard emanating from the back row and the upper galleries.

I keep singing, swaying my hips and wafting my arm at the musicians to encourage them to speed up. Some of them have cottoned on and are doing what I need them to do; others are religiously following the Maestro out of fear. It is painstakingly clear that he has no such plans to speed anything up.

It's a complete disaster. The more we try to attune ourselves, the worse it gets. The rumbling gets louder and louder until even the Maestro begins to peer about to see what is happening.

Please let the ceiling be caving in, I think to myself. *Anything to end this humiliation.*

The rumbling is nothing to do with the place being on the verge of collapse, unfortunately. But it does have everything to do with the audience belly-laughing at us. I stop singing. They are howling with laughter. Some of them have tears running down their cheeks. They are creased up. They are nudging one another and shaking their heads in disbelief. Slowly, the hilarity of the situation dawns on me, and I begin laughing too. Most of the string section have had to put down their bows and are joining in until, eventually, the laughter fizzles to a stop.

'I'm sorry,' I say to the audience. 'Artists are always told to picture the audience naked. I guess this takes things in a whole different direction.' Another wave of laughter engulfs the theatre. 'I'm going to get changed into something less distracting... and let's see if we can't start this evening all over again. How would you like that?'

The audience goes wild, clapping and cheering.

'But I must warn you that my next outfit might not be much better. While York is a magnificent city, your dry-cleaners leave a lot to be desired. They are quite "The Shambles". Thank goodness you have so many charming boutiques that are willing to oblige.'

My little joke goes down very well. The Shambles is the best preserved medieval cobbled street in the whole world. The audience will be familiar with its plethora of atmospheric independent shops and bakeries.

'Thank you for your patience. I'm sure Maestro has something he can have the orchestra play for you until my return.'

In response, the Maestro makes a big show of taking the sheet music from the lectern in front of him as he swivels to face the audience, and rips it into tiny shreds. Millions of tiny flakes of paper curl their way down to the ground. There's an audible gasp before silence descends.

I'm not even going to make eye contact with him as I dash off stage. Dolly is there waiting. She scurries beside me as we run down the corridors.

'Never in all my years,' she says, shaking her head at me. 'But I'm not really sure what else you could have done.'

I give her a grateful smile as we burst into my dressing room.

'Good Lord,' she exclaims when she sees me diving head first into the elaborately ruffled, peacock-blue, feathery creation. 'Why does it have a life-size peacock stuck to the bustle at the back? Were Disney Studios having a clearout? I'm not even sure you'll fit through the door in that.'

She's right. I get immediately stuck in the dressing room doorway, and she has to push me out using her foot on my backside. Good job she's built like a Navy SEAL. We race back to the stage area, her helping me with the dress as it is ridiculously heavy, just as the Maestro is finishing a soothing Mozart clarinet concerto. It has calmed the audience right down.

I chew my lip, nervous as to how he will react to my over-the-top, wildlife-themed, Cinderella-style outfit. It's as though I am deliberately bringing the shame.

He takes one horrified look at me waiting in the wings and rolls his eyes dramatically. He pinches the bridge of his nose and gently shakes his head in defeat. The audience falls still, and we wait. Maestro taps his nose four times with his baton while I refrain from yelling any spells at him.

I get the sense that the audience knows that if one tiny chuckle escapes from any of them, the whole show will be cancelled.

He opens his eyes slowly as though hoping this is all some hideous hallucinatory nightmare. The disappointed look that falls across his face when he sees me tells him this is not a dream. I dread to think what he'll do when I twirl around during the waltz section, and he spots a whole stuffed bird poking out the back.

My heart begins to thump loudly in my chest. I could do with some encouragement right about now. I see Luke staring at me. He looks me up and down from the far side of the stage, a huge grin spreading across his face.

'I preferred the other dress,' he mouths to me. It's okay for him. He's already built his reputation. I'm sure if the situation was reversed, he'd be having a huge diva fit. Well, luckily for me, I have a long history of things going pear-shaped. It's as though my whole career has led to this moment, preparing me to rise above it and show resilience.

I inhale a deep calming breath. I'm ready to steal the show. I walk confidently onto the stage and thank the Maestro, the chorus and the ensemble, for their kindness and patience. They all look shocked as I praise them profusely before turning to butter up the audience.

'How do you like my gown? I was going for *Bridgerton* meets endangered peafowl.' I twirl around to show off the peacock. 'Just doing my bit to raise awareness.'

They return a deafening response, cheering, stomping, clapping. I am going to give them the best performance they have ever seen.

* * *

'You've done it again,' Luke says, making his way to me at breakfast the following day. He sits down at my table and places a copy of *The York Press* in front of me.

I glance at the picture of me on stage and try not to react. I'm so disappointed with myself. The champagne-mist gown is nowhere to be seen. Like actual mist, it appears to have evaporated. All you can see is the outline of my figure and a shocked Maestro with his mouth hanging open. Words from the article are dancing around, leaping out at me. Controversial. Attention-seeking. Stunning. Jaw-dropping. And every girl's dream, they've gone with the headline, *Barely Heir! – Just how far will one woman go to bag an heir to the throne?* and an article entirely dedicated to linking my desperate 'naked' singing stunt to the non-existent love triangle with a Norwegian count and his royal cousin.

Luke's lips are twitching. 'You certainly know how to make a splash, don't you?'

'Whatever do you mean?' I will not be drawn into any more dramas.

'You've been with us for three days, and we've had more publicity than we've had in a decade.'

'Hardly deliberate,' I say between mouthfuls of delicious avocado prawn mousse with beads of smoked salmon foam on toasted, almost see-through sourdough wafers. 'If it wasn't for you being famous, they wouldn't be interested in me in the first place, would they?' My voice cracks unintentionally.

'I feel guilty,' Luke says, sighing. 'I feel guilty at dragging you into the tabloids. You're right. It's my fault. After a while you get used to the papers printing whatever lies they want. I should have warned you.'

I stop picking at my mousse and put my cutlery down. 'Or the Sinfonia could have warned me. It's kind of their responsibility. And I'm not used to this sort of attention. Besides, I'd like to know who's encouraging the press to come along to our concerts. Where are they getting their information from? How would they even know about you and Hermione in the first place?'

Luke shrugs. 'Honestly, I have no idea. I'll ask my father to pull some strings and find out.'

I give him a grateful half-smile. 'Thanks.' I wish he didn't look so handsome and sorry for himself.

'Maybe this will cheer you up,' he says, handing me a small package. It's a miniature velvet-covered box neatly tied with a bow. It is the perfect size for a ring.

An uncomfortable silence swirls between us as I remember us joking about him getting wed to avoid marrying his lesbian.

Alarmed, I quip, 'Bit early for a proposal, isn't it?'

Luke's eyes immediately brighten. 'Why?' he says, dryly. 'Would you wait until at least lunchtime?' He pushes the box towards me.

'I don't need gifts. This isn't your fault. If I had been better organised and... less distracted... then none of this would have happened.'

Luke regards me in a thoughtful manner. 'Please take it. I had it commissioned before you started with us. I was going to wait until the end of the tour to give it to you, but I think, considering what I've put you through, it seems like a good idea to give it to you early.'

I frown at the box. It looks very elegant, which makes me exceedingly uncomfortable. And it's a very personal gesture to make.

'Open it.'

I sigh loudly. 'Okay. But it better not be expensive.'

Gah! First-world problems. Hark at me, having to endure free Michelin-star cuisine and five-star luxury accommodation. And now gifts! Poor me.

I pick at the ribbon, pulling it gently apart. I can feel Luke watching my every move. I slowly pry open the lid and stare.

Inside is a silver locket. It looks antique.

'Open it,' he says again.

Jesus. He's so bossy. I let out a huff of exasperation, which makes him grin even more. I take the delicate locket and chain out of the box and hold it up. It has exquisite markings and is extraordinarily pretty. I undo a tiny clasp at the side, and it springs open.

Oh my God.

My hand flies to my mouth as tears spring to my eyes. I stare down at the picture inside. It's my mother. She's holding flowers on stage at the end of a performance.

I frown quizzically at Luke.

'That's her first-ever performance with the Royal Northern Sinfonia. Dolly found it in the archives. She said you'd probably love to have it.'

I don't know what to say.

'And Dolly said that the pressed flower next to it is from the bunch your mother is holding in the picture. She knows because your mother asked her to press it as a souvenir. This was all her idea actually. Well, mostly.'

I swallow loudly and blink back my tears.

'Thank you. This is the most thoughtful gift anyone has ever given me.'

'Dolly says she lit up the stage. She sounds like an amazing woman. Just like you.'

I take a second to compose myself before I tear my glassy eyes away from the locket. I hear Luke scraping his chair back. 'I'll help you put it on. The necklace has an unusual clasp. It's a family heirloom.'

'I can't accept it,' I gasp. 'It's too precious.'

Luke studies me. 'Yes, you can.'

I swallow a lump the size of Wales lodged in my throat. The next minute plays out in slow motion as I hold up my thick, heavy hair to expose my neck. Luke takes the locket and places it carefully on me. His soft touch and close proximity are causing a ripple of tingles down my spine as he brings the two silver clasps together. The world falls silent, except for our breathing. My heart is thumping rhythmically in time with my quick breaths.

Luke trails his fingers leisurely down one side of my neck, causing me to inhale sharply. I feel him tense behind me. I'm not sure either of us knows what to do next. Without turning around, I say, 'I should go.'

15

I return to my room after breakfast in a daze. Luke has taken the wind out of my sails. I was hoping to remain at a platonic distance from him for the remainder of the tour, but now he has spoiled it by being so... so... desirable.

I slap the newspaper down on the bed and remind myself of why I am here. I'm at work. Luke and I are work colleagues. I pick up my phone, suddenly anxious to speak to my dad. I feel for the locket on my chest as I wait for him to answer. I wonder if he has seen this picture. I wonder if he was at my mother's first ever performance. Was she nervous? Did she ever walk naked onto the stage and cause the audience to gasp before they collapsed into bawling sobs of laughter?

No answer.

I hang up and notice that I have a missed call.

It's from Matteo!

I quickly ring his number back. I'd love to speak to him. Tell him all about the tour. Well, perhaps not everything. But I do want to explain why I'm in the newspapers making an exhibition of myself, why I appear naked on the front page today and why I'm staying in a room next door to my leading man.

It goes straight to voicemail. The message tells me Matteo won't be monitoring his messages and to try calling again in a week's time.

I'm so disappointed.

My phone beeps. It's the Dollz WhatsApp group. Tash has posted a pic of me on the online news and a caption that simply says, 'STUNNING'.

Then Liberty replies.

> Look at that thigh gap.

Apparently, she is beyond jealous of the way my inner thigh triangle has been amplified against the backdrop of the orchestra, thanks to the stage lights – it's all very classy.

> INCREDIBLE BOOBS – they look fake but without the price tag.

Cherry, the only Doll to be a reluctant mother (the world's first person to have birthed two oversized, pointy-headed babies nine months apart), is also jealous as she has paid a small fortune, the price of a much-needed second car, to transform her saggy spaniel's ears into perky breasts post breastfeeding.

Sometimes, their priorities are misplaced. I am anything but body obsessed. That's the opposite of what I am. But I miss them terribly.

Big Sue has posted:

> Diva the shit out of it babe #bodyconfidence #womensupportwomen #nakedandproud #muffsout

Big Mand has love-heart-hands emojied them all. If anyone has body confidence it's her.

My phone springs to life. It's my dad. I should probably explain the newspaper headlines to him as well. He must be so confused.

* * *

There's a knock at my door just as I'm saying goodbye to my dad. Thank goodness he was okay about it all. He laughed off the suggestions of the Royal Family being annoyed with me and the fact that my dress had attracted uncomplimentary accusations. He said, 'Connie, love. If you can't embarrass yourself in public when you're young, when can you?'

Which was sweet but didn't really cut the mustard in terms of me needing reassurance that I haven't just killed my career before it has even begun.

I open the door, bracing myself that it is Luke armed with any flimsy excuse to see me, but it is the concierge. He is holding all of my costumes.

'Oh, thank God,' I cry, launching myself at them. 'Thank you so much. Thank you, thank you, thank you!' I never want to wear that awful peacock dress ever again.

'My pleasure, madam.' His kindly expression is all that is needed to open the floodgates.

'And just in time for the matinee performance today,' I tell him as he waits politely to be excused. 'Hopefully, nothing will go wrong this time, and the Maestro won't have me sacked, and the chorus girls will finally get over themselves and treat me with the respect I deserve. Because... because at the end of the day...' I take a deep breath in. 'I don't deserve any of this shit!'

The concierge waits for me to catch my breath. 'Your car is ready, madam.'

'Sorry. Yes. I'll be right down.'

Luke appears in the doorway. He fills the entire frame as he leans casually against it. 'I heard shouting. Are you okay?'

I take a huge inhale. 'Yes. Just letting off some steam. Things seem to be running away with me, but I'm fine. I'm fine.'

He turns to the concierge. 'Can you book us both a table in the private dining room for seven thirty tonight, please?' He smiles questioningly at me. 'That okay with you, Connie?'

'Oh, I, erm, hadn't thought that far ahead.'

Why can't he see that he's the cause of things running wildly off track? I'm not sure we should be allowed anywhere near each other off stage. He's too much of a distraction.

'I thought, considering your present notoriety, you'd appreciate a little privacy after the matinee performance today,' Luke says in quite a matter-of-fact way. 'Plus, we have a rare night off. We might as well use it to relax here at the hotel without any press lurking around corners. We can recharge our batteries, ready for tomorrow's York finale.'

I dither over my answer.

First the hot tub, then the locket and now private fine dining. On the surface it seems very much like he is wining and dining me, but I'm really hoping it is more of a kind-hearted, innocent gesture. Which is how I will be explaining myself to Ged later on. He is hugely suspicious of all of this, especially now

Liam seems to be Team Luke. It's the frilly sleeves and buttocks thing. *Bridgerton* has a lot to answer for.

'I will make the necessary arrangements, sir. Will you require full butler service for this dining experience, sir, madam?'

What?

'No. No, we won't because,' I say, looking from Luke to the concierge. They wait for me to spit it out. 'Because the dinner, it's just... erm, food. Not a dining *experience* as such. More of a food arrangement. Between colleagues.'

'Yes, madam. Food will be served. We will make it very special.'

What I mean is that this is not a *date date* requiring anything special!

'Seven thirty it is. Table for two,' says the concierge, disappearing down the corridor before I have time to reply.

Oh, what's the point?

'Need a hand with those?' Luke indicates the costumes draped over my arms. He is trying not to smile. 'My outfits are already at the theatre.'

'Yes, please. I only need a few minutes to get all my stuff together.'

Luke nods and waits at the door. I go back in, but it feels rude to shut the door on him and even ruder to leave him standing there holding all my gowns.

'It's okay. You can come in,' I tell him.

'No, really. I'm fine here.'

He's certainly quite the gentleman. I immediately soften. It's not his fault I'm finding him attractive. And I'm certain I can ignore whatever feelings I'm having and not act on them. 'No. It's fine. Come in.'

As soon as he is through the door, I immediately regret it. He looks from me to the huge four-poster bed with its many cushions, sumptuous quilts and blankets and swirls of silk, and back to me. His cheeks have pink spots growing by the second.

We stand for a beat too long.

He clears his throat, laying the gowns out carefully on the bed. 'I think I'll wait outside for you. Wouldn't want any rumours to spread, would we?'

Now he's made the mood awkward by insinuating that something untoward might happen if he didn't step outside. It's not like I'm going to rip his clothes off with my teeth and milk him dry. I must stop using that vulgar phrase.

But it is so handy.

'I'll only be a second.' I must make it clear that this is nothing but a platonic working relationship. 'Besides, you're quite safe.'

'I am?' He half smiles. He must be so used to women constantly throwing themselves at him.

'I mean, nothing will happen. I have no sexual interest in you whatsoever.'

God. Matteo said the same exact thing to me the night we first met. And look how that turned out.

Luke seems surprised. 'Good to know. That's just what every man wants to hear.'

A nervous laugh escapes my lips.

I'm relieved to see Luke jokes along. 'I get that a lot.'

'I really can't imagine you do.' *Oh, God.* It just slipped out. Now Luke is giving me cow eyes. I'm going to tell him I'm spoken for as soon as we get the next performance over with. It's time to clear the air so that his obvious attraction does not get out of hand. I will add it to the list of all the other things that also need doing immediately: nipple tassels, Barbie-pink waistcoat with fringing, tell Luke that I'm practically a married woman.

* * *

The ride to the theatre is fraught with tension. We are sitting in the back of a limousine. There is a screen between us and the driver. Luke is sitting next to me on the spacious leather seat, but I am keeping as much distance between us as I can, sharp bends in the road notwithstanding. He leans towards me and in a low voice he says, 'You know I've been thinking about your idea.'

'What idea?'

'To ask someone else to marry me. To stop this ridiculous fake wedding going ahead.'

'Was that my idea?' I cast my mind back. I'm not sure who said what.

'Whatever,' he says, quickly dismissing it. 'The point is I think you might be right.'

I blow my cheeks out. 'Luke. I'm not sure I did come up with that idea, but anyway, what are you saying?'

'I think I'm running out of time. I need to do something, and I need to do it quickly.'

I swallow. 'And you're asking me to help?'

He nods.

'As in, find someone for you to marry?' I had jokingly mentioned Liberty, but in all honesty, I can't see them making a good match. She'd eat him alive.

Luke shakes his head slowly. He's about to say something when the car pulls up outside of the theatre and the driver jumps out to open the door.

* * *

We are just about to go back on stage for the matinee finale and the big 'Mi Amore Mi Amore' number when Luke drops a bombshell.

'My parents just messaged me. The palace has been in touch to begin tentative protocols and background checks on my suitability for Hermione, and this "delicate situation", as they've put it. I guess this shit is getting real now.'

He sounds unbelievably down. Not a great frame of mind to be in, considering the song we are about to sing together.

I reach for his fingertips. 'Try not to worry. No one will make you marry someone you don't love.'

He gives me an intense look, and it's a moment before we realise the Maestro is calling us onto the stage.

Our duet of 'Mi Amore Mi Amore' is turbocharged with emotion. Luke is belting out the lyrics as though this is his final performance as a free man. The emotion in the tone and delivery is his best yet. When it comes to the part where we sing together, and he holds me in his arms, the electricity crackles between us. It throws me completely off guard. His lips hover over mine as he sings the final lament.

He is literally taking my breath away. It's as though he has become the character, and I am caught up in his spell, enthralled by him. I am his one true love, and he must leave me to go off and fight in a war he doesn't believe in, knowing he will never see me again.

In response, I can't help but be swept along. I give such a soulful rendition of the aria that you can hear a pin drop at the end.

He has me clamped to him. His heart is beating out of control. Our lungs are contracting and expanding against each other. His lips are millimetres from mine, while his eyes frantically search my own. I feel his hand on the small of my back, bringing me closer. He wants to kiss me. I can feel it. There's an energy drawing us together. I look up at him through my huge fake stuck-on lashes. My lips are parted and primed for action, and my boobs, crushed against his chest, are bursting to be free of this corset.

'Christ,' he growls in a low voice that only I can hear.

For a second, it is as though we are lost in our own little world, before the audience erupts into applause and brings us back to reality.

Luke gazes lustfully at me before a look of panic spreads slowly across his face. I feel something gently nudge my thigh.

Nudge. Nudge. Nudge.

My eyes snap wide open.

Nudge. Nudge. Nudge.

Luke whimpers quietly.

Good God Almighty.

We're on stage, and Luke has a raging hard-on.

'What do I do?' he whispers between his clenched teeth.

I have no idea. I've drawn a blank. The moment I move away, his massive cucumber will be on full display. Even the back row will get an eyeful. I dread to think how the Maestro will react. This may well be his tipping point.

Suddenly, I get the giggles. I bite my lips together, but that doesn't stop my shoulders from shaking.

Luke is horrified. 'This isn't funny.'

'Isn't it?' I snort.

The Maestro points his baton, directing the applause our way.

Luke gives me a pleading look. It is time for us to relinquish the embrace and for Luke to hold my hand at arm's length while I curtsy to the audience, and he takes a bow. Instead, we stay facing each other, my bustling skirt hiding his embarrassment, and we try to do a sort of uncomfortable side-bow as though we are conjoined twins. We are met with a sea of confused faces.

As I remain clamped to Luke, my only option is to point behind me so that the audience can direct their applause to our talented musicians, who are now shaking their heads at our weird behaviour.

The Maestro joins us at the front of the stage. I hear him mumble under his breath, 'For fuck's sake.' He faces the audience, takes a swift bow and stomps past us off stage. 'I'm never working with you imbeciles ever again.'

16

'Oh, my goodness,' Luke says, clinking my wine glass later that evening. 'I literally owe you my life. You have no idea what disgrace I would have brought to my family if you hadn't hidden me like you did. Here's to your quick thinking and your billowing petticoats.'

We are dining in the private room. It's breathtakingly elegant with wooden surrounds, a big roaring fire, twinkling lights strung up, candles everywhere and tropical flowers bursting from designer vases. I'm finding it difficult to act like we're not on a romantic date because, with the delicious cuisine and free-flowing wine, it very much feels like one. Instead of just food on a plate in a room.

After the head rush of the performance and then the ridiculous way we had to sidestep off stage to save any further embarrassment, we collapsed into peals of giggles. Dolly took one look at Luke trying to cover his gigantic bulge with a flimsy sheet of music backstage and proclaimed I was just as much to blame. Me! She shooed us both off to our dressing rooms with a huge tut.

We have been laughing like children about it ever since. We've been highly unprofessional. Which just makes it all the more hilarious.

'I'm not sure Dolly will ever speak to me again,' he says, sitting back down. 'Shame because she's been an excellent work-wife. Sorry. "Co-worker".' He does air quotes. 'She really looks after me.'

'It was not your finest hour,' I say.

'I think it is fair to say that you have single-handedly saved both the British monarchy and the House of Glucksburg. On their behalf, Constance Cooper, I salute you.' Luke stands up and does a formal salute.

He is quite tipsy, and so am I. 'That hardly makes up for saving my actual life.'

Luke gives me a bashful look. He still has not mentioned his heroics to a single person. 'Why don't we say this makes us even?'

I raise my glass to his. It's hardly a fair comparison.

'Connie, we are electric on stage.' His face grows serious. 'Tell me it's not just me. Tell me you can feel it too.'

Oh my word. The temperature has just gone up a thousand degrees. I shuffle in my seat. We are only halfway through this tour. It feels a thousand years long. We still have three more performances to get through, this last one in York tomorrow and two in Newcastle.

Luke reaches across to take my hand. 'You do something to me. It's like my entire body bursts into flames whenever you walk into the room.'

He is gazing lustfully at me. I need to nip this in the bud.

'Luke. Please stop. There's no point.'

A knock on the door breaks the tension as the waiter comes in. I whip my hand from Luke's, and we sit in silence as he clears our plates away. When the waiter leaves, we resume the conversation.

Luke sighs loudly. 'Why? Why is there no point?' he asks, reaching over to top up my glass.

I cover the glass with my hand to stop him. 'I'm with someone.'

Luke's jaw falls slightly open. 'You are?' He puts the bottle down with a thump, regarding me for a moment as he visibly recovers his composure. A full range of expressions crosses his face. 'Of course you are,' he says with a huge sigh. 'Look at you. Why wouldn't you be?'

What a relief to finally get that out. I'm glad Matteo is not here to witness how unnecessarily long it has taken me to admit to Luke that I'm in a relation-ship. And hopefully, Luke has mistaken how deeply he feels for me, and we can get back to being co-workers.

Luke glugs back his wine and reaches for the bottle. He looks thoroughly dejected. I am finding this whole scenario quite stressful. It's not in my nature to knowingly upset anyone. 'Actually, I will have some wine, please.' I remove my hand and watch as the dark red liquid sloshes into the oversized carved crystal glass. It's time for a change of subject. 'The weather's been nice so far, hasn't it?' I almost choke on the words.

'Is it serious?' he asks, maintaining eye contact. He's clearly not British enough to be tempted into weather talk.

I nod.

'You love him?'

I nod.

'How long have you been together?'

I gulp down a mouthful of wine. 'Erm...' I say, frowning as though it's been a while. This is not going to sound great. 'A week... and four days.'

'A week and four days?' Luke knocks back his drink and immediately pours himself another. He is trying hard not to look amazed. 'And four of those days you've spent with me?'

'I know it doesn't sound long. But a lot of stuff happened over that week. Benidorm can be a very intense place. And we weren't really *together* together until the very end.' I am babbling.

'So, you met him on holiday? He's a holiday fling?'

I shake my head. 'No. Absolutely not. I met him while singing, for work. We were work colleagues of a sort. It all happened so fast.'

Oh, the irony.

Luke has a strange expression on his face. He places his hands wide to grip the corners of the table. A smile is dancing around his lips. 'How do you know he's the one?'

I fiddle with my napkin. I'm not answering that.

He throws his head back and regards me through thick lashes. His eyes have a look of mischief.

'And if you hadn't met him last week,' he asks, 'would you be interested in me?'

What a question. I look away. 'I think we should change the subject.'

Luke shakes his head very slowly. 'I want you, Connie, like I've never wanted any other woman in my life.'

I gulp nervously. He really fancies me. He could literally have any woman on the planet. It makes no sense.

Luke walks over to the sideboard, a big, dark wooden beast laden with all manner of alcohol, and picks up another bottle of wine. He yanks the cork out with his teeth. I consider the two empty bottles lying on the table in front of me and realise that we are getting through way too much. He fills our glasses up to the brim.

'I'm falling in love with you. There, what do you say to that?' He sways slightly before slumping back into his seat.

'I'd say you are very drunk. That's what I'd say.'

He lifts his glass and drains it in one go, immediately pouring another. 'I'm not. But even if I was very drunk, that wouldn't matter, would it?'

'Kind of, yes.' I'm a bit startled at his declaration. I should nip this conversation in the bud. Besides, I'm in love with Matteo. I know it has only been a week and four days, but when you know, *you know*. And I very much need to give that a chance because I get the impression that Matteo has fallen for me too, despite the lack of a formal relationship status.

'Connie. When this tour is finished, I want you to come away with me.'

'No. I can't do that.'

'I want you to give me the same chance to win you over.'

'No. Sorry. I'm already booked.'

'To go off and be with him?'

'For work.' Not that it is any of his business.

'Cancel it. Come to...' Luke casts his eyes around the room as though the answer lies hidden in the lavish, baroque furniture. 'Santorini. Come to Santorini with me.'

'What's in Santorini?'

'Nothing.'

He's very drunk.

'You make it sound so tempting,' I quip, desperate to lighten the mood.

'Well, obviously it's full of things, beautiful things, but the point is... there's nothing there without you.'

'I can't. I have personal performances to give.'

'Personal performances?' Luke leans towards me, his eyes wide. 'Can I have a personal performance?'

'No. Erm, it's a performance at the Palace. To an audience.'

Why am I making it sound more important than it is?

'Kensington?'

I shake my head, wishing I hadn't gone down this road.

'Ah,' he says, pinching his chin as though he's deep in thought. 'St James's. Nice venue.'

'No. Not quite.'

Just tell him!

'Buckingham Palace?' Luke's jaw has fallen open.

'No, it's the one in Benidorm actually.'

Luke screws his eyes in confusion. 'There's a Spanish royal residence in Benidorm?'

'I'm making it sound very... erm, well, it's Benidorm Palace. It's more of a cabaret place than a royal one.'

Luke flops back in his seat, disappointed. 'But I want you to come away with me. Surely this Benidorm Palace can replace you for a few nights?'

It's time to spell it out for him. 'Look, you're a really sweet guy, and I like you a lot, but...'

He gives me a smouldering stare. 'Honey, the very last thing that I am... is sweet.'

I'm not sure where to go with that. I'll try another adjective. 'Okay, you're a really thoughtful and considerate—'

'No. Try again. I'm selfish to the core. My own mother would tell you that for free.'

'You're really... erm, punctual?'

Luke leans forward, his forehead thumping onto the table. 'Kill me now.'

'The point is, I'm spoken for. I'm in love with someone else. Nothing can happen between us.'

He looks like a teen who has just been told he's not allowed to play any more Xbox games. He lifts his head and examines me thoughtfully as his brows knit together. He drums his fingers on the table as though he's thinking of a solution to this problem of me not willing to give things a go with him.

'I'm not a fool. We have chemistry whether you like it or not. I can tell that you can feel it too. The way you look at me. The way your hand is trembling now.'

I hurriedly put down my glass. 'I'm sorry. Maybe I should have told you earlier,' I say. 'I mean, I'm sorry you have those feelings for me but, truly, they are not reciprocated.'

He mulls over my words, not taking his eyes from mine for a second. 'Marry me.'

'Excuse me?' I can't believe he just asked me that.

'Marry me. Be my wife.'

'But we haven't even kissed!' *Dear God, is that the only reason I can come up with?* 'I mean, we barely know each other.'

'You've known me almost as long as *him*.'

'We're work colleagues. We should keep it that way.'

'Lots of couples meet at work. You said it yourself. You and he are work colleagues.'

'We *were* colleagues. Now we are in a relationship. I'm spoken for.'

'You've known him a week,' he says. 'Don't be ridiculous. Marry me.'

'You're the one being ridiculous.'

'I'd make a great husband. You'd make me a great wife. What's the problem here? I need to marry someone, and you need a leg-up with your career. It's a win-win.'

Oh. My. God. I am not liking the way this evening is going.

'No,' I say, leaning back on my chair as I put my napkin on the table. 'I'm pretty sure you can avoid marrying a lesbian some other way.'

'I can't believe you're rejecting me.' Luke lets out a long sigh of frustration. He reaches into his dinner jacket and pulls out a small packet with white powder in it.

Oh God. Such an obvious red flag. I'm rapidly going off him by the second. He flings it down on the table, his face serious. 'We need to get high.'

'No thank you,' I say. I'm no prude but I really am shocked.

He shrugs before deftly ripping a corner from the menu. He rolls it into a small tube, empties a substantial mound of the powder onto the back of his phone and bends to sniff it straight up his nostril. Then he does the same thing again with his other nostril.

I am speechless. Those menus look bespoke. They have gold edging!

Luke shakes his head, his hair flopping into his eyes, and blinks a few times. He leans so close to me across the table that I can see a ring of white powder round his nostrils. 'Come on, Connie. I know you want me. I see it in your eyes. All women want me.'

Whaaat?

'Not me,' I hiss, pushing my chair back. 'What if the waiter comes in and sees you with drugs?'

He laughs as if I've made a huge joke. 'It's just harmless fun.' He sniffs unattractively and leans back in the chair. He gives me a hopeful look.

I huff. 'Absolutely not.'

'I could lock the door to make sure we're not disturbed.' He studies the rug on the floor in front of the fire. I can see his mind ticking over. He is not quite getting it.

'You're drunk and high, and I'm going,' I say, reaching down to retrieve my handbag. Not quite the wholesome dinner conversation I had originally imagined. However, he's done a brilliant job of putting me off him forever.

'No. Wait! Don't go.' Luke leaps up, desperately clawing at his shirt and trying to kick his shoes off at the same time. 'Stay. I'll show you how good we can be together. I have a ten-pack.'

'I don't care how ripped you are.' It's quite pathetic really, the way he is assuming I'll simply lie down and think of England. Or Norway. Or whatever post-Brexit free trade agreement we've put in place.

'But I love you,' he says, hopping on one leg as he yanks off a sock.

Hop. Hop. Hop.

'I'm in love with you,' he declares, all without so much as eye contact. 'Why are these socks... so goddamn difficult... to get off?'

'Luke!' I bark. 'Put your clothes back on.'

He freezes as though I've pulled out a knife and threatened to stab him with it. He suddenly looks tearful standing there with his trousers round his ankles, his shirt ripped open, a raging hard-on and a sock in his hand. 'But what about milking me dry?' he pleads.

How dare he.

Seconds tick slowly by while I march across the room and he processes what is actually happening. 'But I thought...' He lifts the sock towards me as though it'll make all the difference.

'You thought wrong,' I say firmly, slamming the door on my way out.

17

'Things escalated exponentially,' Luke is whispering to me the following evening. 'I can only apologise. I wasn't myself. It was the drugs. Please forgive me.'

We are standing at the side of the stage ready to embark on the final performance in York. I have been ignoring Luke's persistent stream of apologies all day. He has been sending them in the form of bouquets of roses, a giant cookie with 'I'm sorry' spelled out in chocolate, and Lord knows how he managed it, but I received a ten-second voicemail from Justin Bieber singing his 'Sorry' lyrics down the phone.

It doesn't matter how secretly impressed I could tell Ged and Liam were, I am never speaking to him ever again.

I am furious.

And I am not the only one.

The Maestro is also furious. He is still recovering from our shambles of a finale yesterday. Dolly told me he was on the verge of quitting. He has erupted in boils. He is complaining of hair loss, and his twitch has become more pronounced.

I refuse to make eye contact with either of them, which will rather impact on the performance, but I'm past caring. I'm tired, hungover and homesick. I need my friends around me. Thank goodness we will be going back home to Newcastle tomorrow for our final performances of the tour.

'I couldn't sleep for feeling so guilty,' Luke persists. 'Well, that and because of the cocaine. It was an unusually high grade.'

He couldn't sleep? What about me?

'Please, let me make it up to you.'

Dolly races over to tell him off. 'Keep your voices down. What is going on?' she hisses.

I stare straight ahead. I am not getting involved.

'Well?' she asks Luke but gets no response. She lets out an audible sigh. I hear her muttering under her breath before bustling away. 'Every time, Luke. Every frigging time.'

It does nothing to cheer me up.

'She's wrong,' Luke hisses to me. 'I'm not like that.'

The Maestro introduces us on stage to enthusiastic applause. Poor audience.

* * *

An hour later, during the interval, I am backstage in my dressing room. 'I can't work with him,' I say to Dolly. She is helping me out of one gown and into my grand finale costume before she needs to race off. 'Thanks for this. I know it's not your job to help me get dressed. Or to listen to me moan on.'

'I did try to warn you, didn't I?' She is yanking my dress down my legs so that I can step out of it. 'Didn't I say, "Stay away from Luke"?'

'Yes,' I sigh as I go over the memories of last night. How over the course of minutes, we went from harmless flirting to him flinging drugs and marriage proposals at me. Ending in him holding out a sock begging for a handjob. Bizarre doesn't even begin to cover it.

Dolly stops what she is doing. 'Is this about the hotel?' Her tone has changed to very serious.

I let out a frustrated groan. 'If only the Sinfonia had never bloody upgraded me and Luke in the first place, I'd have been with everyone else and none of this would have happened.' My voice is rising along with my blood pressure.

Dolly looks shocked at my outburst, but I am sick of always being caught up in other people's messes, so I continue my rant while she helps me into the finale gown. 'I didn't ask to be upgraded. I didn't ask to be part of a love triangle. I didn't ask for Luke to fancy me instead of the chorus girls.' I plop down into my seat at the dressing table. 'I just want to do my job without all this drama.'

Dolly purses her lips. 'I see. I see.' She clips a few strands of hair away from my face. Her hands land with a heavy thump on my shoulders as she talks to me through the mirror.

'So, Luke told you that the Sinfonia was paying for the hotel upgrade, did he?'

'Yes. Aren't they?'

She raises an eyebrow at me. 'You didn't think that was strange? That only the two of you are staying there? Alone?'

'What do you mean?'

'The Sinfonia would never upgrade the talent. Not even the Maestro. The bottom line comes first. Always.'

'So why did they upgrade me and Luke this time?'

Dolly rolls her eyes at me.

'If it wasn't the Sinfonia then...'

'Wait, don't tell me. Even at such short notice, the hotel "managed" to get you two adjoining rooms?' She does air quotes. 'What a coincidence.'

Oh. My. Fucking. Word.

I've been played like a fiddle.

'You mean...?'

Dolly nods. 'I thought you knew.'

I'm speechless.

She doesn't wait for me to answer. She helps me put on the finale costume and says simply, 'Leave him to me.'

'Thank you. I really appreciate it. I'd rather not have to speak to him,' I say, my fingers going to the locket round my neck. It comforts me to know I have my mother near me. Dolly's eyes are immediately drawn to it.

'Where did you get that?'

I hold it out, the delicate chain tugging at my neck. 'Luke gave it to me. How can someone be so despicable on the one hand and yet so thoughtful on the other?'

Dolly tuts. 'That's because he isn't. The Maestro gave me the locket and I had it made up for you as a surprise. We were *all* going to surprise you with it on the last night at the farewell party. Krzysztof will be so disappointed.'

'Luke made out it was from him.'

She screws her eyes, sighing. 'I bet he did. Typical. Well, I hope you like it.'

'I love it, Dolly. I love it so much. Thank you,' I gush, twisting to give her a hug.

She hugs me briefly before her face hardens. 'I'll leave you to do the rest. I have some unfinished business to attend to.'

* * *

Minutes later, the grand finale is a huge flop. I couldn't summon up an ounce of enthusiasm and nor could Luke. We avoided eye contact. I refused to go anywhere near him. When he reached for my hand to take the final bow, I ignored it and left him hanging.

I'm also quite certain that my face was fused into an angry expression throughout the entire performance.

The only people overjoyed at me and Luke giving the worst performance of all time were the three lead chorus girls. Once we were off stage, they pounced all over him. I watched them drag him off to his changing room and file in after him, slamming the door shut behind them.

Dolly came up behind me. 'You won't get any more bother out of him.'

* * *

I woke up super early this morning following another restless night. There's only one thing on my mind. I ring Matteo. I really need to hear his voice. He picks up within a few rings. 'I'm really sorry to wake you,' I say, 'but I just needed to ask you something.'

'I wasn't asleep. We're still up working. It's great to hear from you,' he says, sounding pleased. There's music playing in the background. 'Let me just step outside a moment.' I hear muffled sounds before he comes back to the phone. 'Is anything wrong?'

'No. I'm fine. It's just that I wanted to ask...' It sounds stupid now that I'm saying it out loud. 'I just needed to ask you if this is real. What we have. It's only been a week...'

'It's real,' he says quickly. 'Very real. And I know it might seem stupid but...' He takes a deep breath in. 'I can't stop thinking about you.'

I sigh softly, my whole being immediately lighter.

'You're my muse,' he says. 'All the musicians I'm working with have noticed a fire and passion that wasn't there before, apparently.' He sounds excited and it fills me with joy to think it's because of me.

'I have to go but... I really can't wait to see you,' he says in a low voice. His meaning is unmistakably clear.

'I can't wait to see you too,' I say. 'There's something I need to tell you.' I take a deep breath ready to rip off the band-aid. I am going to tell him that Ged and Liam and the Dollz are also coming to Vegas, and that I have to squeeze some other activities into the trip. I'm going to suggest we meet earlier or stay later after they have gone.

There's a loud blast of music and some voices yelling his name.

'I'm sorry, Connie!' he yells over the noise. 'I have to go. Can we speak later?'

'Sure,' I say as Matteo clicks abruptly off the call. 'Bye then.'

* * *

After breakfast in my room, reading the local newspapers that were delivered with it, the concierge helps me carry all my cases and costumes down to the waiting coach. As I climb the steps, Dolly greets me with a warm smile. As I pass the Maestro, I avoid eye contact. I'm not in the mood for any hostility today.

The York Press ran with the obvious headline this morning of *Royal Rift?* and an article claiming that the whole of the Royal Northern Sinfonia have fallen out. *Stiff. Wooden. Out of key.* That we are all at war with one another. *Ugly energy.* That we are all having affairs behind each other's backs. *Obvious sexual tension.* That I am jealous and upset. *Cooper devastated.* That the Maestro has lost all control and respect. *Appalling. No clue what is going on.* That the leading man has also been dumped by his royal suitor and is humping the entire chorus line every which way imaginable. *Spurned Count seeks comfort in arms of lowly backing singers.* And finally, that we all must think we are in a Jilly Cooper bonk-buster. Cooper by name, Cooper by nature. I have created a *hotbed of sinfonia.* All according to an anonymous source within the Sinfonia itself.

Dolly walks up the aisle doing a headcount before we set off. She stops briefly, leaning down to murmur to me, 'I bet I can guess who the anonymous source is, can you?' And without waiting for a reply, she shuffles back down the aisle.

I don't care. I really don't care.

This is the final leg of the tour and I have two performances to make everything right. No more ridiculous headlines. No more ridiculous shenanigans on stage. No more naive idiot. I am a part-time professional classical music singer. It's time I grew up and acted like one.

* * *

It is a huge relief to see the familiar landmarks of my beloved Newcastle appear in the distance. The Glasshouse glittering against the skyline on the Gateshead Quayside, St James' Park towering over the city, the mirrored windows of the high-rise hotels reflecting the late morning sunshine, the seven bridges of all shapes and sizes crossing the river. As we pass by the Gateshead Angel welcoming us back up north, and the coach turns off the road just before the Tyne Bridge to dip down to the quayside, I know I am home.

I text Ged and Liam to announce I am back. They are dying to hear all my news and will meet me off the coach as today is Saturday, and they are off work.

A shadow falls over me. I look up to see Luke standing in the aisle by my seat. His eyes are bloodshot. His skin is the kind of full-on mottled grey you'd find on someone who died of cholera back in the day. His hair is sticking up all over the place as though he spent the night hanging upside down like a bat.

'I'm so, so sorry,' he blurts. 'I've never behaved like that in my life. I'm so ashamed. I'm so, so ashamed of the way I acted. I can't believe I put you through that. Please. I beg you. Forgive me.'

His eyes are wild and desperate. His breathing is raspy, and judging by the alcoholic fumes, he's at least 700 per cent proof. He steadies himself by grabbing on to the back of my seat.

I turn to stare out of the window, ignoring him.

He hovers silently beside me for a few seconds before exhaling heavily and walking back down the aisle.

We will never recover from this. I'm certain of that.

When the coach pulls up at The Glasshouse, I see Ged and Liam waving at me from the path. Relief floods through me at the sight of them, causing me to instantly burst into tears. All the anxiety of the last few days manifests as big fat teardrops. They stop waving as confusion clouds their faces.

They rush to meet me as I come down the steps.

'Dear God. You were crying when you got on. Have you been crying this whole time?' Liam asks, taking my handbag from me while Ged smothers me in a hug.

A tiny burst of laughter escapes my lips.

'I admit this does look bad,' I tell them, sniffing up my tears.

'We don't care, hun. As long as you're okay.' Ged keeps his arm wrapped round my shoulder and guides me away to one side to sit down on a nearby bench. 'How are you? What can we do?'

I wipe my cheeks, instantly cheering now that I'm back home and in the safe and reassuring company of my dearest friends. 'I'm just relieved to be back. I'll tell you all about it when we get—'

I'm interrupted by Luke clearing his throat. 'I can explain.' He is standing over us with a pleading expression on his face. I immediately stiffen and grab tightly on to Ged's arm.

Like lightning, Ged springs up. 'Don't bother. You've done enough damage by the looks of things. Take your toxic masculinity elsewhere.'

The two men square up to one another. Luke is towering over Ged. Nostrils are flaring. Chests are puffing.

A few prickly seconds go by before Luke seems to deflate. He gives me one last mournful look and hangs his head, before walking back to the coach.

I watch him go.

'Do not fall for it,' warns Ged. 'I can see right through him. It's all an act,' he says firmly.

18

I decide, under the circumstances, and because I live so close to The Glasshouse, to go home with Ged and Liam, rather than stay in the hotel and risk bumping into Luke.

'I've got a couple of hours before I have to go back for the soundcheck and set up,' I explain as I stuff all of my costumes and cases into the car. 'I might pop over to see Dad.'

'Great idea,' says Liam, giving Ged a look I immediately find suspicious. 'A lot has happened since you left.'

'What do you mean? I've only been away five days.' It feels like a lifetime. 'What's happened to Dad?' I panic. When you are down to your last parent, you feel overly protective towards them.

'Oh, nothing major. Nothing to worry about. Probably best if you see it for yourself.' Ged is biting his lips as though trying not to laugh.

'Okay. Take me straight to his house, please,' I say, whipping out my phone to give my dad a ring.

* * *

Two hours later, I'm back home. I burst through the door and flop straight down onto the sofa.

'Do you need wine?' Liam offers. 'A lot of wine?'

I nod. 'Unfortunately, I'll have to wait until after the show.'

'Ged,' Liam yells through to the kitchen. 'Do we have anything we can give Connie for the shock that doesn't include alcohol?'

Ged bustles through holding a tray laden with hot chocolates with squirty cream and a tower of cookies. 'Way ahead of you.'

We take a mug each and dive in.

'How long do you think it'll last?' I say, shaking my head in disbelief. 'He could barely move his face. He couldn't speak without drooling.'

'He's only had a tweakment, so maybe another two weeks,' Liam says, taking a slurp of his hot chocolate. His face lights up. 'Brandy?'

Ged winks at him. 'Yes. I put a medicinal shot in each one. For the shock. Now, Connie. Forget all about your dad's botched Botox job and tell us about Luke and these rumours online about the two of you. What is going on?'

I try to articulate what happened this week but, somehow, it doesn't sound right.

'So,' Liam sums up for me. 'The two of you realised you had amazing chemistry on stage, yes?'

I nod.

'Then you realised there's chemistry off stage?'

'Uh-huh.'

'Did you act on this chemistry?'

'No.'

'But he books the two of you into a luxurious five-star hotel and attempts to sweep you off your feet?'

'Correct. Is this off the record? Because it's starting to sound like another police inter—'

'But conceals that he was the one paying for it?' Liam holds up a hand to stop me. 'And then he showers you with expensive gifts and propositions you while disgustingly drunk and high on class-A narcotics?' He looks to Ged. 'It sounds rather like how you proposed to me, darling.'

'Classic love-bombing from your typical pompous opera weirdo. What did I tell you?' Ged says, ignoring him. 'We've got you, Connie, hun. Just get through these last two performances and then you never have to see him again. Liam and I will come to both shows. We'll keep guard.'

My phone pings.

> What time is the Sinfonia show? We want to come and
> show our support.

It's almost as though Tash was listening in.

Liberty wades in with immediate excuses to say that she'd love to show her support, but listening to classical music makes her feel queasy.

Then Cherry says:

> Listening to classical music is no different to really bad
> morning sickness. Just stay calm, go to a happy place
> in your mind and try to remember that you're not
> actually being tortured on purpose.

Liberty informs us that her happy place is Timothée Chalamet with his *come-to-bed* eyes. But as he's not performing with me tonight, there's not much I can do.

Big Sue says that she will attend but that she will have to wear noise-cancelling earphones because she has an irrational fear that classical music causes early onset narcolepsy. Big Mand then agrees to wear hers too so that Big Sue doesn't feel like the odd one out.

Another text arrives from Tash:

> And will the bar remain open throughout the entire
> performance? Because we might just listen from there.

I can't help smiling to myself. They would rather be anywhere else, but they are making the effort just for me. They can all be so lovely when they try.

* * *

A few short hours later, I'm backstage at the north's iconic musical hub. I stare at myself in the dressing room mirror.

'Connie, you're as white as a ghost,' Dolly is saying. Her voice seems strangely distant. She clicks her fingers in front of my face to snap me to attention.

I'm nervous as anything. All my loved ones are sitting in the audience and I am desperate to give them my best performance, yet the heaviness of the last two days is weighing on me. I can't summon the will or the enthusiasm.

'When your mother was homesick, she had the exact same look as you've got now,' Dolly tells me. 'And do you know what I used to say?'

I shake my head.

'I used to say, "Think of him. Think of your father," and she used to perk right up and go out on stage and give her all.'

'My mother used to think of her father?' I say, confused. 'My grandad?' I never knew him, God rest his soul.

'No. Not her father, *your* father. She was madly in love with him. Her eyes would glaze over at the mention of him. They were head over heels for each other.'

I wonder what she'd make of Dad's – let's face it – midlife-crisis hummus-coloured hairdo, his shirt-tie-jeans combo and his newly frozen face. Dating the second time around has not agreed with him, but you couldn't accuse him of not trying. He is panicking and jumping on board with what seems like all the trends. He has the beginnings of a moustache and is letting his hair grow out at the back to cultivate a mullet. Madge has introduced him to the wonders of Botox, and he has embraced it in a foolhardy fashion because he has been swept up in the early bloom of an exciting, new romance. But at least he seems happy. It has been a long and painful road to recovery for both of us.

'They were so in love. Until you came along.' Dolly laughs, bringing me back to the present. 'Then they just seemed knackered all the time! But those were her happiest days, she'd always say. Love conquers all.'

That's it. A light bulb pings to life in my brain. All I need to do is think of Matteo. It has worked before. It will work tonight.

'Thank you, Dolly,' I say. 'Great advice.'

I finish off slapping make-up on my face and Dolly helps me into the first gown before whizzing off to check on the chorus girls and the rest of the choir. Who cares about Luke? I must put it all behind me and move on. I'm a grown woman. I'm on a mission to rebuild my reputation and make a successful career out of singing.

My phone pings. It is Big Sue. She has taken over command of 'Operation LoveBomb'. She has assembled a crack team. They will cover both nights' performances. She will make sure I am safe.

Ping.

Tash is messaging to say that she has already issued a warning to Luke via social media.

Ping.

Cherry has sent him a GIF of someone being waterboarded.

Ping.

Liberty will be running interference with Big Mand. They have me covered. One wrong move and they will jettison Luke from the stage faster than he can blink. Apparently, they are standing guard right outside my door.

I turn my phone off with a sigh. It's lovely to know they all have my back, but sometimes… a girl just has to fight her own battles.

There's a knock at the door. A voice yells through, 'Two minutes to showtime. Coast is clear. Roger that.'

I'd recognise Big Mand's no-nonsense voice anywhere. I'm instantly lifted. It's great to know they are there. I will fight my own battles another time.

'How would you know the coast is clear? You've been outside having a ciggie,' Liberty argues outside the door. 'I've been the one keeping guard.'

Big Mand sounds quick to retaliate. 'Cheeky cow. You just spent thirty minutes at the bar. And you forgot my pint of pale ale.'

'I didn't forget it,' I hear Liberty defending herself. 'I was sick of holding it, so I drank it while you were outside smoking.'

I fling open the door to prevent the argument from escalating. Their faces break into wide smiles, and it is lovely to see them. They have come dressed as crack-whores, and Big Mand still has her arm in a sling from Benidorm – don't ask.

As we bustle down the corridor, we pass Luke coming out of his dressing room. Big Mand booms, 'Do not engage.' She has a hand to her earpiece.

'You have earpieces?' I ask, astounded.

'Target in sight,' she roars, ignoring me. 'Repeat. Target in sight.'

There's a crackling sound followed by a muffled response from Big Mand's earpiece. 'Roger that. What's your twenty? Over.'

Luke's bewildered face falls a hundred feet. He steps aside and has the decency not to make eye contact as we charge past. He leaves a few seconds before I hear him follow cautiously behind.

We can be civil with each other. We both have to rise above this and be professional. That reminds me; I need to speak with the Maestro.

When we pass through the back of the stage, Big Mand and Liberty are squabbling over who will get the next round in if Liberty drank both drinks.

'I'll take it from here,' I say, keen to get them back to their seats. 'Why don't you go now quickly? The show's about to start, and they'll close the bar.'

As they tear off at lightning speed, I spot the Maestro hovering at the side of the stage ready to go on. When he sees me, he swivels around to avoid my gaze. I can't say I blame him.

'I'm going to speak to him,' I whisper to Dolly.

'Who?'

'Krzystzof.'

'Please don't,' she says. 'He's developed hives with all the stress. He's scratching himself raw.'

I take a sly glance over to see the Maestro twitching and clawing at himself like a scabby rat and instantly feel sorry for him. His limp hair is swept over a pointy head. His skinny frame is sagging at the shoulders. His arm hangs down by his side, fingers drumming nervously against his leg. He is the best conductor on the planet and I am responsible for doing this to him.

'Is he single?' I ask Dolly.

'Of course. Why do you ask?'

Yes, why am I asking?

'No reason. I just feel a bit guilty that I've reduced him to... well, that.'

'You're not entirely to blame. His partner, Bernard, passed away last year after thirty-one years together. They had weathered some storms along the way. Not just Bernard's illness towards the end, but their families never acknowledged the union. You can imagine how difficult keeping it a secret has been until recent years.'

My heart lurches for him.

'Then, of course, their beloved dog died. Horatio was all he had left after Bernard passed. Run over while he was away on tour last month. So there was guilt over that.'

Oh my God. Tragic.

'Then, of course, the Inland Revenue came last week and took his house off him. Apparently, Bernard hadn't been paying his taxes. He'd been spending it all on young men in Thailand, every time the Maestro was away on tour.'

My mouth drops open. I think I'd tap my nose and look miserable if that happened to me. It certainly puts my troubles into perspective.

I approach quietly and tap the Maestro on the shoulder. He jumps a mile, a fearful glint in his eye.

'I just wanted to—'

'No,' he snaps.

'But I—'

'Don't. You've done quite enough already.'

'I'm sorry,' I whisper. 'I'm sorry for everything. I promise I'll be better.'

His eyes flick to my locket as I instinctively put my fingertips to it. His entire body sags as he exhales slowly, a melancholy smile tugging briefly at the corner of his mouth before he nods stiffly and walks away from me.

Seconds later, the spotlight shines down onto centre stage, and the Maestro strolls out to take a bow. He looks so downbeat. He has no sparkle. I must, must, must do something about it.

I glance over to the chorus girls smirking viciously at me and whispering to one another.

I glance sideways at Luke. His eyes are fixed on the audience. He seems petrified. I follow his gaze to Big Sue. She is sitting with all the others a few rows from the front with a menacing expression on her face. She turns briefly to wink at me. Liam and Ged are sitting between her and my dad and Madge. My dad tries his best to smile, but his frozen cheeks and forehead won't allow it. Cherry and Tash, also in the same row, have enormous cocktails in their hands and raise their glasses to me just as Big Mand and Liberty return from the bar with three drinks each and packets of crisps under their arms. I can see that Big Mand's sling is filled with bags of nuts.

Liberty's bum cheeks are hanging out of her hot pants as she bends over to pass the drinks along the row. There are multiple pairs of eyes out on stalks in the seats behind.

'Please don't ruin this performance,' Dolly begs me. 'I'm not sure any of us can take any more drama.'

I pat her arm. 'Don't worry. I've got this,' I say confidently, because I am imagining the time Matteo first saw me on the plane. He tried to hide the fact that he was checking me out, but his eyes told me everything I needed to know.

By the time the Maestro invites me to sing the opening song, I am determined to give the performance of a lifetime. And while I'm at it, I might as well let Luke know who he is messing with. And those chorus girls. I'll put them all to shame.

I am going to shine so brightly I'll blind the lot of them.

19

Luke says nothing to me as we take our final bow. He has the decency not to attempt any physical contact. The audience is on its feet, stamping, cheering and clapping. The show has been a hit. The Maestro gives me my first genuine smile. He is happy with me. And so he should be. I did absolutely everything he instructed me to do, and I was better for it.

Once we are off stage, he approaches me.

'Thank you,' he says curtly in his Swiss accent.

I'm dying to tell him that I get it now. I get why I need to follow his lead. How he is the golden thread that weaves between the musicians and the choir and me. He creates the synergy; he creates one beautifully orchestrated sound. I'm only one part of a much bigger picture.

Oooh. That would make a great speech. I open my mouth to tell him of my new-found wisdom, but I am met with a knowing look.

He raises his hand to stop me talking. He must have seen the penny drop with a thousand singers. He arches a stern eyebrow as if to say *About bloody time!* and walks off to his dressing room.

I am immediately surrounded by the Dollz.

'Eeeh, Connie, babes, that was proper mint. It really was.'

'Thanks, Liberty,' I say, giving her a quick hug.

'You totally stole the show, pet, although you're still a bit wooden. Would it kill you to move your hips?'

'I'll try, Cherry. I'll try.' I will absolutely not try; this isn't Benidorm and she knows it. Cherry gives me a pat on the shoulder because she's not a hugger. She even struggles to hug her own children because they are always so sticky. She has confided that her daughter has a permanent runny nose, and every time she spots it dribbling to her lips, it makes Cherry gag. Her thinning-haired husband has accused Cherry of causing attachment issues.

Tash has brought Sister Kevin along. She is hoping to get some clarity around whether their weeks-old relationship is exclusive or not, because she has been in two minds as to whether to propose to him. I clocked him coming in late after the interval and them doing tongues throughout the performance. Tash's lips are swollen as though someone has stuck a couple of pink bananas on her face. Or it could be filler. But at least her ankle has returned to its original girth, and she can comfortably get back into her six-inch stilettos.

'We thought you were the best by a mile,' she says loudly, just as the chorus girls pass by. She stops to eyeball them. 'That stuck-up lot can't sing for toffee.'

I can't help but smile. The Dollz have an unsubstantiated theory that the chorus girls are behind the tabloid leaks and have been selling their stories to the press out of jealousy.

'It's Kev's first time doing classical, isn't it, Kev?' Tash gushes. 'He hates anything like this usually. I mean, who doesn't, but he says he'll do anything for me. Especially now that we've agreed to change our relationship status on Facebook,' she says, sounding almost shy. 'We became exclusive during the interval, didn't we?' She holds out her phone as though it were an engagement ring, sweeping it around so that we can see her social media profile.

Sister Kevin, even though he has been put on the spot, is grinning down at Tash. He doesn't even look as though he's listening to a word she is saying. He has the same glassy-eyed, loved-up expression she has.

After we have jumped up and down squealing with congratulations, I notice a couple of Dollz are missing. 'Where are Big Mand and Sue?' I ask, scanning the room for them.

'With your dad and Madge. Big Sue is advising him on how to regain his facial movements with an electric toothbrush. Same thing happened to her once.'

'Luke's dead fit, mind. For a posh opera-type, I mean,' says Liberty.

'Yeah. If I wasn't so dry down there at the moment, I'd probably do him,' adds Cherry.

'And if you weren't so married,' I remind her. Sometimes, I think she forgets that she has a husband and two children.

'He looks like he would give good head,' says Liberty to Cherry, as though the rest of us weren't here. 'His tongue looks massive when he sings.'

There's a loud 'AHEM' as we see Luke hovering nearby.

Christ Almighty.

'I wondered if I could have a word,' he says to me. 'In private.'

Tash steps in front of me. 'No, you can't.'

Luke tries to get past her, but muscle-mountain Sister Kevin steps in the way, followed by Cherry and Liberty. Although I can see Liberty is blatantly eyeing Luke up and down like a lioness would a gazelle. She's even licking her lips.

Luke swivels on his heel and walks away.

They all turn to me.

'We've got your back, pet. Now, let's get to your dressing room to freshen up. We're all out on the hoy tonight to celebrate.'

Dear God, no.

* * *

Even though I am completely shattered, Saturday night post-show finds us all in super high spirits. I can barely walk in my too-high strappy sandals and short playsuit. I am still nicely tanned from our week away in Benidorm and the girls are similarly dressed and in full flow.

I take a moment to appreciate the lively dressing room scene before me.

Cherry has put on her playlist and is dancing while also bickering loudly with Liberty. Big Mand and Tash are puffing away on their duty-frees even though smoking is not allowed in the building. They each smuggled eight hundred cigs through Duty Free and are determined to smoke them.

'Who's for lady petrol?' I ask.

They balance drinks in their hands while hair-curling and straightening. Hairpieces are being clipped in, eyebrows are being crayoned on and noses are being contoured. They stop to look me up and down. I giggle as the memories of the Benidorm makeovers flood back and let them loose on me while we drink the six bottles of Prosecco I had delivered from the bar.

I love these girls.

'Connie, where are you at with Hot Stuff getting us into all the fancy clubs in Vegas?' Cherry asks, shimmying at me.

Las Vegas? Oh my God! There's still so much to organise.

'Erm, nowhere yet. Matteo's incommunicado at the moment. I'll ask him next week. But it'll be fine. I'm sure.'

I'm not sure, and it won't be fine, and I haven't yet confessed to Matteo that our much-anticipated romantic minibreak has now become a work trip, as well as Ged and Liam's pre-moon spree.

'Eeeh, I'm so excited for Las Vegas!' she squeals, and they all start jumping up and down.

'Ow! Watch where you're putting the fucking straighteners,' yells Liberty. 'You nearly had me eye out there!'

'Stop moaning. You've still got another one, haven't you?' Big Mand says. Her career as a midwife has hardened her to most life-altering catastrophes. Especially childbirth.

'Drink up, everyone,' says Tash, sticking straws in the bottles of Prosecco as she hands us one each. 'My mate Abi has got us into the VIP at Aveika. They're throwing in a bottle of vodka if we'll do our hot girl twerking routine.'

Adorable. Well, it would be if I didn't have to get up early to shop, pack, do a final tour performance, attend the end-of-tour formal gathering with the Sinfonia stakeholders and get on a plane back to Benidorm the following day.

* * *

We finally pile out of the theatre, over the swing bridge and straight into the club directly across the river. The bouncers greet the girls like ex-girlfriends. And by that, I mean they practically snog each one of them on the way in.

This reminds me of Benidorm. Of Matteo. Of my life-changing, soulful experience. I will never forget how profoundly, how deeply Matteo and I connected. How from the moment we first met, we had this unbelievable bond...

'Connie, hurry up!' Tash bellows, yanking me inside.

The club is already heaving, and we let loose on the dance floor almost immediately. I glance happily around at the girls, flicking their sleek tresses about suggestively, as we dance around to the thumping music. It is a world away from the classical scene. A world away from the quiet calm of songwriting at the piano. Of layering vocals on top of one another in the music studio.

What is my Mr Window Seat doing now? Where is he? Is he thinking about *me* the way I've been thinking about *him*? Has he been tempted by Birdie, the way I was tempted by Luke? Has he learned the hard way that she is not the one for him? Has he, like me, realised that I am not the rebound but most likely the one? Maybe I should—

'Connie! For fuck's sake!'

'What?' I scream.

'Pay attention. There's a special offer on. We've all got three Skanky Ladies each!'

I am so going to regret this in the morning, I think as Tash hands me drink after drink.

The night whizzes past in a haze of cocktails and a whirl of dancing. I see Big Sue and Big Mand dancing together a lot. I join them and say they make a lovely couple. Big Sue seems momentarily rattled and gives me a glare that would freeze the sun. I explain that I didn't mean a couple 'couple', I had meant a couple of good dancers, before she discontinues her death stare.

Big Mand grins. 'Watch this.' She lures Big Sue into doing some choreographed line-dancing moves that only they know how to do.

It looks great, and before we know it, we are all joining in with them, and it becomes a bit like a Texas line-dancing hoedown in the middle of the dance floor. Then Cherry yells 'Slut Drop!' and down we go, coming up very slowly to loads of cheers from those around us. Everyone in the club is extremely pissed.

Eventually, at 1 a.m., I call it a night, and just as I decide to jump in a taxi and go home, Big Sue swoops up behind me. Her head ducks between my legs, and before I know it, she has me on her shoulders, and I am being escorted back to the bar. Apparently, it is my round.

* * *

The next morning, I wake up feeling very rough and make my way into the kitchen. Liam is standing by the Nespresso machine, fussing about with cups, avoiding my gaze and making a huge show of not making a huge show. Ged is glued to his laptop and unusually silent.

'Okay, what is going on?' I ask, yawning.

Ged spins his laptop to face me. It's a copy of the *Evening Chronicle* online.

Oh crap.

20

I lean on the kitchen bench and take a few seconds to get my thoughts in order. The *Evening Chronicle* has posted a series of photos. They have been taken wildly out of context.

One is of Tash pretending to take me from behind. Another is of me being sandwiched between Big Sue and Big Mand with a startled expression on my face. Another is of me standing over Liberty while she does the splits and licks my leg provocatively. The worst one, by a mile, is of me and Cherry. Somehow, we ended up doing the cancan on the bar. The photo shows angry bar staff, bouncers racing towards us and a huge pile of broken glasses on the floor.

The newshounds are speculating whether the Sinfonia's female lead vocalist is on recreational drugs. And spiralling out of control. *Hot mess.* They are wondering if Count Nikolai or the Royals know about this sordid secret life that I am leading. Goody-two-shoes classical diva by day, flamboyant go-go dancer by night. Or is it because I have been dumped by the Count, who has clearly come to his senses at last?

I am never drinking ever, *ever* again. 'Fuck,' I say, putting my head in my hands. 'My classical career is dead.'

I am unusually quiet for the rest of Sunday. My stomach is churning at how to put this right and come up with a win-win scenario before I have to face the entire Sinfonia ensemble, who I may have accidentally upset on our last day of what had been a successful tour, with my shenanigans. It has put me off wanting to go shopping for my Las Vegas outfits. It has put me off contacting Matteo. It has put me right off planning any drunken nights out for Ged and Liam's pre-moon spree. Instead, I run a hot bath and lie there for two hours having a word with myself.

* * *

Luke has a smug look on his face when he joins me on stage that afternoon for the matinee. Apparently, word has got round that I am in big trouble. Bigger trouble than him, so he is pleased that the attention is back on me.

'Touché,' he says simply. 'We all do things we regret when drunk, it seems. Or were you high? You looked very high to me. And to think you gave me such a hard time when I was coked up to the eyeballs, and yet here you are... splashed all over the tabloids once again.'

'No. Of course I wasn't high,' I retort, keeping my voice low.

'But you were inebriated. And you did do things you now regret. I was both. I committed a cocaine-fuelled faux pas which never would have happened if I'd not taken it. What are you not getting?'

'That's still no excuse.'

This seems to have an immediate effect on Luke. 'Christ. It *is* an excuse... Perhaps if you were high, you'd understand how out-of-control horny and obnoxious it can make you. How many times do I need to apologise?' he pleads.

'I don't want your apology. It wouldn't mean anything anyway,' I whisper loudly. 'I can't trust a word you say.'

'That's not true.'

'The locket?'

'It was a joint endeavour but, yes, Dolly did most of the work. But the locket is a family heirloom. That part is true.'

'The hotel?' I add.

'Have you never heard of a grand gesture?' He looks at me with an incredulous expression.

'Telling me that you are being forced into an arranged marriage?' I put my hands on my hips as we square up to each other. 'Asking me to be your fake wife?'

He continues to stare rigidly at me, shaking his head in disbelief. 'Fake? You think I wanted a fake wife?'

I give him a steely look.

'If I wanted a fake wife, I can have Hermione. Why would I want *you* to be my fake wife? I meant what I said.'

Dolly's words about him being full of charm and not to be trusted ring in my ears. 'Let's just get this over with.'

As the Maestro brings the orchestra to life, Luke and I begin to treat the audience to what I'd comfortably describe as the worst performance ever. We are so angry at one another that we can barely get the words out. And once he starts over-singing at me, well, I can't help but retaliate. Then, when he deliberately begins to cut me off, I have no option but to do the same.

We are cutting the songs so short in our attempts to outdo each other that the Maestro's arms are flinging about trying to keep up with us, which sends the brass section into overdrive. The overall effect is a cacophony of screeching and parping, and out-of-time sequencing.

'Dreadful,' the Maestro mutters to the audience at the end. He contemplates me and Luke standing side by side ignoring each other. 'Simply dreadful.'

My blood is boiling as I stomp off stage.

* * *

'What were you thinking?' asks Dolly for the millionth time as she helps me out of the gown. 'We finished over thirty minutes early. That's never happened before.'

'It's not my fault,' I say. 'I was...' How to explain that I now regret my lacklustre performance very much? We were childish and extremely unprofessional. And it very much was my fault.

'There's no denying that the two of you have explosive chemistry,' she says. 'Sure, you hate each other now, but your voices work incredibly well together. Do you know how rare that is?'

'We sounded "dreadful", remember?'

'I'm not even sure the audience noticed, love. You still got a standing ovation.'

This is true.

'Well, at least I won't have to see Luke again after tonight. He'll probably hop on a private jet back to Norway so he can escape having to marry a royal lesbian. If that's even true.'

I sound petty.

Dolly smiles. 'Let's hope so, eh? Just ignore him at the Sinfonia farewell tour do.'

'Oh, God. Do I have to go?'

'Yes.'

'Are you going?' I ask. I don't want to go without her. I'm not sure anyone will be speaking to me.

Dolly does an embarrassed cough. 'It's at an exclusive club. They won't let people who look like me in. Too fat and frumpy, I'm afraid.' She shrugs, her cheeks beginning to redden. 'You go though. It's an important tradition. Besides, no one ever notices that I'm not at these things.'

Oh, Dolly. My hearts slumps in recognition. The lack of confidence. The lack of self-esteem.

'Listen, why don't we go somewhere else to celebrate instead? Besides, they'll be relieved I'm not there to cause a scene.'

Dolly sounds pleased. 'Really? That would be lovely. I'd like to celebrate the end of this crackpot tour before I start my next one with the very down-to-earth Southbank Sinfonia. At least everyone is more friendly there and not as dramatic.'

'Oh, so you manage other classical tours? Not just this one?'

'You have to in this line of work. There's no such thing as full-time, anywhere.'

'True. I start my Benidorm gigs the day after tomorrow.'

'So I guess we'll see each other on the next Royal Northern Sinfonia tour.'

'If they'll still have me.'

There's a loud knock on the door, and in burst the Dollz looking fabulous in full hair, make-up and fake tan.

'Dolly, meet the Dollz,' I say. *How did I not spot this link sooner?*

Their eyes light up.

'We could do so much with you, babes,' says Liberty, making a beeline for Dolly. 'We could do a full face, a high hair and I'm thinking a blurred lip.'

'You definitely need some of these stretchy wonder pants off TikTok. I carry a spare set at all times. Just in case. It would take years off.' Big Mand slings a pair of knickers at her. 'Put them on.'

Dolly regards me with alarm.

'It might be easier to do everything they tell you,' I explain.

While Dolly plonks herself down in the chair, Cherry takes out a brush, Liberty unpacks her make-up, Big Mand sorts through the wardrobe of stuff I brought with me to change into, while Tash launches at Dolly with a giant pair of tweezers.

Twenty-five minutes later, Dolly can barely believe her eyes. She looks fabulous. She's patting her hair and feeling her face as though discovering her cheekbones for the first time. She's smoothing down the dress they have squeezed her into. It's the abandoned green gown from York that I bought. Cherry ripped off the blousy sleeves, put a belt round the waist to hoick up the length and, somehow, made a perfectly lovely dress out of it. Dolly is over the moon with gratitude.

'Constance,' she says. 'I think I would like to go to the end-of-tour celebration after all. If that's okay with you?'

'Is there a free bar?' Tash asks.

Dolly giggles. 'And goody bags.'

'Well, count us in too.'

I'm still hungover from last night. But when I see them fussing over Dolly, the way they once fussed over me, and the way Dolly's face has lit up, and her confidence increased tenfold, I am overwhelmed with love for my friends.

Who wouldn't want the Dollz in their lives?

There's another knock on the door, and in troop Ged, Liam, my dad and Madge. Big Sue puts some music on, and suddenly there's a party in my dressing room. Everyone is chattering away, drinks have been produced, a fuss is being made, and bunches of flowers are being delivered.

My dad puts a gentle arm round my shoulders. 'You were fantastic, love. Wasn't she?' He nudges Madge, who is standing beside him.

'Oh, yes. Oh, yes!' she gushes. 'Astonishing. Especially those bits where you sort of act the song out. So believable. I don't know how you do it.'

She's referring to me and Luke singing angrily at each other and me wanting to slap him because he kept battling me for the high B notes when he sang and throwing his arms wide to make himself seem important. He was grabbing air and pulling it down as though he was singing an eighties rock ballad. Don't even get me started on his legs. He was almost doing the splits. Ridiculous creature. And Liberty is right. He has got a massive fat tongue.

'You sing so beautifully together. Will the two of you tour often?'

I snap to attention. I'd rather poke my eyes out.

'No. Absolutely not.' I give Madge a nice smile. She's trying to say the right things. It's not her fault she's not my mother. She seems nervous to meet me and she's clinging to my dad like he's a horse ready to bolt at any second.

'I could see that the two of you weren't getting along. When your mother didn't like who she was singing with, she'd eat a whole bulb of garlic before she went on stage.' My dad chuckles to himself. 'She'd reek for days, but it was worth it.' His eyes are full of amusement at past memories.

'I didn't know that.' I'm suddenly aware that, for the first time in ages, I'm not distraught at the mention of her. It's comforting getting to hear snippets about her that I never knew. 'Oh, look.' I dig out the locket from my cleavage and open it for my dad to see.

His face clouds over. 'That was her first ever performance. She was so nervous, she vomited over my shoes before she went on.'

We all laugh.

'Who gave you that? It's a beautiful gift,' he asks.

'Luke gave me it. But it was Dolly's idea.'

'Well, technically, it was the Maestro who gave me the photo, and I said it would make a nice gift and then Luke had the idea to put it in one of his family heirlooms,' Dolly says, coming to stand next to us.

There's a lot for me to unpack here but I don't get the chance. Dad's eyes pop at Dolly's glamorous transformation. He kisses her on both cheeks. 'That was very kind of you all. Ah, Dolly. What would we ever do without you? You've been with us through thick and thin. Sorry we've lost touch these past few years.'

They share a knowing look. The past few years have been harrowing, but because of their joint bizarre makeovers (Dolly's high hair and Dad's botched Botox situation), only their eyes carry the sadness. He clears his throat. 'This is Madge... my, erm, my...'

'His friend,' she finishes for him, receiving a bright smile in return.

'I'm very happy for you, Geoff,' Dolly says. 'Now, let's get everyone to this party.'

'We'll let you young ones enjoy it,' says Dad.

Dolly sounds chuffed. 'I'm nearly forty.'

'That's nothing these days,' says Madge. 'You're in your prime. Have a great time.'

'I'm so proud of you, Connie. Your mother would have been over the moon to have seen you on stage. You look just like her, darling. I'm glad you're doing it. It makes me...' His eyes are glassy with tears. 'When I see you up there on stage, it makes me feel like she's still here with us.'

Yikes. I guess that's me not telling him that it's very likely I'll be sacked after tonight because of all the trouble I've caused this week.

I give him a huge hug. 'Thank you, Dad. I love you so much.'

'By the way, Connie, babes,' Cherry interrupts, yelling over the music. 'Nancy said she sent you the itinerary for Vegas a few days ago.'

Christ, did she?

'An itinerary would be great. Will there be a hot-air balloon or any other occasion to wear high-concept casuals?' asks Liam. 'Because Ged and I have invested in some matching gold, glittery dungaree hotpants.'

Of course. Of course they have.

'And what did Matteo say about us all coming over?' Ged says, folding his arms and tilting his head to the side expectedly.

They wait for me to answer.

'He's fine with it, is he?' Ged probes. 'He's fine with having to share you with your work commitments and your best woman duties? Did you tell him that we'll not be taking up all of your time?'

'And we can combine some of the activities such as when he arranges the celebrity meet 'n' greets,' enthuses Liam, his head bobbing with excitement. 'I hope Harry Styles is in town. Can you ask if he knows anyone who knows anything?'

'I'd be happy with a casino full of drunk, emotionally illiterate millionaires,' chips in Liberty. 'Ask him if he knows any, will you, Connie, pet?'

We are all fully aware that while impossibly handsome and kind, Matteo is also the dark-eyed, brooding sort who doesn't suffer fools. He has little patience when people – in other words, me and the Dollz – occasionally let others down professionally due to our amazing ability to wreak havoc wherever we go.

'Yes. Yes, of course. It'll be fine. I'll send you the itinerary first thing tomorrow. There are just a few little things I need to confirm first.'

Lies upon lies upon lies.

I must tell Matteo that we are all coming to Las Vegas. I must. But I will leave it until the end of the Sinfonia farewell party. He is about eight hours behind, so he will get my message when he wakes up.

The thought of seeing him sends an excited shiver right up my spine.

'Oh, and Nancy says Eddie from Talent Star needs us to do him a favour while we're over there. Some sort of birthday surprise,' says Big Sue.

'What do we have to do?' asks Tash.

Big Sue shrugs. 'She didn't say.'

I notice my dad is looking concerned. 'As long as you're safe, love.'

'Of course, Dad. I'd never do anything stupid. It'll be perfectly above board. Probably.'

He takes a moment. Most likely chewing over the fact his daughter has pretty much made a fool of herself in public every single day this week. 'I just worry that' – he casts a quick glance around the room – 'that this is all a bit much for you. It's all happening very fast.'

He's right. It is all happening too fast and I am thriving on it. 'I'm fine, Dad. Don't worry. I've got it all in hand,' I say, ushering everyone out of the dressing room.

Famous last words.

21

The end-of-tour celebration always begins with a speech by one of the founding members of the Sinfonia, apparently. It is being given by a very old gentleman who has come dressed to shoot grouse on a country estate. He keeps stopping at the end of each sentence to noisily suck in a lungful of air as though he should be hooked up to a ventilator as a matter of urgency. After laboriously telling us when and why the company was founded, he thanks the ensemble, the chorists and the tour manager.

'If Dolly were here, I'd tell her what a marvellous—'

'I *am* here, Mr Faberhouse,' Dolly says, standing right next to him. 'I was the one who escorted you in. We had a whole conversation about land inheritance tax and your views on what's wrong with multimillionaires having to pay it, remember?'

He takes a second glance at her. 'Really? Is that you? Why, I barely recognised you, my dear.' He throws his eyes to the ceiling and carries on as though he's baffled by her transformation. Eventually, he gets around to thanking the world's leading conductor, Krzystzof Helmuth, who keeps his own speech mercifully short and to the point.

'I, too, would like to thank everyone for their efforts and look forward to seeing *some* of you doubling them the next time.'

He gains a weak ripple of applause, but he does have a point. I'm glad I don't have to make a speech. The mood has somewhat flattened, and the Dollz are making noises of becoming bored. Just as we think the Maestro is about to tell us all to avail ourselves of the free bar, Luke steps towards him and throws an arm over his bony shoulders.

'Maestro, the Sinfonia would be nothing without you.' Luke sweeps his gaze across the crowd of musicians until it lands on me. 'I'm sorry I messed things up for you, Connie. I'm sorry for lots of things.'

The silence that follows is ear-splitting.

Oh my God. Even the Maestro coughs with embarrassment. I have no idea what to say, and my face is on fire. Why would he apologise so publicly?

When I don't respond, the Maestro shrugs Luke's arm away to face me. 'You are both as bad as each other. However, somehow it works. You are both as equally brilliant as you are competitive, as you are impulsive.' He gazes around. 'We all know it. You create something unique and very special together.' He turns back to Luke. 'Only a fool would not respect that. Whatever you did, do not do it again.'

The Maestro's speech takes the wind out of Luke's sails. He deflates in an instant, shrinking backwards into the crowd as Dolly yells that the bar is now open.

* * *

'God, he's gorgeous,' says Liberty to me for what seems like the billionth time.

'He isn't. You've got your beer goggles on,' I tell her firmly. In my peripheral vision, I can sense Luke staring at me. I make the mistake of looking over to see if I'm correct. Luke is standing with each arm slung over the shoulders of two chorus girls who are gyrating against him. Oh my God, his legs are too far apart again. He's laughing at something they are saying. They take turns to reach up and whisper in his ear. Now he's flicking his hair away from his face, but his eyes are trained on me the whole time. He's trying to make me jealous.

Oh, God. Part of me feels sorry for him. He really needs to stop thinking he is still in with a chance.

'He's rich, good-looking, posh, and he can sing. What's wrong with him again?' Liberty asks.

'He's a manipulative liar,' I say, pointing at him dancing with the chorus girls at the edge of the dance floor. 'And he can't dance.'

'Great idea,' says Liberty, grabbing my hand and dragging me towards him. 'Let's show him how it's done.'

Gah! Let's absolutely not show him anything! I have successfully avoided him all night. The last thing I want is for him to think I'm deliberately cavorting in front of him.

'We'll get his attention, and then he'll be sorry.'

I am aghast. It makes no sense. I watch, horrified, as Liberty bellows over to the other Dollz, 'Hey, lasses! We're doing the Tay Tay.'

What is Liberty doing? The Tay Tay is not for the faint-hearted. Plus, you need to be wearing good supportive knickers because there can be a lot of undercarriage on display. Liberty is bold and adventurous. She does not mind her undercarriage being ogled at. Not one little bit. In fact, she says it is her favourite part of her body.

The Dollz leap into action, and out of nowhere, Ged and Liam appear. Ged yells to Liam, 'I'm so glad we practise this regularly at home!' They had to stand in for Tash and Big Mand on the final night of our Benidorm tour, and they are still buzzing about it.

'It's going to form part of the pre-moon finale,' Liam beckons to me. 'Come on, Connie. We can't do it without you.'

This is the first I'm hearing of a pre-moon finale. I look at the crowd gathering around us and inwardly cringe. The DJ starts playing Taylor Swift, and suddenly we have taken over the dance floor as we get ready to perform our much-talked-about routine from Benidorm.

Luke is watching with interest.

I. AM. MORTIFIED.

We begin standing with our legs apart and our hands on our hips. When the first heavy beat lands, we all swivel our heads to the left in perfect synchronisation. Soon, we are gyrating our hips. We are twerking. We are bending our bodies. We are waving our arms in time. We are rolling our necks round and swinging our hair. We are dragging our hands down our bodies, copping a quick feel of our own boobs, and trying to appear suggestive while we do it. Then – God help me – we are thrusting our undercarriages at the crowd in a sort of splits-meets-downward-dog kind of move. It's very complex choreography. Cherry is a huge fan of mixing her genres, especially when it comes to ballet, pole dancing and the Kama Sutra.

I try not to make eye contact with any of the audience. After all, they are my work colleagues. Fellow classical musicians and singers. They are prim and proper and do not necessarily want to see me flashing the insides of my thighs at regular intervals or Big Sue pretending to reverse-cowgirl me, or how high I can kick my leg above my head while Tash slides down it to the floor like it's a greasy pole.

We are coming to the end of the routine where we all respectfully place our hands on each other's bum cheeks and rub them round in small circles before doing the same thing to our own bum cheeks. We finish the routine in a variety of poses. Splits. Low twerks. Sun salutations. Downward dog. And again, with the bum obsession, our bodies twisted, one hand on a boob with the other on a bum cheek.

The crowd burst into applause as we stand, keeping our poses and panting heavily for a few moments. I have to admit, it is thrilling. My heart rate is through the roof, and I'm sweating. I wipe the hair from my face and make eye contact with Ged and Liam. They are bursting with pride. They have every right to feel pleased with themselves.

'That was so much fun,' Liam mouths to me before we break formation and start hugging each other.

I accidentally lock eyes with Luke. His jaw is hanging open. He is full-on staring at me. He is not even blinking. I see him visibly swallow as he tries to recover himself, pretending to look elsewhere. Someone catches his eye, and he forces a huge smile. I follow his gaze to Liberty, who is batting her lashes at him. She's twirling a long strand of her hair and now she's biting her lip suggestively. He shakes himself free of the chorus girls and strides towards her like a sailor to a siren call. Just as he reaches her, he glances back over his shoulder to check that I'm watching him.

* * *

Over the next hour, Liberty goes nuclear in her attempts to bag Luke at the club. The chorus girls try to put up a fight, but there's no contest against a she-devil on a mission. Liberty is pulling out all the stops.

'What is she playing at?' asks Ged, coming over to me. 'I've been watching them for half an hour. She's all over him.'

'I know. I've warned her off him, but she's not bothered that he is a self-centred moron.'

'She'll love that even more. Besides, it's probably him who will come off worse in that fling. She'll go mental when it all fizzles out.'

As though Luke was listening in, which would have been impossible over the blaring music, his eyes find mine across a sweaty, heaving dance floor full of writhing bodies.

Ged misses nothing. 'He's clearly only flirting with her to make you jealous.'

'He totally is. I'm even starting to feel sorry for him.'

Ged gives me a stern look. 'Are you?'

'If I didn't hate him so much I would.'

He strokes his chin and squints at me. 'There's a very fine line between love and hate.' He's been overdoing it on the Tequila Rose shots, and they have given him a false sense of emotional intelligence. 'This thing between you is clearly still unresolved.'

Whereas the tequila shots have given me a sharp sense of sarcastic wit. 'I didn't realise you'd picked up a PhD in psychotherapy while you were at the bar.' I put my hand on my hip to emphasise my point. 'Do keep explaining to me how I feel.'

'You're obviously torn between the two love interests. I'm not sure you're being entirely honest with yourself about your true feelings.'

I huff, ready to disagree, but he continues loudly, bellowing over the music. 'It's about making the right choices when it comes to love. You should ask yourself whether you're ready to truly love with authenticity and passion.'

'Should I really, professor?' *I'm a child.*

I can see Ged's perfectly shaped eyebrows rise slightly. 'Can you be brave? Can you be vulnerable with someone? Can you be honest and open? Can you forgive?'

This is a ridiculous rhetorical question, and not one that I'm sure I know the answer to.

'Because in my humble opinion' – Ged swings his gaze back to Luke, watching as his backside sways back and forth – 'you've been neither with either of these... these incredibly hot love boats.'

'Wow. I did not expect such a detailed or free therapy session.' I down my shot. I am miffed. Ged is giving me the hump. He is saying things that I do not want to hear. 'I thought you were on my side. I thought you hated Luke, too. What about his fat tongue and standing with his legs too far apart?'

'Seriously? I impart a decade of romantic wisdom and that's what I get back?' says Ged, seeming almost exhausted by me.

He's right. I'm hardly the poster girl for emotional literacy, but when it comes to Matteo, I haven't been open with him at all about what's been going on. And if I'm really honest, I think the reason I won't accept Luke's apology is because I feel as much to blame. I was catching feelings for him early on, and I could see he was growing more attracted to me. I should have put a stop to it earlier. I'm angrier at myself than Luke, I suppose.

'Sorry,' I say, rubbing Ged's arm. 'I don't know what's going on with me. It's been a very weird week. And yes, I hear what you are saying. Maybe I was a little dazzled by Luke at first, but I'm sticking with Matteo. Even if he is a little too magnificent.'

Ged throws an arm around my shoulders to give me a hug.

'What's she playing at?' says Liam as he approaches us with three Skanky Lady cocktails. He points to Liberty. 'Have you sent her on a mission to ruin him, babes?'

'No. She appears to have gone rogue,' Ged answers for me.

'Who's gone rogue?' says Big Sue, eyeing Liberty on the dance floor from her great height. 'That's hardly "hoes before bros", is it?' She shakes her head.

'We do always say no double-dipping, like.' Big Mand is screwing her eyes to get a better view. 'Why has she got her leg up on his shoulder? It's not time for the Strictly. It's way too early for the Strictly.'

'Who's doing the Strictly?' Tash says, looking a bit worse for wear.

'Liberty is doing her Strictly move on Luke. Even though she knows he has a thing for Connie,' explains Big Sue. 'And they clearly have unfinished business.'

'I'm all for her getting her flaps out, but she's breaking the "sisters before misters" sacred code,' Tash says. 'She's a bloody disgrace. Strictly is an end-of-night pulling move, and that girl knows exactly what she's doing.'

We watch Luke slide his hand the full length of Liberty's leg, right down to her rock-solid tiny bum. He pulls her in close so that she is doing a perfect vertical split against him. His eyes are popping out of his head as she slides her leg slowly down so that he can place his hand under her knee. They are grinding their groins together as Liberty expertly bends over backwards to expose most of her chest and neck, her long hair sweeping down to the floor.

'Now she's going straight into the Dirty Dancing move. He'll never be able to resist that.' Cherry has joined us from out of nowhere. 'She does look hot though. I'll give her that.'

It would appear Luke can't resist it. With one hand securing her firmly at the waist, he drags the other from under her knee, up her thigh to linger over her hip, her ribcage, lightly over her breast to her neck. He brings her slowly back up towards him. Just as they look about to kiss, Luke turns sharply towards us. His eyes travel the length of our group as we all stare blatantly back.

Liberty takes the opportunity to roll her eyes at us. But it's Luke's sorrowful expression when his eyes reach mine that has us all thrown. He stands back from Liberty, does a little bow that only aristocratic men can get away with, and disappears into the throng of dancers. By the time it is clear that he has left the building and he is not coming back, Liberty stomps over to us. She is not pleased.

22

The following morning, I'm up and ready to face the music. This has to be one of the most bizarre weeks of my entire life. The Royal Northern Sinfonia have summoned me to attend a briefing. It's a performance review. Like they do with all new staff after their first tour with them. I'm almost certain they've never had a singer cause so much trouble in their seventy-year history.

'What time do you have to be at The Glasshouse today?' Ged asks me, coming into the kitchen. 'Need a lift?'

'No, thanks,' I say, handing him his first coffee of the day. He is a little late for work, and we are all hungover after last night's end-of-tour party, which was then followed by a twenty-seven-minute rant from Liberty about us interfering with her rights to the throne of Norway. She started when we ordered the Ubers and was still ranting as they pulled up and we all piled in. Thankfully, Liberty was in a car with Big Sue, who was having none of it.

'Are you sure? Because I'm driving to work that way?' he says, taking a grateful sip.

'I could do with the fresh air, so I'll walk,' I say. 'And sorry about being stroppy last night. This whole Luke thing has thrown me.'

Ged's face softens into a caring smile. 'I'm getting used to it. Wouldn't have you any other way. You're a diva now. Own it.'

I make him a heart shape with my hands, and he makes one back. 'Good luck. I'm sure it'll all work out for you, honey.'

* * *

I stand in front of the Royal Northern Sinfonia executive board members as they sit around an elaborate semicircle-shaped desk made of highly polished, expensive walnut. The chief exec of the Royal Northern Sinfonia has just outlined his objections to my staying on as lead vocalist, to the stiff-looking colleagues sitting on either side of him. Mr Faberhouse is acting as though he has never seen me before.

'However, after careful consideration... and much deliberation... we have come to a decision.' The chief exec shuffles some papers in front of him. He's really labouring the point even though I have explained many times that the tabloid headlines had nothing to do with me.

In fact, now that I'm here and taking in their pious faces, I'm not sure I really want to go through another tour with them. But I do have bills to pay and the expensive trip to Las Vegas coming up next week. And, hopefully, if all goes well, Matteo and I will be flying back and forth to see one another in Spain, LA and other exciting locations. And, of course, Ged and Liam will want to have their wedding shortly after the pre-moon spree, which I'm sure will be some-where equally as glamorous and expensive.

'You know, we never have any of this bother with our other lead vocalists.' He flaps a dismissive hand in my direction.

His words pinch at my heart. I take a deep breath in. 'It's okay,' I say, holding up my hands. 'I completely understand. Even though none of you seem to accept that the tabloids were not my fault. You seem very eager to blame me in some way. And the irony is that the extra publicity resulted in the first sell-out tour you've had in decades.'

I have their undivided attention.

'Whoever sent in those latest photos must have been doing some major stalking. Because they would have needed to leak them to the press at 2 a.m., in time for the morning news. And the other leaks, who was behind them? It certainly wasn't me. If I were you, I'd be looking into it. You obviously have a mole in the organisation. Unless you are all accomplices. And in it for the profits.'

They furrow their brows as I explain, sliding their eyes back and forth to each other in a concerned manner.

'I think I'd be better off with the London Sinfonia. You never hear of this sort of thing happening down there. They have proper safeguarding in place for their staff. And besides, I've been asked by the London Opera House to consider an exclusive performance in front of the Royal Family for an upcoming anniversary.'

I see their startled faces flush with surprise. The London Sinfonia is their biggest rival. The chief exec suddenly doesn't seem so smug.

'We have decided that in light of your extraordinary talent,' he says, eyeing the other two warily, 'we'd be delighted to keep you on as lead vocalist.'

I'm not sure.

'You are by far the most surprising young voice we've heard for a decade. And you do seem to bring in a younger, more niche audience.'

'Well, that's very nice of you to say.' I can feel myself softening. 'But—'

'And we'd match the salary we are paying the Count, of course.' He scribbles a figure down on his notebook and turns it to face me.

Wow. I can't deny the money and the kudos is very appealing.

'I'd need reassurance that you are going to investigate who is behind all these leaks. I have my own reputation to think about,' I say firmly.

'Of course. Of course. And you'd have full access to wardrobe. Just ask Dolly for whatever you need for the next tour.'

Ooh, that's very tempting.

'Let me think about it. I'll let you know later today.' I watch as they all squirm.

'We look forward to hearing from you,' says the chief executive hopefully. 'The next tour will be across Europe, if that helps you decide.'

Touring Europe! Keeping the excitement from showing on my face, I manage, 'Thank you. I'll bear it in mind.'

I walk out of there a foot taller.

I am a friggin' hashtag boss lady.

* * *

'How did it go?' Dolly asks, sitting opposite me in a nearby coffee shop on the quayside.

I peer out over the River Tyne and the Millenium Bridge arching over it, coming to rest at the feet of the old flour mill, now home to trendy artworks and a rooftop restaurant. It's in stark contrast to the neighbouring Glasshouse, a giant shining dome reflecting the blue sky and dominating the skyline, home to my new career. I see my reflection in the glass. I am vibrant. Strong. Grown up.

'They want me to stay on.'

'They do? That's great,' says Dolly a fraction too quickly.

'Yeah. I kind of pushed them into a corner over investigating the newspaper leaks on tour. I think it changed their minds about sacking me.' I can't help but feel proud for standing up for myself. 'They want to avoid losing me to the London Sinfonia. So, I'm staying. Apparently, the next tour is across Europe. How amazing is that?'

Dolly fiddles with her coffee, stirring sugar into it. 'Good for you, pet. You'll love Europe. The tours are always... I was going to say wild, but after this one, I'm not so sure. But at least the costumes are more elaborate. I have some ideas in mind already.' She's deliberately not making eye contact.

'Wait. You knew they'd keep me?'

She looks up.

'How?' I ask. Her face is a dead giveaway.

'Luke threatened to quit if they didn't.'

'What do you mean?'

'Apparently, Luke told the chief exec that if they fired you, he'd quit.'

I let this sink in.

'But why? Why would he do that for me? I didn't need him to do that. I was bossing the shit out of it.'

Luke is so annoying. I can't even think of a word to describe how infuriated I am with him right now.

She shrugs.

'There has to be more to it. Why would a Royal be remotely interested in me? He could have any woman in the world. Any *royal* woman, in fact. Why would he go to such lengths to sing with me? Why would he threaten to quit?'

Dolly stares blankly back.

'Come on, Dolly. You know him. Why would he give me a family heirloom? He barely knows me.'

'I think you need to speak to Krzystzof about the locket.'

'He's the second to last person I'd want to speak to. Why? What would he have to do with anything?'

'He's Luke's godfather. And, technically, the locket belonged to him. As for Luke defending you to the Board of Trustees, I think he has genuine feelings for you and just wants to make things right.'

* * *

'This day just keeps getting stranger and stranger,' I say to Ged later that evening. He is pacing up and down our living room. All he needs is a pipe and a deerstalker hat.

'So, if Luke is the Maestro's godson, that must mean the Sinfonia are doing the Norwegians a huge favour. Perhaps in return for some generous arts funding? Maybe Luke's parents have asked his godfather to keep an eye on him, and being on tour keeps him out of trouble?'

'Yes. Yes, that's it,' joins in Liam, excitedly. 'Luke is the wild card of the family. The black sheep. The difficult second child. The oddball. They have shipped him off. I wonder what he has done to warrant being sent here to Newcastle.'

'Must be really bad,' Ged agrees.

'You lost me at arts funding,' I say, putting a stop to the speculating and endless clichés. 'But we don't have to worry about Luke, or Count Nikolai or whatever he's really called, because I won't be seeing him again until the next tour. Which, thankfully, is months away. Besides, when we get back from Las Vegas, I'll buy another locket and return the antique one to the Maestro. Let's just forget all about it for now and concentrate on getting these gigs out of the way in Benidorm and then having a great time in Vegas.'

'Quite right. We have much bigger things to worry about.' Liam starts jumping up and down. 'How did you get on shopping today?'

They peer at my cases, all packed and ready to go. We are all flying to Benidorm tomorrow morning with the Dollz. Ged and Liam are going to stay in the supremely gorgeous annexe of the villa because the five-star hotel they were thinking of booking refused to let them sunbathe naked on the balcony. The Dollz will stay in the main villa. I will stay in my new room above Voices.

'Have you got everything?' Ged asks, getting out his checklist to supervise me.

I nod. 'Cherry is bringing all the Barbie and Ken outfits with her to Benidorm for us to try on.'

'What about the pink glitter cowboy hats?' Ged asks.

'Big Sue has those. They have a picture of you two kissing on them,' I assure him.

'And the Elton John big heart sunglasses?'

'Tash is in charge of those. She also has the "last night of freedom" satin sashes, the deeley boppers, the handlebar moustaches and a wide range of inflatables.' Thank God for next-day delivery.

'Good. Good,' says Ged, famous micromanager that he is. 'And I assume it's all vacuum-packed in with the hold luggage? They'll never let us through security with all of that stuff.'

'Yep.' Vague memories come back to me of the Dollz getting stopped at security the last time we flew from Newcastle Airport, and all their sex toys and fake tan being taken off them. They were livid. 'I've hidden them amongst the clothes.'

'So, you and the Dollz will be gigging at Voices and Benidorm Palace while Ged and I do our beauty prepping, before we all fly out to Las Vegas together for the best celebration of our entire lives?'

Could he be any more optimistic? 'Uh-huh.' I nod vaguely, wondering if I'll even survive the magnitude of such pressure.

I open Nancy's email on my phone. She has booked us to do three nights in Vegas over the course of a week, plus the dubious thing we need to do for Eddie at Talent Star. We are also doing Ged and Liam's pre-moon spree by day, and on the alternate nights. While I am also trying to enjoy a romantic break with Matteo, so that we can spend some much-needed time together.

My heart starts racing at the stress of it all. Short of using dark magic to somehow create dual timelines, there just aren't enough hours in the day to squeeze it all in.

I have still not plucked up the courage to tell him.

But I will.

I will.

PING.

Matteo's name flashes onto my screen. He is messaging to let me know that he will be unexpectedly free tomorrow for a few hours if I'm available to FaceTime.

'What's wrong?' Ged asks.

I show him the text.

'But that's a good thing, isn't it?' he says, sounding confused.

I blink rapidly. 'Yes. Yes, absolutely.'

'Then why do you look so worried?' He screws his eyes at me. 'You *have* told him we're all coming to Vegas, haven't you?'

23

After a rather sleepless night, Ged, Liam and I arrive at Newcastle Airport ready to travel to Benidorm. This is the build-up to Ged and Liam's pre-moon spree. With their wedding potentially only months away (they are currently floating the idea of a pop-up ceremony), this is them going out with a bang to celebrate their last weeks of freedom in style. And everything needs to be perfect. And by perfect, I mean micromanaged like a Las Vegas casino heist.

The three of us are waiting at the check-in desk with our luggage trolleys piled impossibly high when we hear an almighty racket coming from the other side of the concourse. I know without even turning around that it is the Dollz. Like us, they have a trolley each, piled high to an excessive degree. They are squabbling over whether they should split the fees for being 'overweight' between the group or whether poor individual packing and case management is to blame.

'We could use my credit card but it'll get declined,' offers Cherry without any further explanation.

'Mine is chocka full,' says Liberty. 'We put all the ciggies and duty-free on it last time, remember? You all still owe me.'

'I don't have one,' says Big Sue. 'On principle.'

'Definitely split all the fees,' I say firmly, bringing an immediate halt to the argument. The costs for this trip are escalating by the second. 'Add them to our

WhatsApp total and I'll work out how much it is for everyone while we are in Vegas. For now, let's dump everything on my credit card.'

This brings a sigh of relief from the girls. Tash swoops towards me in a cloud of perfume and hairspray. 'Thanks, babes. I haven't got the headspace for working things out right now. I just need to focus on what's important.' She flicks Ged and Liam an adoring smile.

'Honey, we love that you're all so invested,' Liam says, beginning to well up. 'Celebrating this happiest time in our lives with us, it means everything.' He swishes his hand over his face. 'Everything.'

Ged steps in. He has been practising a variety of speeches all week. 'You are like family,' he says, taking his fiancé's hand and clamping it to his heart dramatically. 'There's no one we'd rather share our happiness with. This week isn't just about us. Please don't make us the centre of attention the whole time. We just want you all to have an amazing experience.'

Ged and Liam do namaste hands at us. If there's one thing I'm certain of, it's that this week is all about *them*. They absolutely do want us to make sure they are the centre of attention the whole time. And it's *all* about *them* having an amazing experience. And *my* job is to make that happen for them.

'Thank goodness,' says Tash, beaming. 'Because I've invited Sister Kevin to come to Vegas. And we'll need a bit of quality time together now that we've taken our relationship to the next level.'

Ged and Liam's faces fall instantly. 'You've invited him to our pre-moon?'

Tash carries on as though everyone is now riveted at her plans for the week. 'No, don't be silly. I would have asked you first.'

'But he's still coming to Las Vegas at the same time we'll be there celebrating?'

This is a bit rich coming from Ged. Only five minutes ago, everyone was muscling in on my big romantic break away with Matteo, and nobody seemed to mind about that. I'll have to let it go.

'Yes. It's his BIG birthday next week,' Tash says, seemingly oblivious. 'And we are in a mutually exclusive relationship now, remember?'

'How BIG is this birthday?' Liam is quick to ask.

'Big,' Tash says, leaving it at that.

'Couldn't you take him somewhere else afterwards? For his BIG birthday?' Ged asks.

'No.' Tash begins to screw her eyes at him. 'I'm organising a surprise for him. And it needs to be in Vegas.'

This is the first we're all hearing of Tash having alternate plans for the week. This is just what I need. An added complication to factor in.

'He looks about thirty-five to me,' says Cherry, causing us to silently ask via eye contact with one another whether this is, in fact, a BIG birthday. 'What surprise have you got in mind?'

'I thought I'd surprise him...' Tash beams at Cherry and excitedly grabs her hands before looking at each of us in turn. She takes an exaggerated breath in and squeals loudly, '...with a baby!'

We all take a beat to let this land. Questions fly through my mind. They've only been together for a few weeks, and most of that has been under the influence. Where will she get a baby to wrap up? It's not like you can just go into a shop and buy one. Unless she has bought one online already. I hear between Shein and Temu you can get just about anything.

The mystery is revealed.

'You're pregnant?' Cherry chokes on the words.

Very recent memories of Tash, paralytic at the Sinfonia end-of-tour party, making a huge show of downing a bottle of Prosecco and then throwing it dramatically over her shoulder, come flooding back. The crack it made along the entire length of the mirrored wall could be heard over the music. It sounded like gunfire, judging by the screams from the poor people sitting at the tables below.

Tash takes in our shocked expressions and shakes her head, laughing. 'Not yet. No. But nearly. You know. When we get there.'

'So, the plan is to trick him into impregnating you, then you surprise him with the news on his birthday?' asks Big Sue in her stern social worker voice.

I'm also pretty sure that if you're going to raise a family with someone, it's the done thing to at least find out his surname first. Tash has only known him as 'Sister Kevin' since we met him and the rest of the bearded nuns in Benidorm.

'And we'll definitely be naming the baby Vegas!' Sparkles are shooting out of her eyes. 'Whether it's a boy or a girl.'

'That's not really a reason to do the deed in Vegas, love,' says Big Sue. 'You could do the deed back home and still call the baby Vegas.'

Ged and Liam are nodding vigorously at this more than reasonable suggestion.

'Everyone calls their children after where they were conceived these days. I'm not going to name my baby Cowgate or whatever town Sister Kev's from, am I? No. Vegas is the place. I wouldn't dream of anywhere else. Baby Vegas. It sounds so...' Tash sighs happily, unable to find the right word.

Big Sue gives Ged and Liam an apologetic shrug.

'I'm surprised you haven't considered Elvis,' says Big Mand dryly. 'Or Slot-Machine as a fun middle name. You do know I deliver babies for a living, don't you? And they are not all that, I'll tell you that much for free.'

'Or Bellagio sounds nice,' says Tash in a world of her own. 'Baby Bellagio. Baby Vegas. Baby Elvis.' She drums her fingers lightly on her huge bottom lip. 'I can't choose.'

'I don't know what's more disturbing,' says Big Sue, rattling off some stats to do with single mothers, unwanted pregnancies and benefits claims.

Before the rest of us can react, the queue has disappeared, and the airline attendant is beckoning us all forward with our huge towers of luggage. She is calling for assistance and complaining that we should have filled out a notification of excessive luggage online ahead of the journey. There will be hefty financial penalties to pay. Everyone turns towards me.

My poor credit card.

* * *

No one has had the courage during the flight to tackle Tash on her 'surprise' bombshell. It has somewhat put a dampener on the proceedings. I can tell by the way Ged and Liam keep whispering to each other that they are not best pleased. Liberty is still barely talking to any of us after the club incident with Luke. She blames us for him walking out. Cherry is unusually quiet and has not even leapt up to dance in the aisle. Not once.

When we finally pile through the exit at Alicante Airport, the heat hits me, and I am immediately transported back to a few weeks ago. The sizzling heat, the Latino music, the smell of olives mixed with taxi fumes wafting on the hot air. As the warmth of the sun penetrates my bones, I breathe deeply to inhale the familiar scent of Spain. The midday sun is blazing in the cloudless blue sky, and everyone on the bustling concourse appears to be smoking cigarettes as though we have arrived in the 1970s.

I quickly switch on my phone to discover that I have missed four calls from Matteo. I hurriedly text him to say that I've been in flight mode and have just arrived in Alicante. He texts me back immediately to remind me that he is thinking of me and hopes the flight over has gone well. He signs off as Mr Window Seat. I stare at his message as a surge of longing powers through me. This is where we first met. Where our incredible journey of self-discovery and personal growth began. Where passions were ignited, where truths were...

'Connie, for fuck's sake, we haven't got all fucking day!' Tash yells at me.

She's going to make a lovely mother.

They are all loading their cases onto an already overloaded roof rack. Our small, wiry driver from the last trip, Jorge, is visibly sweating as he forces cases into tiny crevices on the minibus. He is bewildered at the amount of luggage we have. His face drops when he sees me lug my trolley over.

'Hoargghhhay says we might have to sit on the cases because he can't get them all in,' says Liberty in a sulky tone. 'Apparently, someone should have notified him beforehand.' She trains her gaze on me.

'When are you going to get over yourself, pet?' booms Big Mand. 'We've just about had enough of your sulking. Haven't we, lasses?'

We all nod.

'It wasn't our fault that your Norwegian prince took off. Double-dipping is what you were doing,' Big Mand says firmly.

'You win some, you lose some. You should know that better than any of us. You're the only person I know to have exhausted your Tinder app,' agrees Tash. 'You didn't sulk when any of them disappeared off.'

'Exactly. You've been through more men than I've had hot dinners. No, wait. More men than I've had...' Cherry loses her train of thought, and no one can be bothered to wait.

'We go! Go now!' bellows Jorge, climbing onto the minibus. He probably can't believe the difference in our arrival compared to last time when we were pissed, barely clothed, and all fun, frolics and giggles. The atmosphere is currently turbocharged with resentments and judgy vibes.

Liberty flicks her hair extensions over her shoulder and gets on the bus with a huge, frustrated sigh.

'Just ignore her,' Tash says. 'She'll come round.'

Ged and Liam give me a worried look.

'It'll be fine,' I reassure them. 'I promise.'

Luckily, Ged and Liam sit together, Tash and Cherry sit together, Big Mand and Big Sue sit together, and Liberty says she needs some alone time to process. That leaves me free to sit at the back and do some emergency googling. I desperately need to sort out where we will eat for the first night we arrive in Las Vegas. I really hope Matteo hasn't made plans for us, and he will be in the mood for a group gathering. I search trending restaurants that have big tables to seat nine of us together.

Ged definitely wants to go to EggSlut for breakfast, so I will book a table there for the following day. Before I run out of data, I also try to quietly book shows and fun activities for us to do in Vegas on the nights we won't be singing. My heart drops when I see that some of them need to be booked months in advance. The Grand Canyon skywalk is much, much cheaper than a helicopter ride over the Canyon, so I'll book that. Then the helicopter ride over Vegas at night comes in much cheaper again, so I will book us all on to that too. The Emerald Cove kayak trip keeps coming up, but I'm not sure I can imagine the Dollz wanting to do that. I've never seen Tash in flat shoes. Same with Death Valley. I couldn't bear the thought of Tash's spikey heels digging into those poor horses as we trek through the dry, dusty mountains. There's a lot of zip-lining through shopping malls on offer, and something happening at the High Roller that might be a thing. In a panic, I book us an unlimited pass for the STRAT Tower rollercoaster where you hang off the edge of the highest building in Vegas, staring death right between the eyes. *Ohgodohgodohgod.* I'm panic-booking. I take a deep breath in, praying my credit card will withstand this amount of pressure, and scroll through the list of which celebs are currently touring. Kylie Minogue or Harry Styles would be ideal. And a meet 'n' greet is essential.

By the time we arrive in Benidorm, I have more or less sorted the pre-moon spree itinerary. I just need to pull it all together into chronological order so that everyone knows when and where they need to be. The last thing I need is anyone getting lost or going AWOL.

A message from Matteo pops up. He will FaceTime me in half an hour. I send a reply before my phone runs out of charge. I'm on 1 per cent. Hopefully, we will be able to get all the luggage off the bus and into the villa so that Jorge can run me and my luggage over to Voices, where I have use of the sweet little apartment above the bar. It has a glorious view from the roof terrace all the way down to the beach. And, of course, a shower cubicle that fits two. I can't wait. I can FaceTime Matteo from there, in private. I want him to know how much I have missed him, and how excited I am to see him in a few days.

I should also tell him that I won't be arriving in Vegas alone. I mean, I *will* tell him.

'No, Cherry. You're wrong,' Tash is arguing as the bus pulls up outside of the villa. 'Connie, isn't Cherry deliberately sabotaging my dreams of happiness with Sister Kev?'

'I'm not,' says Cherry wearily. 'I just think that having children is a terrible thing to do, never mind surprise ones.'

'But *you* have children,' Tash accuses, yanking her cases from the roof.

'Yes. And don't think a day goes by that I don't regret having them.'

There's a collective gasp as her words sink in.

'What? Don't judge me. I'm allowed to change my mind.'

'They're not shoes, hun,' says Big Sue, her voice full of empathy. 'What's going on with you?'

Cherry's eyes fill with tears. 'Nothing.' She points to the biggest suitcase. 'Boys, that one has all the Barbie and Ken outfits in,' she says, changing the topic. 'Take it with you so that you can try them on for size. But don't get them mixed up or get any stains on them. It's taken me days of work to customise them.'

'Which one has the pink glitter cowboy hats and the whips in?' Liam asks, casting his gaze to the piles of bags still on the bus.

'Cowboy hats...' Cherry whispers to herself. 'A pink glitter cowboy hat and sunglasses. Oh Christ.' She chews her lip, her face dropping as though she is having a terrible flashback.

'They're in that one,' Tash says, pointing to the roof rack buckling under the weight of all the oversized cases. 'I refuse to lift any more cases because I've just had my nails done.'

'Me too,' says Liberty, wiggling her sharp talons at us.

'My arm is still in recovery,' adds Big Mand, doing a shoulder roll.

Jorge, with an air of quiet defeat, silently retrieves the remaining cases just as Nacho, or Enreeky as the Dollz call him because he reminds them of a young Enrique Iglesias, arrives. He is the villa owner and Matteo's half-brother. He pulls up on his moped to greet us with the keys. He is still as devastatingly handsome as we all remember. He gives us a wide smile, casting a confused gaze around the grumpy group. This is the exact opposite of how we welcomed him the last time. There's no lining up for kisses. No giggling over whether he's packing a substantial piece. Instead, Cherry takes one look at him and bursts into loud sobs.

Liberty tuts loudly. 'Oh my God, could you be any more attention-seeking?'

Tash is also unimpressed with Cherry, and instead of going to pieces over her crush on Nacho (he is fancied by all women everywhere), shrugs apologetically before following Cherry through the main gate.

'Enreeky, pet. Lovely to see you,' says Liberty, recovering. 'How have you been? Still a filthy slut, I hope?'

Nacho laughs at her flirtatious behaviour. He will not have understood a word she just said. He shakes hands with Ged and Liam, who are trying hard not to swoon. I give him a hug, before he kisses everyone else's cheeks in greeting.

'You have heard from Matteo, no?' he asks me.

I blush instantly. 'Yeah. I'm... like, going out to Las Vegas to... like, erm, go and visit him.'

Why? Why am I like this? Matteo and I are an item. A bona fide item. I should be embracing it, not acting like I can't believe it's not butter.

'That's so good. He likes you a lot,' says Nacho, which causes my face to go full furnace.

'We're all going,' interrupts Liberty, sounding jealous. 'It's a work trip. Connie's not the only one who jet-sets around.'

'You are all going to Las Vegas?' Nacho smiles quizzically at me before he hands out the keys, and because we already know where everything is, he says he will catch up with us at Voices tonight.

My chest tightens at the thought of him blabbing to Matteo before I get a chance to tell him. As we wave him off, I encourage them to help me haul the suitcases off the bus. Big Mand, who has taken a break to do some vaping, has an idea. 'Liberty, babes. Enreeky could be just what you need to get over Luke.'

For the first time today, Liberty perks up. 'Yes. It's like riding a horse. You have to get straight back on it.'

'I bet he's hung like a horse,' quips Liam.

'Hello?' Ged interrupts. He is the only one helping me. 'One dance isn't that much to get over. It's not like Luke and Liberty had a full-blown *love affair*. Can we get some help here, please?'

He sounds catty. And the finger quotation marks have not gone down well. Liberty looks outraged before flinging him the keys to the cottage. She picks up her cases and heads into the villa.

'Don't leave me to drag everyone's cases in,' yells Big Sue.

Jorge gives me a pleading look. He has sweat dripping down his cheeks. It is almost forty degrees. He is clearly exhausted and deeply disappointed that we aren't half drunk and making a huge fuss of him like last time, by fluffing his hair and pinching his cheeks.

I glance at the mountain of cases abandoned on the path outside the villa gate. 'Let's go,' I say to him. 'For once, they can sort their own stuff out.' I glance at the time. I have ten minutes to get across town to my apartment, charge up my phone, and make myself look beautiful before Matteo video-calls.

24

As soon as I step through the door of Voices, it feels like home. I survey the quiet bar. There are cleaners sweeping the wooden floors, wiping down tables and polishing glasses behind the long bar at the back. There are huge posters advertising the tribute acts. The family's son, Jolly Murs, is performing tonight as our warm-up act. Fond memories flood back of how sweet and talented he is. I see posters for P!nk, Howz Trix, Ted Sheeran, by far the most popular – shame about his wired-up chin – and The Rolling Bones who are about a hundred years old but still very popular. The bar is huge with small, round wooden tables and chairs surrounding a large circular stage in the centre. Memories flood back of my first ever appalling performance. I gawp at a life-size poster plastered across the back wall.

'Cool, isn't it?' says a friendly voice. I swing round to see Jolly Murs, real name Dan, grinning as he makes his way through the tables towards me. 'I only get a tiny poster while you and the Dollz get that massive one.'

The striking poster is of me surrounded by the Dollz. We are standing with our legs apart. We have our fists in the air. We are wearing what can only be described as full-on bondage gear. Our hair is massive. Our faces are skilfully painted with make-up. We ooze sex appeal on every level. It has been majorly touched up to give us the Hollywood treatment. Say what you like about Nancy, but she is an expert agent. 'Where's that family nepotism when you need it?' I laugh, pointing to the A4 poster of Jolly Murs beside it as we hug and exchange pleasantries.

'Speaking of which, Mum left you the keys to the flat and said make yourself at home. It's all made up, and she's left some bits in the fridge as we weren't sure what your plans were before the show tonight. Do you need help with anything?'

I point to the massive pile of suitcases that Jorge helped me heave to the bar entrance before he looked like he was about to collapse. Dan strides over and picks up two cases as though they weigh nothing at all.

'Thank you,' I gush. 'I'm expecting a call any second now from... well, an important call and... OH MY GOD... my phone is about to die!'

'No problem. You go up there now,' he says, throwing me a set of keys, 'and I'll follow you up later with the rest of the bags.'

'Lifesaver!' I yell over my shoulder as I bolt up the stairs to the apartment, two at a time, carrying some of my luggage. I fumble at the door with the keys because my bags are getting in the way. I drop one of them to the floor and push the key into the lock. It won't open. I take it out and inspect the small bunch of keys. It's the wrong key. OH MY GOD, I'm going to miss Matteo's call again!

Don't panic. Do not panic.

I'm halfway down the stairs when I remember. It's the other key. Of course. There's the apartment key. The front door of the bar key. And there's a cupboard to all the music equipment key.

The apartment is the middle key.

I hurry back up the stairs and burst through the door just as Matteo video-calls me.

I'm so out of breath and in a hurry to find my charger, I click accept and bellow, 'I'm on 1 per cent!'

Matteo is visibly startled.

I prop the phone up on the sofa and drop to the floor to hurriedly unzip my bag.

Without looking at him, I remember my manners. 'Sorry. I mean, hello. How are you? Great to see you.' I flap wildly about, blowing hair from my face as I rummage roughly through my bag, searching for my charger, in an increasing panic. 'It's here somewhere.'

'How was the end of the tour? Everything go okay?'

'Got it!' I say, yanking the charger out by the lead. 'Shit! The adapter plug!' I dive back in.

Matteo watches me fling things out of the holdall. 'Connie. Wait. It's fine,' he says in that calm, soothing voice of his. 'Look at me.'

I promptly stop what I'm doing and take a deep breath in. I brace for the emotional tsunami as our eyes meet. I blink slowly as his dark, kind gaze draws me in. My heart swells at the sight of him. His slightly overgrown hair that he casually pushes back from his forehead makes my pelvis immediately twang. I've missed him. I've missed him a lot. It's a few seconds before either of us can speak.

'If we don't have much time, then I need to tell you something before I head back into the studio,' he says.

I nod. 'I really need to tell *you* something.'

We stare at each other. I'm feeling all the feels. Matteo's face softens and I see him blush slightly. He opens his mouth to say something, then closes it again, no words forthcoming. I feel my own cheeks heat. Even on screen, from opposite sides of the Atlantic Ocean, the chemistry is palpable.

I'm the first to start giggling. It's ridiculous that we have this effect on one another. We continue smiling like love-struck idiots before he finds his words.

'I can't believe how much I've missed you,' he says.

I nod. 'Me too.'

'I'm really looking forward to you coming over. This project has been pretty full-on. Sorry I haven't been able to keep in touch. We've only been outside the studio once. And unfortunately, we've got to quickly redo a whole section, so I doubt I'll be able to talk much over the next couple of days either.'

'That's okay. It's been pretty full-on here too.'

'What did you want to tell me?' he asks. We are still grinning at each other. He fancies me so much. It's written all over his face.

I find his attraction to me so utterly overwhelming that my mind is a complete blank. 'What did *you* want to tell *me*?'

I'm basically just copying whatever he says because I am so entranced by his gorgeous face that I have lost the power to articulate. Plus, I just can't bear to disappoint him with the news that everyone I know will be invading Las Vegas alongside me.

Matteo clears his throat. 'It's not great, which is why I didn't want to just leave a message.'

'Sorry?' Maybe I misheard.

He's just about to tell me when my phone dies.

'Shit!' I yell at my dead phone. What does he mean 'it's not great'? I pick up the holdall and empty everything out onto the floor. I spot the adapter immediately and race over to the plug socket with my phone and charger, ramming it into the wall. I see the circle tell me that I'm good to go with 1 per cent. Now 2 per cent. 'COME ON!' I yell, my pulse racing. At 4 per cent, I make the swift decision to ring Matteo back. His phone instantly clicks to his voicemail. 'The person you have reached cannot take your call right now. Please hang up and try again later.'

* * *

I manage to unpack a few things, go for a run and get changed for the evening performance, all in a bit of a muddle. Matteo's words have really thrown me. I sit with Ged and Liam and the Dollz at a table downstairs in Voices and tell them my worries.

'It could be anything. I wouldn't worry, babes,' Tash says, just before the Dollz are about to perform. We are all enjoying Jolly Murs prancing around on stage. He has the crowd totally warmed up and in the mood for some excellent entertainment.

'This Prosecco tastes off to me,' says Cherry, putting her glass down. 'You know I'm better at dancing when I've had my two Prosecco chasers.'

It takes nothing for them to stray off-topic.

'And you don't think the something "not great" was Vegas- or me-related?' I press, watching them all limber up.

'He probably just wanted to tell you that he couldn't get us all tix to see Kylie backstage,' says Big Sue, dropping into a lunge. 'Me and Mandeep have first dibs if he could only get two.'

'Imagine being that close to her,' Big Mand says, lighting up. 'We're her biggest fans.'

Oh, Christ. They are going to be so disappointed when I break the news that these *fake* memories of promises being made by me aren't going to be kept. I haven't even warned Matteo that I am best woman, never mind asked him to line up a load of celebrities for them all to meet.

'No!' cries Liam. 'I'll be devastated if we can't all get tickets. *We're* her biggest fans. We love Kylie. You don't think that's it, Connie, do you?'

'We'll be gutted,' says Ged. 'So gutted. Any celebrity will do at this point.'

Any celebrity will most certainly *not* do. I've seen their list of acceptable celebrity selfies. As I've said, Ged is a famous micromanager. I need to lower their expectations immediately. 'We'll still have a great time even if we don't get invited to any VIP parties or front row seats. It's Vegas. There are endless ways to have a great time. There's kayaking on the... the what's-it-called river. And zip-lining through the, erm, shopping mall at the... you know, the, erm, famous place that everyone knows...'

They listen to my voice trailing off in a frosty, unimpressed silence.

'Anyway, we'll be working for most of it. By the time we've performed at night and gambled all day, chances are we won't get time to meet any celebrities,' Cherry drops casually into the conversation.

The expression of horror on my best friends' faces tells me to pivot. 'And in between performing and gambling, we'll have lots of time to do exciting pre-moon stuff.'

'And birthday stuff,' adds Tash, squinting up from squatting as she swishes her knees open and closed.

'If he hasn't bothered to get us VIP tix to any shows, maybe Matteo's not that into you,' says Liberty meanly. '"Not that great" could mean he's calling to lay the groundwork for a split.'

'Surely he'd just tell her not to fly over,' says Tash.

'Not if she's already paid for the flight,' Liberty is surmising. 'Or he wants to do it face to face. He did say he didn't want to leave a message.'

'True,' concedes Tash, straightening up.

Oh, my God. Why are they even going down that road?

'It's definitely not that,' I say forcefully. 'He's very much still into me. I guess I'll find out when I go over.'

'Ahem. When *we* go over,' says Ged. 'Don't forget the whole reason we're going is for our pre-moon spree. Don't get distracted.'

'And for Sister Kevin's BIG birthday,' adds Tash, causing Liam and Ged to yet again exchange pinched looks.

'And for my recovery and well-being,' says Liberty.

This is news to us. We all regard her suspiciously.

'The whole Luke thing has thrown me,' she says. 'None of you have shown

me any support, and it's affected my mental health. I might have residual gener-
alised anxiety disorder.'

'Oh, get over yourself, Libs. You didn't even shag him. You barely had one
dance with him,' says Cherry sharply.

'You're forgetting I am a therapist,' says Liberty. 'I have a PhD in psychology.
Don't try to explain my own feelings to me.'

'You have a degree in mood management,' Tash reminds her. 'It's not the
same thing.'

This appears to be the touchpaper as the Dollz ignite in a blaze of bickering.

'This is about our singing tour of Las Vegas for Nancy,' Big Sue booms. 'Stay
on topic.'

'Yes. But it's mostly about our pre-moon,' agrees Ged. 'You only took the job
so that it paid for the trip to Vegas. That's why we'll be there.'

'But we're also there for Sister Kev's surprise, unplanned pregnancy nightmare, don't forget,' says Liberty cattily. 'We'll all need to pick up the pieces
when the baby bomb goes off.'

Oh, my God. We've come full circle.

'Listen. Can everyone stop hijacking my romantic break, please?' I shout
over the bickering. 'If you remember, this whole bloody trip was about me and
Matteo! I was going to Vegas first. To meet him. Not to do a pre-moon or to do
any bloody work. I just want to see my boyfriend! My boyfriend who has some
not great bloody news to tell me.'

It does not go down very well.

'Cherry, why are you so quiet?' booms Big Mand. 'You're usually the first to
have an opinion, pet.'

Cherry's eyes widen but before she can explain, Nacho appears, walking
through the crowded bar towards us.

He weaves in and out of the tables. '*Hola, chicas.*' He treats us all to his film-
star smile. 'I think they are calling for you.' He points to Jolly Murs, who is
repeatedly trying to welcome the Dollz on stage. One swift glance around
informs me that the entire audience is listening in to our squabble. All eyes are
on us.

'Ladies, as interesting as this all is... I mean, I'm desperate to know what
Matteo could have meant as much as the next man, but if you can just stop
arguing for two minutes,' Jolly says, 'we'd all like to hear some more singing.'

The crowd cheers.

'Bollocks,' yells Big Sue as though she's only just noticed we are surrounded by paying customers and there's a job to do. She is army-trained, in a loose sense (she spends a lot of time wearing cargo pants), and therefore meticulous about timekeeping. 'Showtime!'

As the Dollz flick their internal switches to perform mode, I just have time to see Nacho give Cherry a shy smile. Her lip quivers in response, but instead of swooning like she usually does, she bursts into tears again.

Nacho, clearly horrified, reaches out to comfort her. She pushes him away and runs over to the stage. Liberty then throws up her arms in exasperation and yells, 'I don't fucking believe this!' and gives Nacho an angry look before stomping away.

He spins round to face me with a bewildered expression.

I shrug. I have no idea what is going on with either of them. Last time we were here, they wanted to know the ins and outs of how big his cock was, along with the rest of us – I mean *them*, the rest of *them*. Poor Cherry. How is she going to get through this show?

Nacho hovers next to us, his eyes glued to the Dollz as they disappear round the back of the narrow ceiling-to-floor curtain.

Then Cherry astounds us even more by leaping onto stage, not a tear in sight, as though she is in a big Vegas hotel doing her two-hundredth back-to-back show and, like a pro, yells, 'One, two, one, two, three, four!' and launches into the opening routine, the girls falling swiftly in behind her.

'And we're off,' says Ged, settling back down into his seat. 'Nacho, care to join us?'

'We're one big happy dysfunctional family at the moment,' Liam tells Nacho, pulling him down to sit between them. 'You wouldn't believe the drama. Did Connie tell you we are also going to Las Vegas for our pre-wedding celebration?'

Nacho shakes his head as he takes a seat next to us. 'No, she has not told me. You are not going to meet my brother, Connie?'

'Yes,' I say quickly. 'Yes, I am. I just haven't told him that' – I make circles with my finger as I point to Ged and Liam and then the Dollz – 'that we're *all* going.'

Nacho looks suitably mystified. As do we all. *How have I not told Matteo? How?*

'But I will. As soon as he is finished in the studio. He's locked in again.' I deliberately avoid meeting Ged and Liam's annoyed glares. 'He is working with a very important client.'

Nacho lights up. 'Yes. He says it is one of the biggest pop singers he has worked with.'

Ged and Liam both perk up at this. 'Who? Nacho, who is it? Harry Styles?'

Nacho laughs. 'Maybe. I don't know. Matteo cannot say me. It is big secret, but you know he works with French producer? She works with all the famous stars. She is very beautiful.'

I bristle. 'Yes. Yes, she is.'

This causes Nacho to laugh more. 'Don't worry. My brother only has the eyes for you.'

I smile tightly. Let's hope that is true. I turn my attention back to the stage where, for some reason, Liberty is glaring at me in an unfriendly way. *What now? What is her problem?*

I'm vaguely aware of Nacho leaning across to yell in my ear, 'Matteo has no interest in Birdie. He would never date her again. Not after last time.'

What the actual...!

25

We stare open-mouthed at Nacho's bombshell. How did Matteo fail to tell me that he is working with an ex-girlfriend? Surely he has had plenty of opportunities to tell me (yes, yes, I can hear myself).

'So, I think we can guess what the "not great" news is that he was trying to tell you,' Ged says dryly.

I spend the rest of the Dollz' set in a daze. Horrible delusional fantasies of Matteo and Birdie together are poking me in the brain, taunting me (she's in a clingy vest top without a bra, constantly fanning herself because the studio is baking hot, and Matteo has yet to realise that it's because she has tampered with the heating controls). I'm dying to probe Nacho more, but we have received numerous frosty glares from the Dollz for not paying enough attention. Plus, Ged and Liam are annoyed with me because I finally admitted to not yet telling Matteo that they are all gatecrashing our romantic break.

Matteo is working with his ex-girlfriend. His hotter-than-average ex-girlfriend. His sexy, *French*, ex-frigging-girlfriend.

All too soon, the Dollz have given a stellar performance, as usual, and now it is time for me, in my bewildered state, to give them a less crowd-pleasing and far less energetic show. We clap them off stage, but they do not seem impressed.

'What's so bloody important that you couldn't be bothered to watch us?' yells Tash. 'You missed every single one of my vertical splits.'

'We were watching. We didn't miss anything,' I say. 'You were great. Very bendy.'

'You know that hot French music producer that Matteo is locked away in the studio with?' Liam supplies readily. 'Turns out Birdie is his ex-girlfriend. And Connie is having a giant meltdown over it.'

My best friend, the uncontrollable gossip.

'Understandable,' says Liberty. 'Connie is the rebound from Alex, the cheating ex, remember? So, naturally, that makes Birdie the one that got away.'

I am speechless.

'Don't blame me for having a degree in psychology. Blame Sigmund Freud.' Liberty gives me a mean smile.

'It's a friggin' mood management degree,' says Cherry, tutting. 'Don't listen to her, pet. She's just jealous.'

'And she hasn't even told Matteo that we are coming,' Liam says, clearly miffed.

'My God. Are we twelve? Why are you telling tales like this?' I don't mean to snap, but it's like my feelings don't matter now that my best friend has become consumed with all things weddings and pre-moons.

'Is that true?' Big Sue booms. 'What about Kylie? I promised Mandeep that we'd see her.'

Big Mand gives her a doting look.

'And what about all the VIP tickets to the best clubs? The hottest parties? The frows?' Ged is asking. His voice rises to a shriek. 'Or did you forget about being best woman?'

'Connie!' yells Jolly Murs from the stage. 'Ladies and gentlemen, put your hands together for Connie Cooper!'

Perfect timing. I dash away to the side of the stage and immediately apologise to Dan.

'I've put your set list up for you. You're good to go. Is everything okay?' he asks.

'Fine. Fine,' I say. 'It's all fine.' I quickly grab the microphone off him, snap into professional mode (in many ways this is no different to the many Sinfonia dramas) and prepare to dazzle the crowd. All that opera singing has really sharpened my vocal range, and it shows. I launch into a power ballad to smooth the transition from the electric sizzle of the Dollz' sexy performance. It instantly casts a wave of calm across the sea of bald heads. I lure them in with my hypnotic sounds until you can hear a pin drop, before I build the song up and bring it to a crashing and dramatic crescendo. Halfway in and the crowd seem over the moon with my set. I've put loads of singalong tunes in there, as well as some of the Benidorm favourites from last time.

All the way through, I can see my friends bickering among themselves. It's all I can do to keep my mind from reflecting on Liberty's comments. Technically speaking, I *am* Matteo's rebound. What if she is right, and Birdie is his 'one that got away', which caused him to almost go down the aisle with his cheating ex in the first place? It's another reminder of how much Matteo and I don't know each other. A movement distracts me from this depressing thought. Nacho, trapped between Liberty and Cherry, appears to have had enough and stands up to leave, looking mystified at them both. I'm going to have some serious damage control to do when I get off stage. I finish my set to rapturous applause – thank goodness. Martha and Rody, the bar owners and Dan's parents, come over to greet us.

'Wonderful, wonderful,' Martha says excitedly. 'So lovely to have you all here.' She sweeps her gaze across the group after hugging me tight. 'Are you all pleased to be back again?'

Tash smiles weakly. 'Yeah. I suppose so.' She lets out an enormous sigh, which makes everything uncomfortable. 'It would be better if some of us would grow a pair and stop sulking.'

She screws her eyes at Liberty, who is quick to retaliate. 'It would be better if some of us would *grow* the fuck up.'

'Maybe it would be better if some of us would just *shut* the fuck up.' Tash is furious.

'No, pet. It would be better if some of us learned to live in the real world.' Liberty squares up to Tash. 'And FYI, an unplanned baby is not a friggin' surprise. It's a friggin' honeytrap.'

'I think you'll find that some of us need to chill the fuck out,' says Big Mand, stepping in between them. 'Although she's right about the honeytrap.'

Cherry scrapes her chair back noisily and clambers onto it. Towering over us, she puts her hands on her hips and flicks her flaming-red hair before turning her thin, wiry frame in our direction.

'I think some of us should take some responsibility instead of living in a dreamworld where they think having a baby will solve all their problems. They don't always lead to eternal bloody bliss. And FYI, being sliced open to have a screaming human yanked out of you *while fully fucking awake* is not as *fun* as it sounds!'

We all turn to see Cherry, her face bright red, her eyes filled with tears, her voice filled with pain. But she is not finished. She rounds on me. 'Connie, stop procrastinating. Do what you need to fucking do and stop people pleasing.'

She faces Liam and Ged. 'Boys, I love you, but chill the fuck out about this stag do.'

They inhale sharply.

'Yeah, I said it. It's a fucking stag do. Get over it.'

The whole bar has gone quiet.

'You're like a couple of extremely needy bridezillas,' she adds unnecessarily. 'We all saw it coming.'

She spins round. 'And Liberty. Luke is not fucking interested in you. He wants Connie, and he can't have her. End of. So back off.'

Tash blinks slowly as Cherry swivels round to pin her with a steely gaze, her voice low. 'And you. Babies are for life. You better be fucking sure it's what you *both* want.'

We all stare mutely while she clambers down off the chair and charges to the doors at the back of the room, scarlet hair swishing violently, everyone in the place scraping their seats to make room and clear a path through the crowd. All in complete and utter silence. She stops briefly at the bar to give Nacho a disappointed look before disappearing outside. It's a few moments before any of us can speak.

'That's it. I've had enough of her stealing the limelight.' Liberty marches off towards the doors too. 'None of you care about me. None of you!' she yells as she dramatically picks her way through the tables. You can hear a pin drop. The crowd seems very invested in the scene. No one has moved a muscle.

I shrug apologetically at Martha. 'It's fine. We're just having a few issues. I'll make sure everything is good for the next performance.'

* * *

The following morning, I wake up after yet another horrendous night's sleep. Not only have I missed another call from Matteo because I'd gone to sleep with my phone on silent, but no one has dared comment in the WhatsApp group about anything. Radio silence and plenty of it. We all pretty much went our separate ways after the show. I made the grave mistake of googling Birdie and discovered that she has a habit of becoming romantically involved with co-workers and singer-songwriters. There was an article in the LA entertainment section of the What's Hot website saying she was locked away in production in a secret location because the star she's working with is HUGE. There's a photo of her going through a doorway with a denim jacket over her head. Her long, lean body is all you can see underneath. And I'm not proud, but I signed up to notifications so that if any articles appear about her, I will get pinged.

I'm just about to put my breakfast dishes away when there's a knock on my door. Cherry is standing there looking very rough and stinking of booze.

'Have you been out all night?'

She shakes her head gloomily. 'Not really. Just until four. Can I come in?'

'Of course.' I step aside. This is most unusual. 'Fancy a coffee on the roof terrace?'

She nods, and I take her up the few steps to the sweetest little outside space. It has potted plants and baby palm trees, a rustic, olive-green wooden table and chairs, and a couple of white plastic sunloungers, but the best thing about it is the view from the veranda. She stands clutching the white balustrade, staring down the pedestrianised strip to the sea. The sun sparkles on the water like diamonds. It is a glorious, calm morning. I take in a deep breath of fresh salty air and wait for Cherry to tell me what's wrong.

It takes her a few minutes.

'I'm pregnant,' she says, her voice dull, her face wretched.

'Congratulations...?' I venture, unsure if that's the right thing to say. 'I guess you're feeling pretty ill with morning sickness.' That would explain the mood swings, but not why she's boozing.

Cherry shrugs. 'I haven't taken a test, but I'm pretty sure.'

'How does...' *Dear God, what's her poor husband called again?* She's constantly slagging him off. I should know his name. 'Erm, how has the news gone down with...'

'He doesn't know. I haven't told him. And to be honest, I'm not sure if he's the—'

BANG. BANG. BANG.

We jump as someone thumps loudly on the door.

'Wait here,' I say, running down the steps and through the tiny living area to the front door. 'Who is it?'

'It's Tash. Hurry up, I'm bursting!'

I fling open the door to see Tash looking very worse for wear. 'The bog, babes,' she announces. 'Where's the bog?'

I point to the bathroom through a little archway. 'First on the left.'

While she's in there, I race up to the roof terrace. Cherry has overheard and is trying to hide behind a potted plant. 'Don't tell her I'm here.'

I sigh. 'Okay. Got it. I'll see if I can persuade her to go back to the villa. Looks like she's been out all night too. Weren't you together?'

Cherry shakes her head forlornly. 'No.'

I dash back inside just in time to see Tash emerge from the bathroom, pulling at her bum-skimming dress. 'Sorry about that. I didn't quite make it.'

Good God.

'What do you mean?' I ask warily. She is as white as a sheet. It could have been either end or both.

'Doesn't matter. Where's your mop and bucket?' She appears slightly cross-eyed and not entirely sober. 'And we'll need some bleach. A lot of bleach. And a new bath mat.'

Sweet Jesus.

'Wouldn't you rather go back to the villa and rest?' I say, fearful that she will hurl chunks all over the rest of my lovely, currently rent-free apartment.

'No.' Tash wipes her finger under her eyes to remove some of the mascara smudges. 'I came to see you. For some advice.'

Advice? She probably needs some advice on how to stop binge-drinking. We may be here a while. 'Well, erm, I'll nip downstairs and get a mop. You just...'

'I'll get some fresh air on the balcony...'

'No!' I say forcefully. Tash stops, surprised. 'Because... because you need to rest. Lie down.' I grab her arm gently and guide her towards the sofa.

'Okay,' she sighs. 'You're right.'

'What do you think is wrong with you?' I ask. *Ten pints too many?*

'Isn't it obvious?' she says in a small voice. Her lip trembles. 'I'm pregnant, aren't I?'

Oh my God. Can everyone just stop being pregnant for five minutes while I get my head round it all?

'Pregnant?' I squeak.

Tash nods glumly. 'Probably.'

'Or maybe it's food poisoning? Or a bad pint?' I suggest. 'Or a sickness bug from the plane?'

'Who's to know? But I feel pregnant.' She rubs her tummy.

'Why don't you do a test?' I ask. 'Just to be sure.'

She is horrified. 'No! Not here!'

I don't understand. 'Why not here? They have great chemists in Spain.'

She shakes her head. 'No. No way. Not here.'

'I could go and get you a test right now,' I say gently. 'I'll even wait with you. You can do it here. In the bathroom.'

Once you've cleared a path through your own vomit.

She smiles thinly. 'Thanks, but I'll have to wait until Vegas.'

'Why?'

She sighs, elaborately throwing her arm up to her forehead. 'Because if I do the test here, then I'll have to call my baby Beni or Benners, won't I? And I specifically told you I want to call it Vegas. Or Casino Royale.'

'Right. Right. Yes. Of course.' *She is fucking insane.* 'Makes sense.'

'You best get that mop because I was drinking Bloody Valentines last night, and they tend to stain. Plus, I had extra chilli and garlic sauce on my kebab this morning. I imagine that'll be tough to get off the blinds.'

I try not to think of the hellhole she has made of my pristine bathroom. 'Why were you drinking when you think you're pregnant?'

'I didn't think I *was* pregnant until just now when I threw up. By the way, get some stepladders while you're at it and a hose. For the ceiling.'

'What?' I say, aghast.

Tash swings her legs off the sofa. 'Perhaps you're right. I should go sleep this off at the villa. We have that big gig tonight at Benidorm Palace.'

She's going to leave me to clean up her vomit. It's like history repeating itself all over again. But if she doesn't go then Cherry is stuck on the roof terrace. It's lose-lose.

'Fine,' I say through gritted teeth. 'I'll swing by later to see how you're doing. Leave the bathroom to me.'

Tash softens. 'Thank you, Connie. You're a real friend. Please don't tell anyone about the baby.' Garlicky fumes mixed with rancid alcohol burn my eyeballs.

'It might not be a baby. It could be a food baby.'

'Christ, what if I *do* have to call it Baby Beni? Remember our last night in Benidorm, when I disappeared with Kev for twenty minutes?'

I don't, but whatever...

'We were in The Knee Trembler doing an upside-down pretzel over the beer barrels out the back. No, I just couldn't...' Her hand flies back to her forehead. She tears up. 'I just couldn't bear it. I couldn't. Pretzel. That's no name for a baby.'

Yep. She's still drunk. Tash throws herself into my arms, enveloping me in a waft of pungent kebab meat. 'You're the best.'

I watch her pick her way down the stairs before closing the door.

'She's fucking pregnant?' Cherry yells. 'And drinking? How irresponsible.'

We take a second to let this land. Cherry looks like she has just emerged from a collapsed brewery. She stinks of stale booze. She has a vape pen behind her ear and mascara down to her chin.

She sniffs the air and retches. 'It smells like she's shat over a bed of rotting garlic.' She retches a bit more.

'Quick, get to the bath—' I yell, but it's too late. Cherry leans over and throws up in my lovely potted plant.

'Sorry,' she says, wiping her mouth on her sleeve. 'I can't stay here with that stench. I'll have to get back to the villa.'

'But what about the...'

Cherry pauses at the door. 'And not a word to anyone about the baby.'

'Which one?' I say, not entirely impressed that I'm being left to mop up after these two.

Again.

26

Two bloody hours later, having borrowed a mop, bucket and two bottles of heavy-duty cleaning spray from downstairs, my bathroom no longer looks like a scene from *The Exorcist* and is back to being pristine. Except for a blue stain on the ceiling that I fear will need painting over.

I've had to have three showers just to remove the smell of it all from my skin and nostrils. I also left a voicemail for Matteo saying to call me with the 'not great news'. But I have yet to hear anything back. I take a deep breath in as I head over to the villa to offer an olive branch to Ged and Liam, who have still not replied to my WhatsApp about what everyone is up to this morning. I'm going in my Lycras with the intention of asking them to go jogging along the beach.

My suspicions are immediately aroused when I arrive at the villa to find it deathly quiet. I let myself in the gate and wander round to the pool area. It is empty. There's a loud snoring from an upstairs bedroom that I take to be Tash or Cherry, but there's no sign of Big Mand, Big Sue or Liberty. I slide the doors open and go into the kitchen. Nothing. No signs of life or anyone having eaten or thrown up.

I head back to the pool area and slide round by the hot tub. An instant flashback of Matteo and me making out in the cottage hot tub sears my brain, causing an involuntary twinge of excitement. In three days, we will be face to face. I'm so nervous and excited to see him. I just wish I knew what he was trying to tell me. As if he has sensed my worry, my phone pings. Matteo has messaged to say that he is sorry he missed my call again. Things are so hectic there. He will try again later today. He has ended with a message in Spanish saying he is counting down the days and calling me Cenicienta. Butterflies tingle in my stomach as a smile spreads across my face.

The white walls round the pool appear seamless until you look up close from a certain angle and see there is a break in it. I marvel at how well concealed it is. Fitted in the narrow gap in the walls is a white gate arched with pink blossom that leads to the luxurious, picture-perfect cottage that Ged and Liam are staying in. I unlatch the gate quietly and pick my way along the path, picturing that first night when Matteo ran me over on his moped and stayed over to make sure I was okay. I knock gently on the door, and it swings open. At least they are home.

I sweep my gaze around the room. There's the kitchenette where Matteo frightened the life out of me when I thought he'd gone home but he just went to get pizza. The bathroom where he took a shower completely naked because he was covered in Fanta. I laugh at how he told me many times that he wasn't sexually attracted to me and that I was quite safe, and how disappointed I felt. How we ended up talking all night and confiding in each other. I remember becoming lost in his eyes. Whirlpools of darkness and worldliness. He was the perfect gentleman that evening. So caring, so—

'What the actual…?' I hear Ged shriek at the same time Liam screams.

I snap to attention, immediately joining in the screaming. I don't know where to look.

'Hide your eyes!' bellows Ged. 'For God's sake. Look away! Look away, woman!'

'I'm trying to!' I say, but my eyes are glued to the scene as though I'm witnessing some horrific natural disaster, like an avalanche hurtling towards me or a major tectonic plate opening up to swallow an entire city.

'Connie. Close your eyes!'

I clamp them shut and instinctively hold out my palms to steady myself. 'What is happening? What did I just see? I don't understand.'

Images swim before me of my best friends standing completely bollock naked, arms and legs spreadeagled in the garden, covered in a substance not unlike a glossy wood stain for garden fencing. Whatever it was, steam was rising from them.

'Who did this to you? Were you held hostage? What happened?' *What sort of monster would do this to two kind, caring, harmless individuals?*

There's a silence.

'TikTok made us do it,' I hear Liam say in a low voice.

I'm still holding out my arms in front of me as I walk carefully, eyes tightly closed, towards his voice. 'Sorry. Who?'

'It's a new hack,' says Ged. 'It's tan accelerator. For the pre-moon.' As though it needs any explanation. 'We have to stand here for six hours and then wash it off.'

'Six hours?'

'Yes. You get a tan equivalent to a whole year but in only six hours.'

'An all-over tan by the looks of things,' I say from behind closed eyelids. 'Why are you steaming? Are you sure that stuff is safe?'

'Of course it is. It's off TikTok. Anyway, we're only three hours in so we can't go anywhere as it dries rock hard, but would you be a love and bring us something to eat, please? We're starving. But don't look at us.'

I hurry to the kitchenette to make sandwiches for them, and see the pot of treacle-like substance dripping onto the bench. I wipe up the spills and notice it stains the tea cloth immediately. I can see where they've brushed past the fridge on their way out to the garden. I wipe that up too and follow a trail of tan accelerator along the wall to the dining table.

I take a sharp inhale.

The Ken and Barbie costumes are piled high on the table. Either Ged or Liam has accidentally bumped against them, causing some dark brown staining against the white and pink fabrics. My stomach drops.

'Guys,' I say, taking hastily made cheese salad rolls out to them with a hand over my eyes. 'Are you sure about the tan treatments? Because it has dripped all over and left stains everywhere.'

'I'm sure it will rub off or wash out,' says Liam.

'And it's definitely six hours, is it? Not six minutes?' I ask.

Ged gives Liam a momentary look of alarm. 'What does the packaging say?' he asks me.

'I don't know,' I shoot back. 'I'll go check.'

I can hear them beginning to panic. I take a deep breath and yell behind me, 'I'm sure it'll be okay. I'll check the tin.'

I race into the kitchen and gingerly pick up the pot, scanning the small print.

Oh no.

It will not be okay.

* * *

'Where are Ged and Liam?' Tash asks later that evening as we get ready in the villa kitchen for the biggest show of the trip. Benidorm Palace hosts thousands of people every night of the week and is renowned for putting on the highest quality shows on the whole of the Costa Blanca. The audience are treated to a five-course dinner and dazzling original performances, dance, acrobatics, magic and cabaret-style music. They pride themselves on having the best costumes, the best staging and the best light and sound to create unforgettable and captivating entertainment. They have launched many a singing career. It's quite nerve-wracking.

'Oh, Ged and Liam?' I say, images floating before me.

It has been a very harrowing afternoon involving me helping to pull, peel, chip and lever off the second skin that was welded onto their bodies. I found myself performing unintentional head-to-toe depilation and ended up using the patio power shower to hose what was basically industrial-strength road tarmac off the boys. 'They'll meet us there. What time is Jorge picking us up?'

Before anyone can answer there is a familiar beep-beeping outside. 'He came half an hour ago,' says Tash. The Dollz turn towards the door with nods of acknowledgement, but none of them move. Poor Jorge.

'Don't we look fabulous?' says Big Mand, surveying the group as we stand around the kitchen table. It is piled high with make-up, hair tools, brushes, pots of paint and jars of glitter.

'No. We don't,' says Liberty. 'We need more. We need to stand out. Tonight has to be perfect.'

'No, it doesn't,' argues Tash, who still seems a little worse for wear. Like Cherry, despite the heavy make-up, she has dark circles underneath her eyes. 'They'll take what we give them.'

'You mean what they're given,' corrects Cherry.

Tash tuts loudly. 'Whatever. If they don't like it, they can just fuck off and die.'

'I mean it,' says Liberty. 'Come on, girls. Don't let me down.'

I can feel everyone tense. This seems wildly inappropriate, even for Liberty, who everyone has the hump with. If I've learnt anything at all, it's that the Dollz thrive on their 'who gives two flying shits' attitude.

'Don't be a dick,' says Big Sue. 'Pull yourself together, Libs. You're not normally like this.'

'The taxi is here,' I say to lighten the mood. 'Ooh, get us. On time for once.'

'She's right. Let's ship out. Move it, people.' We all do what Big Sue says and scurry out to a waiting Jorge. He is lounging against his minibus, peering anxiously down the street and smoking a ciggie. There is a small pile of cigarette butts at his feet. They have kept him waiting for way more than half an hour.

Just as we're about to pile on to the minibus, my phone pings with an alert. It's for the LA entertainment Facebook page. I glance at the image and halt midway up the steps, causing Big Mand to bump into me.

'Is that Matteo?' she says, peering over my shoulder. She whips my phone off me to wave it at the girls. 'Matteo is having an affair with Birdie. It says right here.'

They are quick to pass round the image of Birdie looking impossibly glamorous, and Matteo looking dishevelled and sexy, leaving the studio together. 'We'll kill him,' threatens Big Sue.

'They're describing them as the ultimate music power couple,' bellows Liberty, turning straight to me. 'And speculating as to who they are working with. They've thrown Ryan Gosling and Mark Ronson in the mix after their performance at the Oscars.'

'There's no way Matteo is cheating on me with Birdie. It'll be clickbait,' I snap, grabbing my phone back. 'Come on. We have a job to do.'

* * *

Jorge starts the engine and turns the music up loud. Smooth ballads waft from the speakers to complement the low mood. Tash sits, staring out of the window on one side, while Cherry sits at the opposite end doing the same. Both probably thinking of the small lives they are potentially creating within their hungover, booze-addled bodies. Liberty is uncharacteristically chewing on her talons and checking her phone constantly. Big Sue and Big Mand keep whispering to each other and occasionally nodding towards each of the girls. The ambience is nothing short of glum as we hurtle through the army of cyclists enjoying their new cycle path in the centre of the main road in Benidorm. There's a lot of beeping and screeching of brakes going on. By the time we arrive, there's a clear need for some leadership and a pep talk. As the headline act, I feel the responsibility lies with me. But Liberty beats me to it as we stand at the entrance.

'Come on, girls. I know we're all in a difficult place right now, but let's bring our A game. This is Benidorm Palace. The crème de la crème of forced entertainment. The crowd are literally trapped in there for four hours, and it's our job to make at least seventy minutes of it bearable. Let's go in there and knock it out of the park.'

We take a moment to consider this. It seems Liberty has never before tried to chivvy the Dollz on, by the confused looks they are giving her. Liberty is fussing around, making sure everyone knows what they are doing and insisting on a quick soundcheck, which is very out of character.

'We don't need a soundcheck,' moans Big Mand. 'I'm going to stay outside for a vape.'

'But I've already told them that we are doing it,' says Liberty, putting a hand on her hip.

I suppose it's sweet that she is trying to earn their forgiveness. She has been a pain in the neck since we arrived.

'Okay,' booms Big Sue. 'Liberty, pet, want to tell us what is really going on?'

Liberty peers down at her high, strappy sandals and pretends to smooth down her pleather minidress. She looks spectacular. I take in her showstopping, limelight-stealing, outrageously skimpy outfit. I'm not the only one admiring what she has done with her hair and make-up.

'Are those my hold-up Lycra stockings?' asks Tash.

Liberty reaches down and slowly adjusts one of the stocking tops. They somehow make her shiny legs seem even longer. 'No.'

Tash screws her eyes. 'And that's my lip gloss. The mega-plumper in Violent Rouge. I've been looking everywhere for it.'

'So what?' Liberty says, pouting back.

'Don't start,' booms Big Sue. 'Let's just get the fuck on with it. But as soon as we've finished, Liberty, you have some explaining to do.'

We troop into Benidorm Palace, barely speaking, like a group of disappointed schoolkids on a day trip to Butterfly World. While the organisers are falling over themselves to accommodate a group rehearsal, I take a moment to pluck up the courage to leave a WhatsApp voice note for Matteo to tell him I've seen the news headlines. I'm going to tell him that I am fully understanding, and that he is not to worry one little bit, because I'm not the sort to believe salacious gossip. After all, it would be a bit rich coming from the woman who, only last week, was splashed over the UK tabloids as the Norwegian Count's bit of rough.

I find a quiet space away from the Dollz doing their soundcheck on stage, but just as I take out my phone, Matteo FaceTimes me. I accept the call and hold the phone up to a flattering angle.

'Oh wow,' he says, his eyes mushrooming.

I blush instantly.

'Good luck for tonight,' he says, realising where I am. 'I'm just calling to explain... in case you saw, erm, some news about...'

'It's okay. I understand.' We smile goofily at one another. 'I had the same issues last week in the tabloids. It's all rubbish. Comes with the territory, I suppose.'

Pah! Like we're minor celebrities!

He sighs with relief and gives me another incredulous look. 'I thought you'd be angry or upset, but anyway, it's good to see you again.' His eyes sparkle, and his whole face is lit up. He totally has the hots for me.

'How long have you got?' I ask.

'A few minutes.'

I come over all Dollz-like and daring. I'm going to execute what the Dollz frequently call their Hot Garbage routine. Apparently, it never fails. After a quick peek around to make sure no one is watching, I smile in a flirty way. 'How do you like my outfit?' I tilt the phone and trail it slowly down to my cleavage, which is squashed into the world's tightest spandex dress. Down over my flat, bare stomach to my legs. I perch the phone on a nearby table while I place my high-heeled sandal provocatively on the chair and run my hand the length of my stocking, just like in my Birdie nightmares. The phone is pointing straight up my skirt to give Matteo a tantalising glimpse of the goods. I slip my finger into the suspender strap at the top of my stocking before snapping it back into place French floozy-style. I drag the phone sexily back up to my face. Matteo's jaw is hanging open. But not in a good way.

I peer at the screen. Something feels odd. There's an arm over his shoulder and some salmon-pink hair hanging down.

Oh my God. I instantly bristle. He's not alone.

I hide my surprise as Birdie's beautiful, large, turquoise-blue eyes, slender nose, and full lips come into view. 'You must be Connie,' she says in an utterly charming French accent.

'I, erm, well...' I stammer. *Why didn't Matteo tell me we weren't alone? Wouldn't you start with that?*

'Good to meet you at last,' says Birdie with a laugh, coming back into view, cool pink hair piled messily up on her head. 'Great legs.'

I feel my face flame.

'I guess you need to get some air to yourself,' she says. 'Rubber skirts? Am I right?'

I close my eyes and pray for an early death. But when I open them a second later, she's still there smiling at me. She has perfect teeth and a smile twice as wide as any normal human woman.

I hear Matteo clear his throat as he muscles back into the shot. I notice Birdie leaves her arm draped over him. 'Sorry. She snuck up on me while you were... doing the tour of the outfit,' he says. I must look shell-shocked. 'So, we have to go. But it was great to see you.'

He sounds all brisk and formal. I am mortified. There's no mention of my sexy leg stroking. *Why? Why did I do it?*

'Matty told me you were very talented, but he didn't tell me how gorgeous you are,' she says, licking her lips playfully. 'He'd better watch out. I'm an insufferable sapiosexual.'

I have no idea what she means but she appears to be flirting with me. Matteo shoves her out of the way, rolls his eyes and gives me an embarrassed look before I am cut off and the screen goes blank.

I have never felt so disheartened. Just in time for rehearsals.

* * *

An hour later, we are standing backstage. Big Sue and Big Mand have become leading authorities on different types of sexuality.

'She's attracted to brains and talent,' Big Sue is explaining. 'She doesn't care for gender. She's after you for your looks *and* your mind.'

'Oh. And I suppose, therefore, she could be after Matteo for his enormous brain too?' I say, feeling disheartened.

Big Mand laughs. 'I'm not sure it's his enormous *brain* she's after.'

This causes a ripple of laughter from the Dollz.

'Don't worry, Connie, pet. French women might have all the sex appeal, but they have no sense of humour, and they all have flat chests,' Tash says knowingly to the nodding heads around her.

'And we will show you how to weaponise your sexuality in time for Vegas,' offers Big Mand.

'Enough of that, let's get out there and show Benidorm Palace how lucky they are to have us,' says Liberty, hurrying everyone along.

I put all thoughts of what's *not* going on between Matteo and Birdie right out of my mind and peek through the stage curtain to see Ged and Liam right at the front of the audience at a table set for two. They look a worrying shade of burnt orange. I bite my lips to refrain from laughing. I'd best get it over with now, otherwise they'll have a hissy fit if any of us pretend not to notice.

'What? Who have you seen?' Liberty says, grabbing the curtain and peering out across the crowd. 'Fuck me.' She fixes us with wide eyes. 'Ged and Liam have gone the colour of turmeric.' She bursts out laughing. 'They'll be the only yellow Kens in Vegas.'

The Dollz take turns to peer at them.

'Shit the fucking bed,' whispers Tash. 'That's so bad.'

'They look severely jaundiced. I'm surprised no one has called the emergency doctor. They need some vitamin K.' Big Mand puts a fist to her mouth. 'K for Kenergy. Get it? Kenergy.'

We all stifle our giggles in case they can hear us. It's the first time we have shared a laugh since we got here. It feels nice. And I'm sure I'll be able to find something to rub the rest of that tan off with.

'Group hug,' Big Sue commands as we all gather together. 'Let's give them a show they'll never forget.'

Finally, we all seem to be in the right headspace. It's showtime.

It isn't until halfway through their set that the first hiccup occurs. I'm busy watching the Dollz from the side of the stage. They are nailing the complex choreography. They look and sound amazing. The crowd is joining in with every song and watching their every move. Then Liberty, who has been on fire since we arrived, belts out the midpoint banger as though she is Mariah Carey circa 1994 and makes the mistake of pointing into the crowd. I see the rest of the Dollz follow her gaze, and one by one their faces drop. I crane my neck around to see who has caught her attention.

If I know Liberty, it will be a man. A very attractive man. I skim the crowd and spot the back of someone tall sitting down. Staff are fussing over him, and they have given him a whole table to himself. He looks up and smiles back at Liberty. I'd know that profile anywhere.

It's Luke.

Shitting, shitting hell.

27

I watch as the Dollz struggle to keep formation. They are furious with Liberty, who is not only trying to outsing everyone, but she's also routinely repositioning herself at the front so that Luke can get a good view of her. I slide my eyes over to him. He casually picks up the menu, perusing it with increasing abject terror. He's eyeing his surroundings warily then with bemusement. The waiter is bringing him a bottle of wine and, after a double glance, Luke is politely handing it back and laughingly waving him away.

Why would Luke be here?

My whole being sinks at the thought of going on stage and singing in front of him, which is ridiculous because we've spent the last week performing an inch from each other's noses. I take a few deep breaths as the Dollz wrap up their set.

The last hour has been a bit much, what with Matteo ringing and Birdie practically hanging off him while I did my less-than-impressive leg wafting thing. What an epic fail. Ged and Liam have turned up as a pair of Oompa-Loompas, and now Luke, the last man on earth that I would want to see, is sitting waiting for me to entertain him with my eighties and nineties cheap covers. I bitterly regret telling him I was coming to Benidorm.

'He'd better not be stalking you,' barks Big Sue, snapping me from my thoughts, as the Dollz run off stage. 'Did you see him sitting there, clicking his fingers for the waiters to come running? Posh bastard.'

The Dollz rally round.

'Babes. Ignore him. Don't give him the effing time of day,' Tash says. 'It's the attention he's after.' She turns to give Liberty a sharp look. 'Much like someone else we know.'

'He must be after Connie because I doubt he's here for the magic show, the warm wine or the frozen calamari.' Cherry strokes my arm as she is speaking. 'He's obviously been following you.'

'They always do that before a kill,' says Big Mand, chewing a worried lip. 'Stalking. First, they abduct cats, then they move on to humans.'

Oh my word.

'I'll note the day and time,' says Cherry, our resident paralegal. 'For the inquiry.'

There is no need for this level of escalation.

'I'll cover the rear if you can do surveillance on the stage area while she's on,' barks Big Sue to Big Mand, who has already snapped into SWAT team mode.

'I'm sure he's not here to stalk me. He's probably here to...' I say, running out of reasons why Luke might be here. *Is he stalking me?*

'For God's sake, calm down, everyone. It's not *The Bodyguard*. He's not even here for Connie!' shouts Liberty.

'Explain yourself. And make it good because we specifically told you to back off,' Big Mand reasons.

'I invited him here. And he kindly said he'd come and watch me perform. From a professional point of view. He has connections.'

FFS.

'What?' says Big Mand, stepping right up to her. 'Sisters before misters, remember?'

Liberty rises to her full height. 'I haven't broken the code.'

I am speechless at the audacity of her.

'You are bang out of order, Libs. Bang out of order.' Tash stomps away from her.

'Professional point of view, my fat, hairy backside,' snaps Big Mand. 'What utter bollocks.'

'This will all backfire,' says Cherry, flicking her flaming-red hair over her shoulder and following after them.

I can't even look Liberty in the eye. I push past and make my way to the stage. *How could she do this?* Of all the selfish... stupid... idiotic... *Gah!*

As soon as I walk out on stage, I'm on the back foot. I have the Dollz squawking to Ged and Liam at the front. They are constantly turning around with gaping mouths and yelling things to me while I'm trying to introduce myself to the throng of people in the audience. The most distracting is Liberty, who is marching towards Luke. I can see her indicating they leave and Luke staying firmly where he is with his eyes trained on me. Liberty doesn't appear to be taking it well and has plonked herself huffily down next to him.

I have no option but to get on with it. I sweep my gaze around the crowded two-thousand-seater venue. The lights dim, causing a hush to fall. A spotlight blinks and shines down. All eyes are on me. They are waiting for me to deliver the goods. As I put the microphone to my lips, a surge of anticipation fills me.

This is what I do.

When I sing, I have the ability to whisk people off to places they haven't been for decades. I unlock memories, feelings and passion. I inspire people to want to sing along, to dance, to move in time with me. There is no other buzz like it. It doesn't matter what I'm singing or where, it's all about connecting with my audience, and that's exactly what I'm going to do.

'Hello, everyone. Are you having a good time?' The crowd responds immediately. There's an excited buzz in the air from the Dollz, making my job so much easier. 'I'm gonna need you all on your feet dancing for this one,' I encourage, walking up and down the stage while I begin to sing, belting out the lyrics and making eye contact with groups of people who, fortunately, look keen to take me up on my offer. Within seconds, the whole place is up and joining in. I wave my arms in the air, and they copy my moves as two thousand lively patrons become my personal backing singers. 'Benidorm Palace, you are on fire tonight!'

* * *

'Connie, that was electrifying,' gushes Ged. 'What a performance. Well done, babe.'

'Thanks,' I say. I'm still breathless. Nancy has already been on the phone to say the management have rebooked me and the Dollz for next season because they were so impressed. But the Dollz are in a state of flux over Liberty as we ready ourselves to leave. 'I can't believe she's disappeared off with him,' Cherry is saying to Tash.

'I can. Liberty by name, liberty by nature. Don't I always say that?' she replies.

'She's always been a slave to that runaway libido of hers. Always. Remember Turkish Brad? And his brother Greek Alan?' Big Mand says, shaking her head. 'There's no boundary she won't cross.'

'Well, she hasn't got a set of keys to get in, so I hope she doesn't come back too late. I'm going straight to bed,' says Big Sue.

'Me too,' says Cherry, yawning. I contemplate the dark circles under her eyes. She's doing well for being pregnant, but something is niggling at the back of my mind. 'I still have the last-minute adjustments to do. Has everyone tried on their costumes? We're travelling in them, so tomorrow is your last chance.'

Las Vegas! Matteo! The pre-moon! The work gigs!

'I need my beauty sleep too,' agrees Tash. She has bounced back from her unconfirmed-sickness-bug-slash-phantom-pregnancy extremely well. 'Sister Kevin flies in to meet us tomorrow. I need to look glowing. So, FYI, I am staying in bed all day. Do not disturb.'

I'm surprised to see Ged and Liam not rolling their eyes. I suppose they have bigger fish to fry, what with them being the colour of ripe pumpkins.

'We've only got one day left to get sorted,' says Liam, lighting up. 'It's Voices tomorrow night, and then we're all off to Vegas, baby!'

There's a sudden shift in mood as we all realise that, in a day's time, we'll be flying to the party capital of the world. Tash leads with an almighty squeal as we group hug and leap up and down excitedly.

* * *

The following day, I rise early to go for a jog along the beach. Just before I leave, I catch my reflection in the mirror. I look surprisingly vibrant. My skin and hair are sun-kissed. My body is firm and healthy. I put my hand to the locket that houses the image of my mother and trace its delicate engraving. My mind flashes back to last week. It feels like months ago. Almost like it's an alternate life. Luke's sudden appearance has me rattled though. My two worlds are colliding. On the one hand, we are work colleagues. He and I will tour with the Sinfonia together in future. We must retain a polite, professional relationship. But on the other, there are so many questions left unanswered from the last tour. Dolly told me that the Maestro is Luke's godfather. This locket is a precious heirloom that must be returned to his family; surely he has no right to give it away so carelessly? And the rumours in the press about us, what do I do about them? How much of what Luke told me about his imminent arranged marriage is true? None of it? And his behaviour at the hotel, which he'd switched us to without my consent. Expecting to sleep with me just because he was high on drugs and proposing a fake marriage to lure me in. He's not shown himself in any great light. No wonder the Maestro seems fed up with him.

A sudden pang to call Dolly comes over me. She picks up immediately.

'Hello, love,' she says. 'How's it going in sunny Benidorm? It's hoicking it down here. It's rained non-stop since you left.'

After a few minutes of weather-related chat, I tell her about Luke turning up.

'He *what*?' she bellows down the phone. 'That is too far. He's crossing a major line there. What's he playing at?'

'I was hoping you could tell me,' I say. My hand is still on the locket round my neck. 'Why do you think Luke wanted me to have this locket?'

Dolly remains quiet for a few seconds before I hear her sigh. 'It wasn't just Luke's idea.'

'What do you mean?' I ask.

'It actually belonged to Krzystzof. He is Luke's father's cousin. Their grandmother gave him it because Luke's parents had a royal marriage of convenience. Or so I believe the tradition goes.'

'What tradition?'

'It is handed by the men in the family to the woman they love, who in turn hands it down to a male in the next generation to hand it to whoever they fall in love with.'

'I'm confused.'

Dolly sighs gently. 'I think the Maestro was saving the locket for his true love but didn't get the chance to give her it.'

'Her? Don't you mean him?'

'Bernard was his rebound.'

'Oh, that's sad. What happened?'

'She died.'

It's like a penny dropping. 'My mother? The Maestro was in love with my mother? For how long?'

'From the day they met until the day she died.'

'But what about Bernard?'

'I think Bernard knew he'd always be second best. That's probably why he cheated on the Maestro so much. But your mother only ever had eyes for your father.'

'Poor Maestro. So, he was the one who wanted me to have the locket?'

'Yes.'

'So that's why Luke said it was a family heirloom?'

'Yes. I have to say, even though Luke charms every woman he meets, he's been acting very out of character since the day you arrived.'

'He has? I wondered if it was his spoiled, pampered upbringing. Expecting everyone to be at his beck and call.'

'The opposite probably. From what I've heard.'

'He's rich Norwegian royalty,' I say in a disbelieving tone. 'How bad can it have been?'

'He was shipped off to boarding school at a very early age, then more or less left to his own devices until he started to act out. After that, they sent him to Switzerland and palmed him off on Krzystzof who, really, is the only family member to ever take care of him in any meaningful way.'

'Sounds lonely.'

'I know. And even now, his mother is always doing charity work while his father is into politics. He barely knows or sees his parents other than at royal engagements. Do you know, they've never once been to hear him sing? Makes you wonder why they had him in the first place.'

'Blimey. It sounds so depressing when you put it like that.'

Dolly laughs. 'It makes me grateful for the friends and family I have, put it that way. And I know it's not for me to say...' She leaves the sentence hanging before continuing. 'I know he's been awful, and Lord knows he has attachment issues, but... upgrading the hotel, the locket... and I'm pretty sure he must have pulled in some big favours to kill the royal love triangle story. It's as though he genuinely has feelings for you. Real feelings.'

'What are you saying?'

'I just think... that Luke may be... or at least in his mind... he thinks he is in love with you. Unrequited love seems to run in the family.'

A nauseous feeling swells in my stomach as I remember him asking to marry me and then snorting cocaine like it was going out of fashion. 'No. It's a crush. It will pass. He's into Liberty now anyway.'

'Well, let's hope it is a crush and not history repeating itself like Krzystzof. But I know one thing for sure. He's not after your friend. Luke might be a nice guy underneath it all, but he is ruthless when it comes to breaking hearts. Besides, he's a sapiosexual.'

'Christ Almighty. Who isn't these days?'

'So unless she has a string of first-class degrees and is on track to win some industry accolades like Luke, you'd best warn her off him.'

My mind flicks to Liberty and her degree in mood management.

I click off the call, no better off. I have no idea how to handle this situation. Taking the locket from around my neck, I flick the catch open and admire the picture of my mother staring back at me with my eyes. I marvel at how much I don't know about her. Her life before I came into it. Did she know about the Maestro's unrequited love? How did she handle it?

I place the locket carefully on the console table under the mirror and go off for my run. I need to go through my mental checklist of what needs to happen in Las Vegas for every minute of every day that we are there because the list of additional problems is growing by the second.

* * *

After an hour of running the length of both beaches in Benidorm, I arrive at the Dollz' villa to find almost everyone around the kitchen table.

'She's not come back home,' states Ged immediately. 'I say she's fine and probably with Luke.'

'She could also be murdered somewhere, stashed behind a bin,' says Cherry, waving her phone around. 'That's why she's not picking up.'

'You need to stop listening to those podcasts, hun. You really do.' Big Sue is shaking her head at Cherry. 'She's a big girl. She'll ring if she's in any trouble.'

'Wait. Are you saying Liberty didn't come home last night?' I say, catching up. They all nod at me. 'Big Sue's right.' I shrug my shoulders. 'Liberty and Luke can do what they like. They're both consenting adults.' There's a thorny silence while we digest this information. 'I know it feels off, but I suppose we just have to let them get on with it.'

'Okay. Let's not waste the whole day debating whether to track her down. Me and Ged are going to Algar Falls to wash this bloody orange stain off,' Liam says briskly. 'Apparently, the waters there contain the same minerals that you find in washing powder.'

Liam and Ged have turned a few shades darker since yesterday. Any more, and they will be undetectable against the terracotta tiles.

'I've always fancied going to the waterfalls up there,' says Big Mand.

'Me too,' agrees Big Sue.

'Come with us,' says Ged. 'The more the merrier.'

Cherry looks green and pale. 'I'll skip it if that's okay. I might rest up so that I'm good for tonight,' she says. 'Plus, I need to take up some of the costumes.'

'And I have so much shopping still to do,' I say, holding up my hands. 'Ready for tomorrow and...'

'LAS VEGAS!' we all shout together.

'So that's settled then,' sums up Big Sue. 'Me and Mandeep will take the bridezillas to the waterfall to scrub them clean. Cherry, you do a recon of the costumes and accessories. Connie, we still need a pink sequined suit and pink shirt for the Oscars Ken outfit. We're short on one white fluffy coat too. Here's the list. And Tash, you... Where's Tash?'

'She's gone back to bed. I heard her throwing up earlier,' says Big Mand.

'All the more reason to get out of here,' yells Ged, already crossing the patio towards the cottage. 'I can't afford to catch any pre-moon bugs.'

Cherry and I make eye contact. I can't believe she and Tash might both be pregnant in the middle of all this chaos.

'See you tonight, babes,' says Liam to me, chasing after Ged. The Dollz follow suit and scatter, leaving me alone in the kitchen.

'Okay,' I say, unfolding the huge shopping list. 'I guess I'll just have to go shopping for a pink sparkly suit and these other impossible-to-get items alone then.'

28

After returning to my apartment to shower and change into my denim shorts, flip-flops and a T-shirt, I walk into town to go shopping. It's not long before playful photos of Big Mand, Big Sue, Ged and Liam flood the WhatsApp group. They are having a great time up at Algar Falls. I laugh at the photo where Big Mand and Big Sue have Ged and Liam on their shoulders as they wrestle under the waterfall. There's a video of an incredibly tanned Ged jumping off the ledge into the rock pool below. He looks impossibly shredded. It must be all that juice cleansing and intermittent fasting he does. There are photos of each couple gazing adoringly at each other, endless group selfies and a brilliant one of all four of them sitting cross-legged on a rock ledge, with their backs to the camera, as they face the imposing mountains that the waterfalls are nestled in.

I love-heart emoji the photos while I troop from one shop in the old town to the next, hunting for a pink sequined pantsuit.

PING. Big Sue reveals that Ged had actually painted abs on his chest, but that the water has now washed it off. We all laugh emoji it.

PING. There's a message from Tash saying thanks a bunch for leaving her behind. Asking why they didn't have the decency to wake her up and invite her.

PING. Big Sue reminds Tash that she bit her arm the last time she tried to wake her and she still has the scars to prove it. Besides, Tash was very clear about not being disturbed today.

PING. Seconds later, Cherry posts that Tash can help her with the costumes as there are still lots of adjustments to make and hems to sew, and bizarre brown stains that are proving difficult to remove.

PING. Tash is too busy to help all of a sudden. Something unexpected has come up.

PING. Big Mand guesses that the unexpected thing to come up is another four hours in bed. We all cry-laugh emoji it.

PING. Dan warns me that we are following Bongos Bingo tonight at Voices, which means that the crowd will be extra rowdy. I inform the group that he has invited us all to join in, if we fancy it.

PING. Everyone is up for Bongos Bingo. We agree to meet at Voices at 5 p.m. for food and happy hour before it starts.

* * *

After trailing around what seems like every shop in Benidorm, I'm not in the slightest bit surprised that I cannot find a pink sparkly suit anywhere. I've done a DuckDuckGo search, and the only shop to come up is a drag-costume warehouse nestled in the heart of the cobbled old town.

I stop for a quick break in the vibrant Tapas Alley, breathe in the enticing aromas and marvel at how quaint it is compared to the British end of Benidorm. The restaurant-lined narrow lane is bustling with lively chatter from people sitting outside with beers, bottles of wine, plates of fresh, fragrant seafood, tiny fried fish, and baskets of crusty bread. The smells drifting on the air are incredible. I lose myself in the selection of quintessentially Spanish light bites behind the glass counters on top of each bar, stretching as far as you can see down the street. There are almost too many *pinchos* to choose from. I run my gaze over the small slices of baguette with multiple ingredients creatively stacked on top of one another, bursting with colour and held by a cocktail stick. The bright yellow cheeses contrasting against the richness of the salamis and meats, the vibrant reds and greens of the grilled peppers, the juicy pink prawns and the thick slabs of warm tortilla fill the trays. Just as I'm about to decide which of these charming bars to sit in, I get the sudden sixth sense that I'm being watched. I immediately spin round and spot Luke in the crowd, because he is a foot taller than your average tourist. He is laughing at something someone is saying. That someone is not Liberty. It is an older woman who looks very sophisticated. I watch as they exchange cheek kisses before she leaves him. I'm still staring at him when he catches sight of me. The surprise on his face seems genuine, which immediately throws me off guard. We stand rigid as people bustle around us. Neither of us seems to know how to react.

A few seconds go by while I assess the situation. We should really clear the air. Luke bites his lip and frowns as though contemplating whether our speaking is a good idea. I decide to take matters into my own hands and walk towards him. 'Are you following me?'

'I swear this is a coincidence,' he blurts at the same time, while I'm still a few feet away, pushing through the crowd. He holds his palms up. 'I know this looks bad, but I had no idea you'd be here.'

'You had no idea I'd be here. In Benidorm? I literally told you I was coming here.'

'I mean I had no idea you'd be in this street... at this time... on this day. Honestly. Obviously, generally speaking, I did come here to Benidorm... to see you. To apologise properly.'

I don't believe him. 'Then why not just text me?' I shout back above the heads.

He visibly swallows. 'Because I deleted your number from my phone after the tour, and Dolly wouldn't give it to me again because of the way I behaved towards you. Then when I came to Benidorm Palace, Liberty said you didn't want to have anything to do with me and that I should forget it.'

People are beginning to push their way between us as we jostle to talk to each other in the centre of the throng. We couldn't be standing in a more inconvenient place.

'I just wanted the chance to say I'm sorry. Sorry for tricking you into staying at the hotel in York. I wasn't thinking straight. I was just so excited to... Sorry. Excuse me. Let me help you with that.'

I watch as Luke, all politeness, bends to help a young woman pushing a buggy through the crowd. The wheel has jammed in the cobbled stones. He lifts the pram up and sets it down again. She thanks him and after he answers her in what sounds like impeccable Spanish, he continues as though it didn't happen.

'I was just so excited to get to know you. We had this chemistry on stage. And instead, I messed it all up. I had my chance to impress you, and I blew it.'

He's not wrong there.

This time a large and very lively walking tour group come to stand in the same spot we are in. They are instructed to admire the architecture of the old buildings. The guide points to the famous sign for Calle Santo Domingo and sweeps his arm around the compact square leading down to several narrow pedestrianised lanes crammed with foodies taking delight in the famous culinary treasure trove of authentic Spanish cuisine.

Luke nods towards one of the empty alleyways. I make my way to the side of the lane, squeezing through the crowd. Luke follows me, keeping a respectable distance.

'I was awful. I was trying to seduce you with big romantic gestures and... I got it all terribly wrong.' He is shoegazing, and his cheeks are flaming with embarrassment.

He sounds genuine. I just wish he would look me in the eye while he is rambling. Instead, he's talking nervously to the palms of his hands that he is waving around like a politician.

'But the proposal was genuine. Yes, it was spur of the moment... and totally weird and I was horrendously drunk and high, but I'll always regret the way I messed that up.' His eyes finally meet mine. 'I completely blew my chance with you, didn't I?'

I nod back. 'And who jumps on a plane just to say sorry? And threatening to quit your job unless the Sinfonia kept me on board? Can't you see that's all a bit stalkery?'

Luke's face drops a mile. 'Oh, my God. No. Please. That's not what I intended. Not at all. Sorry. I'm just making things worse. I see that. I thought that if there was some way I could make it up to you, you'd forgive me, and then when we tour together for the Sinfonia, everything would be okay. I just didn't want to leave things so awkward between us for months and months until then.' He rakes a hand through his hair. He is flustered. His eyes are pools of disappointment. 'I'll get on the next flight out of here. I promise. And you won't see me again until the next tour. And you don't even have to speak to me then. I'll be professional and courteous, and we can put this whole nightmare that I created behind us.'

They say the eyes are the window to the soul. He still has strong feelings for me despite everything he's saying. 'Okay,' I say stiffly. This has been a lot to process. 'But what have you done with Liberty?'

'Wait. What?'

I'm not buying it. 'Liberty. The woman you were with before that other one, evidently.'

'That was a family friend. She and her husband own property out here,' he says. 'Up in Denia. We met for coffee. I haven't seen Liberty.'

'Sure you have,' I say, my hands on my hips. 'Did she stay the night with you?'

Luke is surprised. 'Certainly not. No.'

'No?' It's very unlike Liberty to *not* get her man. 'We all saw you leave Benidorm Palace together, and she hasn't come back home yet.'

Luke frowns, trying to remember. 'Yes, we left the show together. I could see that my presence was causing some, um, some arguments. So we took a cab to the old town. We went for a nightcap so that I could explain why I was there, and I asked her to let you know that I only came here to apologise. Not to cause any trouble. Then I went back to my hotel.'

I take a moment to think my answer through. He must think I'm an idiot.

'I swear she hasn't been with me. Should we be calling the police?' he asks.

Good point. Should we?

'She definitely did not stay the night with you?'

He shakes his head.

'Oh. I guess in that case we have no further need to...' Now it's my turn to shoegaze.

'I should head back to my hotel,' he says.

'Right. Well, I guess we'll see each other in a few months then.'

'I guess we will. Bye, Connie. And again, I'm so very sorry.' We lock eyes and it's as though he's willing me to say something kind to him. Something hopeful and promising. He gives me a dejected smile.

Suddenly, I feel stifled. 'Goodbye, Luke.' I dart across the promenade, pushing past the tourists, into the main shopping square, to catch my breath. That was so intense. I scan the crowd to make sure he hasn't followed me. He hasn't.

I sit down on the nearest bench to take a moment. I suppose it was good to clear the air, but it means I've run out of time to get even half of what we need on this shopping list.

PING. Instagram. Ged has posted a gorgeous photo of the four of them under the waterfall with a caption – *Just had the best double date ever* – and tagged us all in. My hearts swells for them. Part of me wishes I had gone with them. They all seem deliriously happy. Thank God things are starting to get back on track.

PING. Big Sue is *fecking* furious on WhatsApp. Big Mand is also *livid*. How dare Ged 'out' them when they aren't even 'out'.

Oh shit.

29

'What in the name of fuck is going on?' squeaks Liam tearfully. I hurried back to their cottage at the villa as quickly as I could, post the WhatsApp spat. It has escalated into a massive online argument, even though I suspect that all the people involved are a few yards from each other, texting from their bedrooms, and could easily do it face to face to clear up the 'misunderstanding' much quicker.

Ged is also visibly upset.

I try to broach the 'unexpected outing' of Big Mand and Big Sue. 'What were you thinking? You know they are very protective of their friendship and whatever may be developing between them,' I say.

'I know that *now*, don't I?' says Ged. 'It was an accident. Anyway, they are soooo a couple. A blind man could see it. They vibe off each other the same way Liam and I do. We had a great day.'

'Did you see them being a couple? As in kissing or anything?'

'No.'

'Well then, you have to assume that they're just good friends.'

'Are you mansplaining being gay to us?' Liam asks. 'You're not even a man, or gay! And they are not just good friends. Why are they making a huge deal out of this? We've said sorry. What more can we do?'

'We need them to come over so that you can explain face to face and apologise,' I say.

'We've done that already. We went straight over to the villa as soon as Big Sue WhatsApped. And they won't accept our apology no matter what we say,' Ged moans. 'We told them it was an honest mistake. We'd never intentionally out anyone.'

'Wait. I have an idea.' I message the group and say we need an emergency meeting in their kitchen immediately. It's to do with the Ken and Barbie costumes. Fortunately for me, it's actually true.

It takes five minutes for everyone to scramble into the kitchen. Ged, Liam and I are sitting round the giant kitchen table waiting for them. The pile of newly altered clothes that Cherry has been working on is neatly laid out. I have added the new outfits that I picked up today.

Once everyone has arrived, we sit for a moment, peering at each other.

'Let me address the elephant in the room,' I offer.

'Which one?' says Liberty, coming in last. She is giving me a stern look.

'Yes, which elephant would that be?' says Big Sue, sounding very angry. She throws a heated glance across to Ged and Liam, creating a strained silence. Big Sue, although something of a giantess, is also the voice of reason within the group. Without her on side, I dread to think how we'll get through this.

'Where have you been?' I gasp, staring at Liberty. 'Your phone has been off all day. We were worried sick.'

'Were you?' she asks, arms folded. 'Did any of you ring the police because you were so "worried sick"?'

Ah. She has a valid point. We all take a moment to inspect the table, the floor, our nails.

'I don't care which elephant it is, but could you address it quickly, please?' says Tash, the awkwardness seemingly going right over her head. 'Sister Kevin will be arriving any second now. And please, don't forget, none of you are to mention Las Vegas. I don't want you ruining his BIG birthday surprise.'

Liam breaks from Big Sue's death stare to roll his eyes at Ged. 'It's like she's forgotten the whole reason for the trip.'

'Touché,' I say without thinking.

'That's the sort of thing Luke says.' Liberty is quick to pounce. She picks up the few items that I managed to buy. 'Do you mind telling us what you've been doing all afternoon? Instead of shopping for costumes?'

It is my turn to be stared at.

'Nothing. I mean, I bumped into Luke. It was a chance encounter. He apologised. He left. And I continued shopping.'

'Walk us through this chance encounter,' says Ged. 'I'd like to know what was more important than our outfits for Vegas.' He has gone full bridezilla in the wake of the Big Sue/Big Mand disaster. He is projecting.

I try my best to explain but it is having a negative effect on the group as they begin rifling through the poor assortment of costumes that I was able to get hold of at short notice. Suddenly, it's as though the 'accidental gay outing', 'the accidental hijacking of the pre-moon for a BIG birthday surprise', the 'accidental lying about inviting the Count over to Benidorm for career purposes' and the 'two secret accidental pregnancies' are yesterday's news. Suddenly, the poor selection of Ken and Barbie outfits is the most upsetting issue. And I'm to blame.

'It was all they had. At least it's pink,' I say, trying to soothe a horrified Liam as he holds up the outfit I got for him.

'Ryan Gosling did not turn up to the Oscars in a hot pink spandex onesie!' Liam cries. 'Did he?'

He's right. The onesie isn't quite the sophisticated, glittery pink two-piece suit, but it was all they had at the drag warehouse in Barbie pink for a man his size.

'You'll still look hot to me,' says Ged earnestly. That's true love for you. Liam will look like a raw hot dog. And we all know it.

'Telling white lies to your partner is one thing,' blurts Big Mand, 'but telling the whole world things that blatantly aren't true is quite another.' She looks at Big Sue and we all fall silent. Instead of agreeing, Big Sue's eyes fill with tears. She gets up from the table and races up to her room. Big Mand looks crushed.

PING. 'That's Sister Kevin. He's at the gate. I think I'll just take him straight to my room. I'll meet you at Voices for Bongos Bingo.' Tash dashes off, leaving the rest of us to stare at the pile of clothes in stony silence.

'Who's next? Who wants to try on their costumes?' Cherry asks, trying to smile through the heavy circles around her eyes, the pale skin and the gloomy expression.

Big Mand lets out a muffled cry, scrapes back her chair and runs off.

With a huge, elaborate sigh, Liberty informs us that she, too, would rather not try on costumes. 'Read the room, Cherry, babe. What's the point anyway? It'll all end in disaster. It always does.'

'Wow. Rude,' says Ged as we watch Liberty sashay away, bum cheeks bouncing like a pair of jellies.

Cherry looks forlorn as I feign enthusiasm for trying on my outfits. 'It's fine,' she says. 'I only spent two whole weeks making them. Every minute of every bloody day. I missed my child's first birthday and my own wedding anniversary, but who cares, right?'

'Cherry, I'm so sorry...' I say as she bursts into tears and races off. I can't even say it's pregnancy hormones because I'd be upset too if everyone simply threw my efforts back in my face.

Ged and Liam look gutted. 'We might give tonight a miss, if you don't mind, Connie, love.'

'Sure. Not at all. Sure. No. I totally understand. But hey, listen. Everything will work out. I promise. We just need to get through tonight's gig, and things will be better in the morning. We'll sort everything out before we fly to Vegas.'

They nod sadly and disappear through the patio doors back to their love nest. I put my head in my hands. How has everything fallen apart so quickly? My nerves are fraught enough as it is.

PING. Big Sue is dropping out of the performance tonight. She has to try and explain things to her parents, her family, her friends and work colleagues who suddenly think that she has been leading a double life and are hurt and confused as to why she thinks they would not understand and be supportive.

PING. Big Mand is dropping out. No reason is given.

PING. Cherry is unwell and will not be making tonight's performance.

PING. Tash argues that she feels uncomfortable leaving Sister Kevin alone when he has only just arrived.

PING. Liberty says we are forgetting what it is like to be *single*. She accuses us all of being too wrapped up in our own happy love lives to care about single people and their worries.

I stare at the texts.

Looks like I will have to tell Martha and Rody that the Dollz have cancelled. A picture of Nancy pops into my brain. She will be furious. I let my forehead drop to the table, which reminds me of Luke.

Oh my God. That's it. Luke. My head springs up. I grab my phone and dial his number.

He answers very quickly. 'Hello, who is it?' he says.

'It's me. Connie,' I say.

'Erm, oh. I, erm... did I...? I wasn't...' he dithers.

'Listen. I haven't got time for the Hugh Grant,' I say quickly. 'You wanted me to forgive you, yes?'

'Why, I... erm, that is to say...'

'I'll take that as a yes. Have you left Benidorm yet?'

'Ah, right. Well, the thing is, I can explain. You see, the flights... um, well, I know I promised—'

'Forget that. I'm dropping you the pin of a place called Voices. I need you to go there. I need a favour.'

'I, well, um, yes of course. I—'

'See you there in half an hour.'

I click off the call. Needs must and I am desperate. I examine the pile of costumes on the kitchen table and grab myself a Barbie wig, pink gingham dress, tights, pink love-heart glasses and a pair of size six white platform sandals and race out of the villa. That'll have to do. We are due at the airport tomorrow morning for our flight to Las Vegas. I will message the Dollz once the gig is over. There's no way in hell that I'm missing my flight because of all their drama. I will arrive back here at the villa first thing, suited and booted and ready to drag them all kicking and screaming on to the minibus... or die trying.

* * *

I arrive at Voices in a sweat. Dan is behind the bar as I race towards the apartment door.

'Oh good. You're here,' I say, before launching into my backup plan for tonight's show.

'I can't see why Mum and Dad wouldn't go for it,' he says. 'Is the guy any good?'

'He's great. But I don't know if he can sing anything other than classical songs. I'll ask him when he gets here, which should be soon. Can you look out for him, please?'

'Sure. I'll let my mother know there's a change of plan.'

I race upstairs and fling myself into the shower, getting ready in double time. I'm not in the slightest bit sure about this but it's the only solution presenting itself at the moment. As soon as I'm ready, I go back downstairs. The bar is already filling up with people coming for Bongos Bingo and to see the

Dollz perform. They are going to be so disappointed. I am really going to have to sassy up my act to deliver something as lively and sexy as the Dollz do. Unfortunately, not much can be done with only an hour to go, so they will have to make do with a few changes to my set list. I'm just flicking through my playlists with Dan when we are aware of someone next to us.

I see Luke's jaw fall open.

'It's intentional,' I explain as he takes in my two-bit stripper outfit. 'The Dollz have dropped out of this evening's performance. And I need to cover their show and mine.'

'Ah. I see. And you need me to be your support act?'

'Kind of. I thought we'd just do the whole lot together. What do you say?'

Luke looks shocked. 'Me? Singing covers?' He surveys the bald heads and the crowds pouring through the doors. 'Here?'

I nod. Christ, I hope he knows some Ed Sheeran songs or Coldplay at least, or anyone from this century would do.

'Does that mean you forgive me?' he asks hopefully.

'Yes,' I say. I'm desperate. 'Now, do you think you can do it?'

He suddenly breaks into a half-smile. 'I wasn't karaoke king three years in a row at university for nothing.' He rolls up his shirtsleeves and whips out his phone. 'Show me the set list. Here's one of mine. I can Bluetooth the songs over. And where's the kit? I need to warm up my voice.'

Dan and I exchange relieved glances. While Bongos Bingo roars to a conclusion in the main bar, Luke and I, sitting outside, have agreed on a lively and sexy set list that should please the growing crowd. He seems overjoyed that I have accepted his apology at last and is full of enthusiasm.

We make our way back inside and over to the stage area. 'Ready?' I ask Luke once we've plugged our phones in and done a quick soundcheck.

He stands on the circular stage with his legs wide apart, a microphone in one hand and the other ready to grab some air. He flicks hair from his eyes and winks at me. 'I was born ready.'

'Sodding hell. You're not going to make me regret this, are you?'

And before I know what's happening, Luke is launching into the best rendition of 'Let Me Entertain You' that I've ever heard. The crowd stop what they're doing. Drinks are paused on lips. Martha's head pops up from behind the bar. Everyone wants to see who this fantastic voice belongs to. Halfway through the song he begins to sing the words to another song over the same tune. It's very clever and obviously well rehearsed, and it drives the crowd wild.

When he finishes the song, he is so comfortable on stage that he introduces himself as Count Nikolai, ninth in line to the Norwegian throne, twelfth in line to the throne of Sweden on his mother's side and second cousin once removed to our own Royal Family.

'We're like rabbits,' he jokes, and the crowd love him even more. 'But seriously. It is a pleasure to be here tonight as the guest of the esteemed and extremely talented Connie Cooper. We have just finished a tour in England with the Royal Northern Sinfonia. Some of you may have heard of it.' He pauses to allow the crowd to laugh. No one has heard of it. 'And we thought you'd appreciate a few highlights this evening.'

OMG. He has them eating out of the palm of his hand. I hear the opening notes of one of our arias.

'Okay. So, we're really doing this, are we?' I say, an involuntary thrill running down my spine. I would rather not look forward to singing with him, but there's no denying that we make incredible music together.

Luke welcomes me on stage, and seconds later, we are blowing the audience's tiny minds with the show to end all shows. By the end, everyone is up dancing and singing along. Luke and I have bantered our way through the evening and shared laughs and jokes with the crowd. Even Dan joined in at one point. We decide to end the night with 'Mi Amore Mi Amore'.

Huge mistake.

I'm not sure whether it's the euphoria of a successful show, or the fact that Luke and I appear to be getting on well, or his overwhelming crush on me, because right at the end, when he's declaring his undying love for me, his lips hovering over mine as per the theatrical want of the piece, Luke leans in a fraction too far, so that for a brief nanosecond, our lips make contact. And because we're mid-song, there's not much I can do about it other than pull back immediately and keep singing.

'What is wrong with you?' I hiss when it's all over.

Luke gulps. 'I lost my balance?'

30

'How did it go last night?' Ged asks me the following morning. We have started gathering in the villa kitchen as per my instructions. He is looking me up and down. 'Did you pick up the right size? I think you might be wearing Big Sue's dress.'

'Yeah. I thought it was too long for me,' I say, hitching it up. I take a look at the kitchen table but all of the wigs, dresses, accessories and shoes have gone. I am also desperate not to divulge what happened at Voices last night in case Ged reads something into it. 'I wonder where everything is.'

'Ged, my darling, are you wearing my Oscars Ken costume? Because I think I've picked up a Barbie one by mistake.' Liam emerges through the patio doors dressed in the Barbie travel outfit. He is wearing a pair of tight-fitting hot-pink trousers that have lace-up sides and pink patterned floral flares from the knee. A pink waistcoat just about fits across his torso, revealing toned arms that are a ridiculous shade of deep mustard (to match the rest of his face and body). He is wearing a neckerchief and a pink Stetson with a picture of himself kissing Ged. It looks amazing. He lifts up a flare to reveal white cowboy boots, earning him a wolf whistle from his fiancé.

'You scrub up well yourself, babes,' Liam says, eyeing Ged up and down. Ged has opted to travel in his Cowboy Ken outfit. He is head to toe in black with elaborate white fringing on the shirt, white cowboy boots and a white Stetson with a picture of him kissing Liam on the front. Together, they look adorable.

'I'm keeping the neon paint-splash Lycra outfit for when we go roller skating. So we can be twinsies,' says Liam. 'Connie, did you manage to pick up the yellow knee pads? They were on the list.'

This is the first I'm hearing of a desire to go roller skating. I hide my shock, thankful that we have successfully skirted over the issue of how last night went, and scramble to check my bag for the shopping list from yesterday. *Oh, no.* There it is, clear as day. I'll have to pick some up in Vegas. There's bound to be a sports shop somewhere.

'Connie, I think you might have Big Sue's dress on, love,' Liam says, looking me over. 'Sick platform sandals. They are massive. Cherry puts such dope costumes together.'

I smile and say nothing. Liam is adopting a slightly American twang. He is really committing to this adventure and I will not be the one to dampen his spirits. He is the colour of a blood moon. He has enough troubles.

'Thanks, you guys,' says Cherry, coming down the stairs looking fabulous in a correctly fitting Barbie outfit. She has opted to keep her flaming-red hair as it complements the colour scheme and has put it up into a high ponytail with a heavy fringe. Her make-up is flawless. Huge black flicky eyeliner, thick lashes, hot pink lips and lots of blusher. Her dark circles are nowhere to be seen. Her neat waist looks even tinier in the bum-skimming pink gingham dress as it swishes provocatively towards us. The white netting underneath provides maximum volume and bounce. She has opted for white knee-high socks with her platform sandals. She looks incredible. Only the tiredness in her eyes gives her away.

She shakes her head at us. 'Nope. This is all wrong.' She rubs her temples. 'Sorry guys, I must have mixed everything up. You're all wearing the wrong clothes. I don't know what's got into me lately.' She flicks me a look that suggests otherwise.

'I could wear the double denim shorts and waistcoat,' suggests Liam, dragging Ged off to help him. 'I'll go get changed.'

Oh no.

Liam has an awful brown creosote streak across his backside. Cherry is about to call out to him, but I shush her. 'There's no time now. He'll want to wash it out before we go and our flight is in three hours. I'll get the stain off when we get to Vegas.'

'Okay,' she agrees. 'We'll do that. Hopefully, he's only shat himself. If it's that fake tan, we're screwed.'

I blink slowly. It's like a different world sometimes.

Cherry and I stand alone, facing each other across the table. She looks so vulnerable for a woman who is always so hard and prickly. 'Do you want to come outside and talk?' I ask her. She hesitates for a moment before nodding. We walk round the pool to the farthest spot and sit down on the luxurious sunbeds, under the shade of a large white canvas parasol.

I wait quietly, not wanting to pressure her. Today is going to be fraught enough without Cherry going to pieces. She chews her nails as she stares into the pool. The sunshine is shimmering on the water in small rhythmic waves. 'I'm late. My period is never late. Ever.'

I have no idea how nerve-wracking it must be to bring a new life into the world.

'I'm not sure who the father is,' she says, putting another finger to her lips.

Chew. Chew. Chew.

'Well, actually, I think I do know who the father is. I'm just not sure how it will work.'

'Oh. I see. Your husband isn't the baby's father?' I must, must, must find out her husband's name. I'm too embarrassed to ask Cherry after all this time. I'll ask Tash when she comes downstairs.

Her eyes fill with tears as she shakes her head.

'And you think you know who the father is?' I say gently. I'd hate for it to sound rude. Like she's having to substantially narrow the field.

A single tear spills from her perfectly made-up eyes and rolls down her cheek. 'Yes,' she whispers. 'It's—'

The sound of the patio doors sliding open alerts us to the arrival of Big Mand. She looks furious. 'Is this some kind of fucking joke?' She stands in the doorway, wearing the world's tiniest gingham dress. It is so short it doesn't even cover her knickers, and the bib top only covers one boob. Thankfully, she is wearing a pink bra, but the overall effect is comical. The tights are too short, so the gusset is hanging low. The wig and the shoes are the only things that fit correctly. She stands with her hands on her hips, sweeping an angry gaze around the pool until it lands on us. Her eyebrows are knitted together underneath the thick white-blonde fringe. Like mine, her Barbie wig is a high pony-tail. It swishes forcefully as she stomps over to us.

'Get in line,' Big Sue barks from the bedroom window. 'Whose idea was it to put me in a Ken outfit? Is this to do with yesterday? Well, I'm telling you now, it's *not* fucking funny!' Big Sue, wearing what looks like a big, shaggy white over-coat and a huge gold medallion hanging from her neck, slams the window closed.

'Oh dear,' I say. 'There's obviously been a mix-up with the costumes. I think I know what's happened.'

It was bloody Ged and Liam and that tin of TikTok creosote. They've stained the outfits, mixed them up and now no one is wearing the right costume for travelling today.

'It's me,' blurts Cherry. 'I must have mixed them up. I don't know how it's happened, but I'll sort it.'

'No,' I say. 'It wasn't you. It was...' *Oh God.* Big Mand and Big Sue are furious enough with Ged and Liam as it is. I have very little hope of repairing the damage before we set off for the airport. 'It was me.'

Cherry gives me a relieved look. 'Thanks, hun, but you don't need to cover for me.'

'I'm not wearing this!' yells Liberty, appearing from nowhere. 'It's like wearing a bloody twenty-man pop-up tent. Mandeep, I think we've got each other's costumes on.'

Big Mand swings around and immediately takes the hump. 'Are you saying I'm a fat cow?'

'How do you know it's not mine?' I ask quickly. 'In fact, it looks like it's my size. Here, Liberty, swap with me.'

Cherry shakes her head at me. 'It won't work. Just let them scrap it out.'

Before either of them can come to blows, Nacho strolls round the corner wearing nothing but a small pair of swimming shorts and a smile. He stops everyone in their tracks. He is so handsome that it causes a soothing wave of calm to ripple out across the patio. He is like a walking meditation gong. Liberty is first to react. She races over to kiss him on both cheeks. He pats her on the butt and winks at her. I think we now know where she has been disappearing off to.

I feel Cherry bristle beside me. 'Look at her. Cheap tramp. Leave him alone.'

I feel my eyes widen with shock. I'm not the only one. Big Mand is standing with her mouth gaping open. Nacho's eyebrows are high on his forehead.

Liberty spins slowly round to face Cherry. 'Excuse me? What did you say?'

Why is everyone falling apart? Why are they all fighting over every tiny thing?

Cherry stands up. 'I said leave him alone.'

'What's it got to do with you?' Liberty says loudly.

The patio door swishes open. Big Sue emerges, a menacing expression on her face. She is taking up the entire frame. Tash pushes out past her to watch the showdown. Sister Kevin yawns, standing next to her in a double denim shorts and waistcoat ensemble that is two sizes too small.

'That's where it is!' yells Liam from the far end of the pool. 'Ged, honey, I've found it. Sister Kev is wearing my Beach Ken travel outfit. What's going on?'

Ged joins Liam as they observe the scene from the secret entrance to their romantic hideaway cottage. All of us are staring at Liberty, who is staring at Cherry, who is staring at Nacho.

'Nacho and I happen to have a thing going on,' says Liberty, licking her lips provocatively.

'What sort of thing?' asks Cherry, sounding equally catty.

'None of your business,' replies Liberty, slinging an arm around Nacho's shoulders as though he's her property.

It's all very playgroundy.

'Well, it *is* my business because...' Cherry nervously twists her hands round and round. 'Because he's my baby daddy.'

You can hear a pin drop.

Liberty's face falls a hundred feet while Nacho is still grinning away. He has not understood what Cherry has said. He thinks two hot gorgeous babes are fighting jealously over him, because that's his normal.

I clear my throat and explain to Nacho in rudimentary Spanish that Cherry is with child. His child.

Nacho goes deathly white. His eyes become like saucers, and his lip begins to tremble.

Sister Kevin is the first to break the silence. 'Oh man. I can't imagine how gutted he must be. Imagine some chick you hardly know traps you into fatherhood. That's his whole life ruined. Poor guy.'

Tash's jaw drops open as her hand flies to her mouth. She lets out a small squeak and races as fast as she can in giant platform sandals and a skintight Barbie dress, back into the villa.

Clop. Clop. Clop. She pushes past Big Sue, and we hear the angry slap of her shoes up the marble stairs and a door slamming. Followed by a blood-curdling scream.

Sister Kevin appears genuinely confused. 'What? What did I say?'

I feign ignorance and shrug back at him.

'Cherry? Is this true?' asks Nacho, his voice breaking.

Cherry nods glumly, too upset to speak.

Oh. My. God.

No one dares say anything.

Nacho tilts his head to the side as though trying to figure something out. 'But we did not do the sex. Did we?'

Liam inhales dramatically. 'Ooh, harsh. He can't even remember it.'

Cherry instantly bursts into tears. Nacho runs to her and flings his arms around her thin shoulders. 'I'm so sorry. I'm so sorry. Please. Stop the crying. It will be okay. I promise. Everything will be okay.'

Cherry looks up at him hopefully. She seems tiny in his arms.

'When? When did you sleep with him?' Big Sue has taken charge of the investigation. She has put aside her own family troubles, her grievances with Ged and Liam, and her disappointment with Big Mand, to come to the aid of her distressed friend. I'm almost welling up watching her. If the world was crashing to an end, it's Big Sue you'd want watching your back. She's all woman. I'm in awe.

I step closer to Cherry and take her hand as Nacho backs away from her. He looks bewildered. He's not ready for this, never mind taking on Cherry and her two feral babies and thinning-haired husband. He'd never cope.

Nacho gives Big Sue a perplexed look. He too would like to know when this night of so-called passion, which resulted in the forming of a new life, occurred. 'After the music festival?' he asks Cherry. 'Is that when?'

Cherry tuts and pinches her nose, trying to retrieve specific details. 'Which-ever night you were wearing the pink glittery Stetson hat and sunglasses.'

'That could have been any night,' says Big Sue. 'Think, Cherry, babes. Can you remember any other details? Were you in a bed? On the beach? Behind a bin? Where did the incident occur?'

This briefest of unmemorable incidents that neither can recall.

'I remember you had a pink heart on your cheek...' Cherry bites her lip, deep in thought. 'No, not a heart. Lips. Big red lips. You were swinging my bra round and round, and you kept yelling "Yeehaw" like a cowboy. I remember you pounding into me, pounding and pounding.' She winces. 'On and on. Pound. Pound. Pound. All night long.'

That's a lot of pounding.

It seems to be jogging her memory. 'I remember thinking we were on a trampoline. I was being thrown around, up and down.' She reaches a hand to her hair. 'That's right. I had my knickers on my head. Like a blindfold.'

It's sounding very kinky.

Nacho looks vacant. He clearly has no recollection of this wild Olympic-style night. I sneak a glance over to Ged and Liam, who are riveted. I slide my gaze to Sister Kevin. He is finding this all highly amusing and is trying not to snigger out loud. I feel sorry for him. He will not be sniggering when Tash gets hold of him. That's just about the worst thing she will have wanted to hear.

Oh my God. Poor Tash. If she really is pregnant then she will be crushed to think Sister Kevin doesn't want the baby. She'll have to think of something else to get him for his BIG birthday.

I don't know what to do.

Stay with Cherry or rush to check on Tash?

We are interrupted by Liberty, who has let out a screeching howl. We all watch as she bends over, double wheezing to catch her breath. Her shoulders are shaking.

Oh God. Poor Liberty. Why must every man she has her eye on be whisked away from her quicker than she can blink? She must be distraught. She straightens up. Tears are streaming down her cheeks. Her wails turn into sobs of laughter.

What is going on?

'It wasn't you,' she says to Cherry. She can barely speak for laughing. 'It was me, you idiot. It was me he was pounding. You were asleep next to us. At least, I thought you were. I tied my thong over your eyes so you wouldn't see us if you woke up.'

Cherry's face falls. 'But that would mean...'

Liberty chokes on her words. 'Yep. Unlucky, Cherry, babes.' She doubles over again, cackling with laughter, while Cherry looks at Nacho, bursts into tears and runs back into the kitchen.

We hear her let out an anguished whine. Somehow, finding out that her thinning-haired husband is the father of her child after all has proven more than deeply upsetting.

31

This is a total nightmare. I cast my gaze around the pool area. Ged and Liam are looking baffled. Liam is still wearing my top but with short denim cut-offs because Sister Kevin is wearing his outfit. It's very half-Ken half-Barbie. I will have to let that go for now. There are far more pressing issues. Such as Jorge is due any minute now to take us, and our many, many suitcases, to the airport. The flight is in less than three hours' time and we need to get on the minibus and on our way. I do a quick mental recap of the current status quo.

Big Sue is still standing where she was in the patio doorway, sweating buckets. She is not speaking to Ged and Liam, nor Big Mand by the looks of things. Her big fluffy white coat, black vest and gold medallion are making her look like Gangster Ken.

Big Mand is not speaking to Ged and Liam either. She keeps throwing them annoyed looks as though they are the root cause of all the upset. Which, to be fair, they totally are.

Nobody is speaking to Liberty because she is still laughing over Cherry.

Tash has locked herself in her room and is refusing to speak to Sister Kevin without telling him why.

Cherry has locked herself in the bathroom and is refusing to come out.

Nacho is standing there, looking guilty. He can't run off because he needs to check the villa before releasing the deposit back to Nancy, and he needs everyone to hand back the sets of keys.

I keep picturing him pounding into Liberty while poor Cherry was being tossed around like a rag doll, asleep right next to them. What were they thinking? They could have at least rolled her onto the floor.

It is awkward. Very awkward. And I feel responsible for at least trying to get everyone back on track. After all, they've all helped me at one time or another. For which I am eternally grateful.

'Big Sue, you were amazing,' I tell her. 'If you hadn't started asking questions, this whole scenario might have gone very differently. You may well have saved a marriage, and even though you have a lot on your plate, you still came to the rescue. Thank you.'

She shrugs and gives me a half-smile.

'She's right,' says Liberty. 'Sisters before misters. You always have our backs. Every single time there's a drama.' She goes over to Big Sue. 'I'm sorry for being such a cow. I'm just sick of being lonely. You lot are all so loved up, and I never seem to find anyone.'

There's a silence where we all wait to see how Big Sue will react.

'I guess we don't make it easy for you either, Libs,' says Big Mand, jumping in to save Big Sue from answering. 'I'm sorry if I always hog Sue to myself but... well, we're...' Big Mand smiles over to Big Sue. They lock eyes for what seems like forever. We all seem to be holding our breath.

BEEP. BEEP. BEEP.

Jorge has arrived just in time to pop the tension like a balloon.

Big Sue smiles shyly back at Big Mand, and they share what appears to be a moment of truce.

'Come here, yer daft slappers,' says Liberty, dragging them both into a hug. 'You don't have to explain anything to anyone. Unless you want to. And FYI, we already know something *is* going on. The walls are pretty thin here... Just saying.'

How is that helping?

'I'll go check on Cherry,' I say, desperate to escape before the situation re-escalates.

'It's okay,' says Liberty. 'I've got this. She was exactly the same the last time she found out she was preggers. She'll be savage for the next twenty-four hours at least.'

Great news. Cherry is going to go nuclear on board the flight to Vegas.

'I'm going to go and find another outfit. I can't travel in this because...' Liam fiddles with the shorts.

'No time!' barks Big Sue. 'Everyone, get your bags and rendezvous outside at the bus. We'll swap costumes at the airport.'

'Good plan. If only Tash could get her shit together, we'd be ready to go,' says Big Mand.

'Leave that to me,' Big Sue volunteers.

* * *

Within minutes, I am staring at a full group.

'Wow,' says Ged. 'They can really move when they need to.' We are standing outside the villa by the minibus. Jorge is smoking his usual cigarette and looking at his watch. We are only running twenty minutes late. A new record for us. He looks pleased.

'Nacho,' I say. 'Could you please take a group photo of us by the bus with our bags ready to go?'

Nacho takes my phone from me. 'No problem.'

I organise everyone into a group. 'I'm going to document the whole journey for scrapbooking purposes, and potentially get it made into rolls of wallpaper and items of clothing.'

No one bats an eyelid at the latest of Ged and Liam's crackpot requests. We shuffle around, ensuring Ged and Liam are front and centre. While Nacho is indicating for us to move an inch to the left, an inch to the right, my phone goes off in his hand.

'*Hola, que pasa, bro?*' he says, his face lighting up. Cripes, it can only be Matteo. I listen to Nacho rapidly explain that he is taking a group photo. I see him fiddle with some buttons and then confirm he has sent him a copy. Then I hear him explain to Matteo that we are all going to the airport.

Shite.

Nacho looks concerned. 'Connie. He wants to speak with you.'

With my stomach plummeting as I make my way over, he lets out a strange noise. 'Ah, sorry. I have sent wrong photo.' He shows me the screen. It is a picture of me and Luke on stage at Voices taken by Dan, who thought it was a good idea to capture the moment and WhatsApp it across. We look very cosy.

We decided because things were going so unbelievably well that we would treat the crowd to 'Mi Amore Mi Amore'. We look about to kiss.

'Is that from last night?' barks Tash. 'Is that who you replaced us with?'

'Of all the singers, you chose your stalker?' Big Mand is not happy.

'Singing isn't all they appear to be doing!' snaps Liberty. She has grabbed the phone from Nacho to get a closer look.

'Connie!' yells Ged. 'What were you thinking?' He snatches the phone from Liberty. 'Look at the way Luke's making cow eyes at you. For Christ's sake. He'll think you're interested in him again.'

'Oh my God!' I shout back. 'You lot dropped me in it. What else was I supposed to do at such short notice?'

Everyone quietens down just enough for us to hear Matteo's muffled voice coming from the phone. Ged gingerly holds it to his ear, nods his head a few times and passes it back to me. 'He says he'd like to speak with you.'

How much has he overheard?

I take the phone, all eyes pinning me to the spot. 'Hi, Matteo. It all looks and sounds much worse than it is. And the good news is that Nacho is no longer the father of Cherry's baby.'

My attempt to change the subject does not work. Matteo is wondering why all nine of us are travelling to the airport.

'Well, er, because we're all coming to Las Vegas... to surprise you,' I finish lamely.

Liberty grabs the phone out of my hand. 'We're coming over for work, if you must know.'

Ged grabs it from Liberty. 'No. Matteo, we're coming over to celebrate mine and Liam's special pre-moon spree. We're hoping you can—'

He doesn't get to finish because Tash's long talons appear from nowhere to grab it off him. 'Matteo, honey, we're also coming to celebrate Sister Kevin's BIG birthday. So if you could get us VIP tix to—'

I grab the phone off her.

'Can everyone stop grabbing my phone, please?' I yell. I'm getting so angry with them all. Matteo is on the receiving end of far too much information. Information that I should have had the guts to tell him two weeks ago.

'Hi, Matteo. It's me. Sorry about all of that...' I say hurriedly. I'm surprised he doesn't just end the call on me right here and now. I listen quietly to what he has to say. 'Uh-huh. Yep. Sure. Yes. And again, I'm sorry.'

I click off that call and immediately accept another, holding it up high. 'He wants to FaceTime us.'

We gather round the phone, all of us huddled close.

Matteo takes one look at us. He looks shocked. I forgot to warn him that we are all wearing blonde ponytail wigs and Barbie costumes. 'Hi, everyone,' Matteo says, recovering quickly. 'It's great to see you all. Nice outfits.'

I sigh in relief as we all shout back. Matteo now looks unfazed by it all.

'He's so fucking fit,' Liberty says, shaking her head. She smiles over at Nacho. 'You're like Hemsworth Hotties.'

Nacho grins back. He has no idea what she means, but he does look smitten with her.

'So, Connie will message me the details of all the celebrations going on. It sounds like I will need to pull some strings to see if we can make this week extra special for all of you. Just let me know what's on the wish list.'

Everyone erupts into cheers while I melt, because Matteo is the loveliest guy on the planet.

'But,' he says firmly, 'Connie and I are also going to need time together... alone. I hope you all understand that.'

I go bright red while the others make cooing noises and obscene suggestions.

'Sorry we hijacked your romantic break!' yells Cherry. 'Of course you two should have time together.'

Tash leans forward. 'Yeah. That was on me, Matteo. I thought I was helping by getting the flights paid for. Sorry. I didn't think to ask first.'

'Same,' says Ged, looking at me. 'We got so swept up in this whole pre-moon spree that we lost sight of why Connie was coming to Vegas in the first place.'

I smile back. 'It's okay, you guys. I'm sure we can work it out.'

'I've got to go,' Matteo says. 'Have a good flight. See you soon. I'll organise a limo to pick you all up.'

Everyone whoops while I say a quiet goodbye to Matteo. His dark eyes burn into mine, making my pulse race. 'I knew what I was signing up to. I should have guessed your entourage would muscle in on the trip. It's no problem. I've handled worse.'

'Thank you,' I say. He really is very understanding. 'And about that photo...'

'Forget it. If you say it's all innocent and there's nothing going on, I believe you.'

Oh, wow. Considering what he went through with his cheating ex, this is a huge deal. It can't be easy to trust someone after something like that. Finding out they are cheating a week before your wedding. I'm amazed it hasn't put him off women and weddings for life.

'I'll make it up to you,' I say, my heart skipping a beat.

He studies me for a second, a kind smile tugging at his lips. 'You already have.'

'What's the not great news?' I ask.

He half laughs. 'It can wait. See you soon.'

BEEP. Jorge is on the minibus. He has started the engine. 'I go now. Not later. Now. *Vamos.*'

I click off the call, my heart much lighter. As we throw our suitcases onto the bus in a somewhat violent frenzy, I hurriedly say goodbye to Nacho. He has an amused grin on his face. I suppose at the very least, there's never a dull moment when the Dollz are in town. We line up to kiss him on the cheeks as they all hand back their villa keys.

'Someone was sick on the bathroom mat, but it'll definitely come out,' Tash tells him.

'Someone also burned a tiny hole on the sunbed mattress with a cigarette, but it wasn't me,' says Cherry, kissing him on the cheek.

'Someone has left brown stains on the kitchen bench and brown footprints on the fake grass. They were already there when we arrived but don't worry, it didn't bother us. You can hardly notice. The place is lovely. We'll five-star it on Tripadvisor,' says Liam.

Good God.

'See you soon,' Nacho says, unsuccessfully trying to mask a worried look. 'Have a great time in Las Vegas.'

He waves us off as the minibus hurtles down the street. We are now very late for our flight. Everyone is quiet. Cherry's immaculate make-up has run down her cheeks with all the hoo-hah over her baby daddy. We are all wearing the wrong outfits. They are ill-fitting and stained. We look uncomfortable and dishevelled. I'm not sure we'll have time to swap clothes. We'll have to do it on the plane somehow. Cherry is blaming her pregnancy brain for the costume mix-up, which is a bit of a relief for now, but I will have to come clean at some point that it was Ged and Liam, who are looking dangerously jaundiced. I'll be surprised if they'll be allowed to fly. At least Big Mand and Big Sue are sitting together. Tash is sitting on her own. She has still not told Sister Kevin, banished to the front next to Jorge, what he has done wrong. She must be hoping that he will read her mind and telepathically ascertain what he has to do to make amends.

Liberty is the only one who looks half decent. But she has the hump with me about Luke and is the first to break the lovely silence.

'So, Connie!' she yells down the bus. 'What exactly happened between you and Luke last night? What was so important that you felt the need to keep it a secret from us? It looked like you were almost kissing on stage. Call me old-fashioned, but aren't you supposed to be avoiding him? You did say he was a stalker weirdo. Or has that changed now?'

She makes it sound like I'm hiding something, even though she was the one who bloody invited him here. But I'd rather not think about it right now. I just want to get to Las Vegas and put this whole week behind me. Including Luke, and the fact that right after that photo of us on stage was taken by Dan, he kissed me. In front of the whole crowd at Voices. I was mortified.

I twist my body to look out of the window. We are passing by signs for the historic Alicante castle and the jumbo sex hypermarket, meaning we are almost at the airport.

'Fine,' Liberty huffs. 'Have it your own way. But just so you know, I'm finding seeing images of the two of you together very triggering.'

* * *

Ten minutes later, we have arrived at the airport looking like the Poundland version of the cast of *Barbie*. Everyone looks like they're masking a lot of trauma. Tempers are fraying as we drag our luggage to the check-in desk. I have my work cut out for me on this flight. I have thirteen hours to turn it all around so that we arrive happy, presentable and ready to party hard, work hard and romance even harder. If anyone can do this, I can.

While we are queuing, Ged sidles up to me. 'Can you please try to speak to Big Sue and Big Mand for us?' he whispers. 'We're gutted we upset them. It was a genuine mistake.'

He has dark circles under his eyes and a stress rash appearing on his yellow cheek. I give him a quick hug. 'Of course. I'll do it straight away. As soon as we are on board.'

He brightens and shuffles back to Liam, who is near the front of the queue.

'Connie,' Tash hisses. 'I need you to speak to Kev.'

Why me?

She looks drained, under all of the fake tan and the huge eyelashes. I really hope for her sake she isn't pregnant. 'I need you to convince him that having a baby is a great idea.'

She can't be serious.

'I'd ask Cherry, but she's raging right now. And I'd do it myself, but I'm not speaking to him. And there's no way I'm asking Libs. She'll probably try and get off with him. That girl has no boundaries.' Tash shakes her head and gives me a desolate look. 'And Big Mand and Big Sue have made their opinions very clear.' She sighs resignedly. 'So that just leaves you. You're literally the last person I can ask.'

I feel so special.

'But given what Kev just said about Nacho, and being forced into father-hood without his knowledge, hasn't that put you off going ahead with the surprise pregnancy? Unless... unless you're...?' My voice is barely audible. Sister Kevin is standing only feet away, and even though he has his back to us, he is so tall his ears are probably picking up all conversations in a five-mile radius. It's a shame she has fallen out with him, because they make a very cute couple. Apart from the fact that he is parenthood-averse and she wants to surprise him with a baby.

Tash shrugs. 'I'm not sure. But is it too much to ask that someone is happy for me? Babes, you want me and Kev to be happy, don't you?'

I nod back even though it is madness. 'I'll talk to him on the plane. No worries. But why don't you lay the foundations for a reconciliation by at least talking to him while we check in? He has come all this way to be with you. He must really like you to want to spend his BIG birthday with you.'

Tash mulls over my pearls of wisdom and finally agrees to let Sister Kevin off the hook for now. I watch her sidle up to him and hug him from behind. Without turning, he reaches for her and sweeps her around to face him. Her eyes light up immediately.

Eventually, all of the bags are placed on the conveyor belt, weighed and tagged, and I am presented with a card reader to pay a massive surcharge for the extra luggage. I take out my credit card with a sweaty palm.

'Don't worry. We'll give you it back once we have the full total,' says Cherry kindly, her maternal streak making a brief appearance before she goes back to resting angry-beast face.

I try to smile. I'm really digging deep to stay calm, to keep a lid on the turbulent mess of excitement over seeing Matteo mixed with anxiety and responsibility swirling around in my stomach. They all need me to step up a notch. And I will. I will.

'Fuck me!' yells Liberty, spinning round to face us. 'I've just seen Luke.'

'Where?' I say. *This cannot be happening.*

'Over there. He just went through to passport control.'

Deep breaths.

Deep breaths.

He could simply be making his way back to England or Norway now that we have cleared up our misunderstandings. Kind of.

They all turn to stare at me.

'I'm going to check the departure board for what flight he might be on,' says Big Sue in an authoritative tone. Big Mand offers to go with her. We watch them race over to the boards at the far end of the concourse.

'He'll be going back home. I'm sure of it,' I tell the group.

PING. It's Big Sue texting. There are no scheduled departures for the UK or Norway today.

PING. It's a message from Matteo telling me he has hired a bright pink limo to pick us up from the airport. He will have it stocked with champagne for all the celebrating. He is so kind and understanding. He is about to board his flight from LA to Vegas, and he can't wait to see me. He thinks the Barbie wig looked sexy. He signs off 'Mr Window Seat'.

I clutch my phone to my chest, my heart thumping and my pulse racing. Everything will be fine just as soon as we are together.

Deep breaths.

Deep breaths.

Matteo is desperate to see me. He knows we have something very special. He also knows that I am very much a work in progress. I hope he clings to that when I turn up in Las Vegas with my two bridezillas, my broken Dollz... and my royal Norwegian sapiosexual stalker.

PING. Matteo has sent a screen grab of Luke kissing me. Actual lip-to-lip contact. Taken from Voices' social media last night. His message is simple.

> As soon as you land, we need to talk.

* * *

MORE FROM JO LYONS

Another book from Jo Lyons, *Girls Take Vegas*, is available to order now here: https://mybook.to/GirlsTakeVegasBackAd

ACKNOWLEDGEMENTS

So many writer and reader friends helped me get this book to publication. Huge thanks to all of them and enormous thanks to my wonderfully talented editor Francesca Best for her brilliant support and the entire Boldwood team for welcoming me into the family. Special thanks to copy editor Jennifer Kay Davies and proofreader Ross Dickinson for helping get it in shape and the clever Alex Allden for making the cover look fabulous.

I'd like to thank all the lovely women at Comedy Women in Print, especially Helen Lederer and my fellow long/shortlisters who have been excellent cheer-leaders. All at Curtis Brown Creative for their support and encouragement during the many, many writing courses that I have become addicted to – yes, I'm looking at you, Jenny Colgan. When I started out, I had no idea about how to save a cat. Now I know things like every character needs an arc and a book will never be finished, only ever abandoned. Constant tinkering is not an option.

Last but not least, my awesome and talented writing tribe and beta readers who help fix all the terrible first drafts: Jayne, Jess, Julia, Farrah, Cristal, Amanda (aka The Coven), Nichelle, Kim, Keith, Claire, Cara, Joanna (my Curtis Brown writing tribe). And a special thanks to all my fabulous friends who cheerlead me on: Alice, Nicky, Linds, Mands, Wendy, Helen, Deb, Genize, Shauna, Mrs B, Mags, Paula, Maria, Scottish Kate (and her fabulous Tillyfruskie farm cabin perfect for writing retreats), my ladies in Spain and all my Hull University friends who have never changed in the 35 years we have been meeting up, Janine, Anna Foster (BBC Radio Newcastle) for narrating the Girls series so brilliantly and my sisters, especially Philippa and my niece Gabs who listen to me go on and on and fecking on (I know, difficult to believe) and my lovely aunties and amazing cousins who encourage me to keep going. And the

Lyons boys who always have my back and never moan that I now live in a crazy fantasy world, talk about my novels incessantly and have completely abandoned all housework. I am living the dream!

I could not do any of this without them.

ABOUT THE AUTHOR

Jo Lyons is the bestselling author of uplifting, laugh-out-loud, warm-hearted romantic comedies, and was shortlisted for the prestigious Comedy Women in Print Awards in 2021. She spent years working abroad in sunny destinations like Turkey, Spain and the south of France at a vineyard (trying her best not to drink them out of business).

Sign up to Jo Lyons' mailing list for news, competitions and updates on future books.

Visit Jo's website: www.jolyonsauthor.com

Follow Jo on social media here:

facebook.com/Jo-Lyons-Author
x.com/JoLyons
instagram.com/hinnywhowrites
goodreads.com/jolyons
tiktok.com/@jo_lyons_author
bsky.app/profile/jolyons.bsky.social

ALSO BY JO LYONS

Standalone Novels

A Billionaire for Christmas

The Girls Series

Girls Just Want to Have Sun

Girls Gone Rogue

Girls Take Vegas

Boldwood

Boldwood Books is an award-winning fiction publishing company seeking out the best stories from around the world.

Find out more at www.boldwoodbooks.com

Join our reader community for brilliant books, competitions and offers!

Follow us
@BoldwoodBooks
@TheBoldBookClub

Sign up to our weekly deals newsletter

https://bit.ly/BoldwoodBNewsletter

9 781806 560325